# SAVING
# JUSTICE

## PETER O'MAHONEY

The truth is one step closer…

Saving Justice A Legal Thriller
Tex Hunter 4

Peter O'Mahoney

Copyright © 2021
Published by Roam Free Publishing.
peteromahoney.com

Cover design by Belu.
https://belu.design

# ALSO BY PETER O'MAHONEY

*In the Tex Hunter series:*

**Power and Justice**
**Faith and Justice**
**Corrupt Justice**
**Deadly Justice**

\*\*\*\*\*

*In the Bill Harvey Legal Thriller Series:*

**Redeeming Justice**
**Will of Justice**
**Fire and Justice**
**A Time for Justice**
**Truth and Justice**

\*\*\*\*\*

*In the Jack Valentine Series:*

**Gates of Power**
**Stolen Power**

# SAVING JUSTICE

## TEX HUNTER LEGAL THRILLER BOOK 5

PETER O'MAHONEY

# CHAPTER 1

"I NEED to do this." Criminal Attorney Tex Hunter gripped the steering wheel. "Stacey Fulbright is innocent. She has to be."

"I just don't think it's a good idea." Assistant Esther Wright stared out the passenger window of the BMW sedan, watching as they weaved in and out of traffic at high speed. The city of Chicago had her heart, but the ever-growing levels of traffic was one of her life's greatest annoyances. "Defending another lawyer is one thing, but defending an ex-lover is something different altogether. I've seen it many times before—you become too personally involved when you know the accused. I can see it happening here. You're too involved to make the right decisions. You're going to become obsessive and lose sight of everything else."

Hunter eased his foot off the accelerator, moving the car into the slow lane of the Stevenson Expressway. It was busy, four lanes of a snake-like beast hustling down the pale gray road, everyone desperate to arrive at some place at some time for some important reason. Nobody gave way to anybody. It was a fight for space and time, all the cars maneuvering for the extra room. The fast lanes were a continuous pretense of bluster, fast moves, stubbornness, and close calls. As Hunter's car slowed, the black SUV following them did the same. Two cars back. New and clean. The black SUV had been two cars back, in that exact position, for the past five minutes.

"Is that what this is about?" Hunter's voice softened as he looked across at his assistant. "You don't want me to defend an ex-girlfriend?"

"I just..." Esther avoided looking at him, keeping her gaze out the window. She brushed a strand of blonde hair behind her ear. "You get too personally involved when you know the people in the case. It becomes your life, your world and everything that you do. That's honorable, and it's commendable, but I'm not sure it's good for your health. The more you're personally involved, the more you drink, and you're almost forty-five. You've got to look after your health."

"My health is fine. I'm not having a heart attack any time soon." Hunter looked in the rear-view mirror as he changed lanes again. The black SUV moved with them. "Is there something more I'm missing?"

"It's nothing. I'm just looking out for you."

Hunter nodded in response. Now wasn't the time to engage in an emotional discussion. He needed to focus. "If Stacey wants me to do it, then I'm going to defend her. This is a woman that I've known for more than twenty-five years. She had my back when I was younger, and I've never forgotten that. She's been charged with murder, and she's asked for my help on the bail hearing. She has two young children, Esther. I can't let the system do to her family what it did to mine."

Esther didn't respond, instead turning her attention to the files on her lap.

Hunter picked up the pace of the car, weaving through traffic as he let out his emotions on the road. The black SUV followed his pace. Hunter adjusted the rearview mirror. The windows of the SUV were tinted. There were no plates.

"The deceased is Joe Fielding, a private investigator." Esther ran her index finger over the page as she read. "Found stabbed in the parking lot outside Stacey Fulbright's office building at five in the morning. Found by a security guard with some of Stacey's possessions. Fielding was known to the police and had a close association with criminal gangs that operate in the west of Chicago. Stacey was arrested because her monogrammed gold letter opener was found next to the body and it's assumed, at this point, that the letter opener is the murder weapon. Fielding was stabbed five times in the neck and bled out."

"Wait. Fielding. Joe Fielding…" Hunter tapped his thumb against the steering wheel. He changed lanes again. The SUV followed. It came closer. "Joe

Fielding is involved in Dr. Mackie's case. His name has come up before."

"That's right." Esther snapped her fingers when she made the connection. "From what we found on that case, Fielding worked for Vandenberg and Wolfe Family Law Offices."

"And often in opposition to Stacey Fulbright and her clients."

Hunter didn't signal as he took the ramp off the expressway. The black SUV veered right and shadowed them.

"I don't think we should get messed up in the world of family law, Tex. And not just family law— Stacey Fulbright specializes in representing domestic abuse victims through their divorce. That's what her whole business model is based on. We're talking about violent people with violent pasts."

"Fear shouldn't dictate our sense of justice."

"Of course not, but you have to do the right thing and let someone else defend Stacey Fulbright. There are many great defense lawyers out there. If Stacey is a good lawyer, like you say, then I'm sure she would even say the same thing. You're too close to it. And when you're too close to something, you make bad decisions."

"If she wants my help, then I need to help her." Hunter said as the traffic on the ramp slowed in front of them. "It may have been twenty years since I dated Stacey Fulbright, but she was good to me at a time in my life when many people weren't. She had my back.

It was young love, but it was an important part of my life. And even after we separated, I always promised myself that I would have her back, as a way to repay her. Without her support, I'm not sure where I'd be." Hunter paused for a long moment. He sighed. "Her son Noah is ten years old. That's the same age I was when my father went through his murder trial, and I won't let the system destroy another family like it did mine."

"This isn't your father's case." Esther's voice softened. "This is different. Your father's case involved the killings of eight teenage girls, and this is the murder of a dodgy private investigator in a parking lot. They're different cases, and her son is going to see the trial differently than you did. There won't be the media circus you had to endure."

"My father's defense lawyers were terrible. With all the media pressure, they abandoned the case too easily. Even when I was ten, I knew they weren't doing their job. I won't let that happen to Stacey Fulbright and her family."

"What about your other cases? Dr. Mackie's case is due in court in five weeks. We have to prepare for it. We're not in a winning position in his case yet. It's going to take a lot of work to prepare for the trial."

"We have time." Hunter grunted. "If not, we'll make time."

Hunter stopped at the red light, five minutes from their destination, the Cook County Jail. The SUV moved into the space behind them.

It didn't stop.

The SUV slammed into the back of Hunter's car. The impact jolted the BMW forward. Esther and Hunter gripped the dashboard. The SUV kept pushing. Tires were screeching. Hunter slammed his foot on the brake and ripped up the parking brake, looking behind him.

"Tex!" Esther shouted as she turned to Hunter. There was confusion in her eyes. "Tex!"

Hunter released the parking brake, gripped the steering wheel, threw the car into gear, and lurched forward, into the oncoming traffic. The traffic passing the intersection broke hard, the sounds of horns reverberating through the air. One car smashed into the back of another. A motorbike slid on the road. A truck pulled to the side. Hunter swerved past an oncoming car, and swerved again, before screeching to a stop on the other side of the intersection.

He bounded out of the car, staring at the SUV on the other side of the road, daring it to come forward. The SUV roared its engine, squealed its tires, but turned right, speeding into the distance.

As Hunter watched the car race away, he knew it wasn't a coincidence. Danger was coming.

And he expected nothing less.

# CHAPTER 2

DEATH WAS Tex Hunter's business. It was where the money was. He didn't want it to be, but it was the reality he faced as a criminal defense attorney. Murder. Attempted murder. Manslaughter. Faced with those charges, a client looked at their future and saw nothing but a life in prison, and was willing to spend every last cent they had to prevent it from happening, guilty or not. Over his decades as a criminal lawyer, he'd become accustomed to detaching from the cases, forgetting about the sickening photos from the crime scenes, the depraved nature of the offenses, or the formal descriptions of the deceased. He had to. It was the only way to deal with seeing the underworld of Chicago on a daily basis. He could look at a photo of a deceased body and not see a life lost, not see the wounds of death, but instead see the clues that lead to identifying the murderer. He could do that with ease. Except when the case was personal. That's when he struggled to switch off. That's when he struggled to forget.

Hunter barely recognized Stacey Fulbright when he first walked into the meeting room. He'd never seen her look so pale. The once vibrant and passionate brunette looked broken and defeated. Her shoulders were slumped forward, her eyes stared at the floor in front of her, and her shoulder length hair was a mess. Even in the twenty-four hours since her arrest, she appeared wrecked.

The room for pre-bail meetings was tight, unemotional, and heartless. It smelled like lost hope, mixed with the stench of body odor and pine-scented cleaning products. It was a room designed to lack personality, designed to appear sterile, and it was succeeding in every aspect. There were five narrow cubicles for lawyers to meet with clients, and only a thin wooden panel to separate each space. There were two other women in the room, talking to their lawyers about their forthcoming felony charges. Hunter recognized both lawyers, and greeted them.

Stacey Fulbright waited at the table, staring at the grains in the wood as Hunter sat down. She knew how this worked. She knew the process. But she never thought she would be on the other side of the table.

"Courtroom 101 of 26th and California Avenue." Stacey Fulbright said as she stared at her hands, still cuffed. "I never thought I'd be the one who was applying for bail. I never thought I'd be here, Tex. Not on this side of the desk. I should be over on the other side, with the lawyers."

"Hello Stacey." Hunter's tone was calm. "We've got a good judge today. Judge Lyon. He's a reasonable guy. Should work in our favor, and the 'D' Bond is likely to be set at half a million, given Judge Lyon's history of similar cases. It means you'll have to put up ten percent of the amount. Can you post it?"

"I can post it. I can put up the house as collateral, if needed." She nodded, still staring at the table. "I've thought about this already."

"Do you need me to explain the procedure? It's been a while since you were in criminal law."

She shook her head, before biting her lip. Their interaction was formal, defaulting to the legal profession protocol they both held so dear. When she looked up at Hunter, he saw a face stained by tears.

"I need to get out of here, Tex. I have to make bail. My children can't know I'm in prison. I can't let them think their mommy is a criminal. I'm not a murderer. I can't let my children grow up like that. They can't think I'm a killer. I have to go home."

"We'll work on that." Hunter rested his elbows on the table. "We'll present a good case at the bail hearing, and then the prelim, but this is a murder charge. They've determined there's enough evidence to charge you in the first degree, and that means they've got something on your intent to kill this man. Even if we're successful in the bail hearing, because of the charge, they may request you wear an electronic home monitor."

"An ankle monitor? I can do that." She whispered, more to herself than to Hunter. "I just need to get out of here. I need to see my babies."

Hunter looked back at the closed door. Esther Wright was waiting outside, still shaken up after the car accident. Hunter reported the incident to the police and his insurance company, and within twenty-five minutes of the collision, his car was towed away. Fifteen minutes later, he was walking through the Cook County Prison entrance preparing for a bail hearing.

"Thank you for coming, Tex. You're the first lawyer I thought of when they arrested me." Stacey muttered. "But this is all just one big mistake. This nightmare will be over soon. I'm sure of it. The cops have made a mistake. That's all. They made a mistake. It happens."

"I will defend you all the way."

"I don't need you to do that. I've got someone else in mind, if it gets that far. John C. Clarke owes me a few favors, and his specialty is murder charges. I'll get him to take it over once I'm out of here. And this will be a simple case, so there's nothing to worry about. It'll be thrown out once they investigate the case and find there's no evidence I did this. This is a simple case of mistaken identity. The cops got the wrong person. It happens. Once they find security footage in the parking lot, I'll be in the clear. I know I didn't kill that man. It'll be over before we know it."

"I want to help you, Stacey. I've always said that if you needed me, I would be there. I've got your back."

The statement caught her by surprise. She looked up and smiled. "You're a good man, Tex. You always do the right thing." She reached out and grabbed his hand, giving it one tight squeeze before letting go. "The best thing you can do for me right now is to get me out of this prison."

"Then let's start with what we know." Hunter reached down, picked up his briefcase and placed it on the table. He opened it, and took out the police file. "Joe Fielding was found in the parking lot outside your office by a security guard at 5am yesterday. They're still working on time of death, but they have evidence that he left his apartment at 10pm the night before, meaning the time of death is between 10pm and 5am. The murder weapon is a gold letter opener with your name engraved on it. You say that you didn't do it, but the evidence is strong." Hunter paused for a moment. "Is there anyone that would want to target you?"

"What do you mean?" She looked confused.

"As I was driving here, I was involved in a minor collision with a black SUV. It didn't seem like an accident, because the person targeted my car and then drove off quickly."

"I'm… I'm not sure what you're asking?" She shook her head. "You think the person in the SUV targeted you because you were coming here?"

"I'm saying we shouldn't rule anything out yet."

Stacey's mouth hung open and her face went blank as she tried to process the thought.

The bailiff opened the door behind Hunter, leaned his head into the room and called the next lot of numbers. Hunter gave Stacey a knowing nod, wished her luck, and then packed up his briefcase.

Twenty-five minutes later, Hunter was walking through the hallways of the George N. Leighton criminal courthouse. The marbled floors echoed the sounds of hurrying footsteps, and the high ceilings carried the hum of whispered conversations. Some people pushed past, desperate to make a court appearance on time, and others lingered against the walls, talking in hushed tones.

"Tex Hunter. It's been a while."

Hunter turned to see the man behind him. "Michael Vandenberg. What are you doing in the halls of criminal justice? Don't you belong over in family court?"

"True." Vandenberg smiled. "But I had a meeting here. Tell me, are you still defending Dr. Mackie on the sexual assault case?"

"I am." Hunter was hesitant. "I'd love to stay and chat but I'm on my way to Bond Court."

"I need one minute of your time. That's all." Vandenberg was tall, slim, and had graying hair. He was awkward, hard to talk to, and had a reputation for being much too touchy feely with the women around him. He was old school, even for a man in his late fifties. He held himself well, but the years of working as a divorce lawyer were beginning to take a toll on his health. "I need you to convince Dr. Mackie to sell his business to Christoph King. It'd make everyone very happy, and I'm sure I can make the sexual assault charges against Dr. Mackie disappear if the sale was made. Just mention it to him for me."

Hunter squinted. "I don't understand the connection."

"You don't have to. Just make the sale happen." Vandenberg said. "What do you have in Bond Court?"

"Murder, but it's a case of mistaken identity. It's one of your rivals. Stacey Fulbright."

"Ha," Vandenberg scoffed. "That woman has dedicated her life to ruining my clients in divorce cases. And now she's here? There's some justice in that." Vandenberg stepped back; a smile still plastered across his face. "Just get Dr. Mackie to sign the deal. If he sells the business, I can guarantee his sexual assault charges will disappear."

Vandenberg turned, laughing to himself as he strutted down the hallway. Hunter waited a moment before he continued to Bond Court.

Mondays were the worst for bail hearings. Although Chicago's Central Bond Court ran seven days a week, the weekends usually saw more than its fair share of felonies. More murders. More assaults. More break-ins. The result of a weekend filled with violence left a backlog of people needing their moment in court. Prosecutor Michelle Law was waiting inside the courtroom, seated in the back row of the pews, waiting for her chance to protect the system. She had a file on her lap, impatiently tapping her finger on the cover while another defendant had their bail paperwork processed.

"Looking good," she said as Hunter's tall figure approached. "Is that a touch of gray in your hair?"

"I like to call it experience." Hunter sat next to her. "You have the Fulbright case?"

"I do. It's always sad when lawyers fall off the wagon like this, but I know what it's like. I've been through my own mid-life crisis, although I didn't kill anyone. It makes me sad that someone like Stacey Fulbright murdered a private investigator, but she's been known to snap before. Got that fiery streak. She might dedicate her life to defending abused women in divorce cases, but she's not an innocent angel, Hunter. There's a long line of people willing to testify against her. She's a prime candidate for stabbing someone in a parking lot late at night."

The bailiff at the front of the courtroom called out the next case number. "Criminal Case 20-CR-2555." The bailiff was loud, but he had to be. Bond court in Cook County moved fast. The hum of the courtroom was busy with lawyers negotiating, preparing, and shuffling through paperwork. Hunter followed Law to the front of the room as Stacey Fulbright was escorted into the dock. Judge Lyon welcomed them. He exhaled as he read the file, and then turned to the defendant. He confirmed the name of the defendant and asked the lawyers to identify themselves. They did so and Judge Lyon moved to the next stage in the process.

"Anything to add before I make a determination?"

Judge Lyon asked. "And if you do, make it quick."

"The prosecution moves to request that bail is denied." Law's response was fast. Her tone was cold, as was her demeanor. "This is a violent and callous murder and deserves to be treated as such. We have evidence that she intended to commit this act, and we cannot let her walk the streets."

"That's inflammatory speech, Your Honor." Hunter argued once his surprise subsided. "Mrs. Fulbright has never been charged with a crime, never been convicted of anything, never even had so much as a speeding ticket. In this case, there are no eyewitnesses, there's no video footage, and there's no motive. Mrs. Fulbright is a lawyer, a graduate of Chicago Law School, and has great respect for the institution of this courthouse."

"Your Honor, the defendant has access to funds, a passport, and a desire not to see her day in court. She's a flight risk and we cannot allow that to happen."

"The presence of a passport does not indicate the intention to use it." Hunter retorted. "She has a family at home, and strong ties to the community. She's been married for more than a decade, has two young children, and all her connections are in Chicago. She's no flight risk."

"All valid statements, Mr. Hunter." Judge Lyon read over the file again. He was in no mood for theatrics. "However, the prosecution has a point. The defendant will need to surrender her passport, wear an electronic home monitor, and will have a curfew to be set at 7pm. She may continue her work; however, she's not to leave the state of Illinois. Due to the defendant's assets, 'D' Bond is set at five hundred thousand dollars." Judge Lyon turned to the bailiff, who then called the next case number.

Hunter looked to Stacey Fulbright in the dock and offered her a smile. She didn't return it. She barely reacted at all. Her fists were clenched, as was her jaw. There was anger in her eyes.

Hunter stared at the woman he used to love and started to question how well he really knew her.

# CHAPTER 3

THE CAB trip from Cook County Prison to Naperville took over an hour, and to Stacey Fulbright, it seemed like an eternity. The cab stunk of stale beer and takeaway, but it was still nicer than the smells she encountered while locked up. Sitting in the back seat of the cab, Stacey was stuck with her own thoughts as they drove past the suburbs of Chicago. She cried the entire time her bail paperwork was being processed. There was so much waiting, and so many lines to stand in. When the cab turned into her street, she wiped her eyes with a tissue and took a number of deep breaths. Still in the same clothes as when she was arrested more than a day earlier, she took a moment to calm herself before exiting the cab.

She wasn't sure how many tears she had left. Life as she had known it had come tumbling down in a matter of hours. When the police arrived at her office the day before, she was sure it was a mistake. It had to be. They asked about her gold-plated letter opener. It seemed unusual, but she answered their questions. It was a graduation gift; she told them. Then they asked where it was.

When she didn't see it on her desk, her legal training knew it was time to shut her mouth. She didn't say another word. The following day, the detectives came to her home with an arrest warrant. She entered the police car without a fuss. Most arrests were lawful, she told herself. It was just a mistake. Whatever evidence they had was wrong.

She didn't have an alibi for that Friday night. She'd been working late, negotiating a divorce settlement over the phone, before she left and walked to the parking lot near her office around 11pm. There was footage of her walking into the parking lot at 11:15pm. She drove out of the parking lot at 11:25pm. That was enough time to stab someone, the police said. The gold-plated letter opener was found next to the victim's body, bloodied and used. Of course, her fingerprints were on it. She had used it only a few days earlier in her office.

The multi-level lot was two doors down from her office in The Loop, but even though the distance was short, she always walked there with her hand on the pepper spray in her bag. She'd been attacked outside the lot only two weeks earlier, and that night, she'd managed to fight the man off. She filed a complaint, but she couldn't identify her attacker, and nobody was arrested.

After she was detained, the detective yelled his theory at her in the police interrogation room. Joe Fielding tried to blackmail you, he yelled. The evidence was in his emails. Fielding had contacted her with an offer. He called her multiple times, and she told him she wasn't interested, but Fielding was insistent. He told her that he would find her. 'I'll meet you in the parking lot one night,' Fielding had messaged her.

When she stepped out of the cab, she saw Carl, her husband, sitting on the front step of the house. He looked like a wreck, although she was sure that she looked worse. After she was arrested, Stacey told her husband to stay away from court. She didn't want her children to have any idea about what was happening.

She could see Noah and Zoe were playing in the front room of their two-story home. Noah was ten, becoming more intelligent and more aware by the day, and Zoe was five, still growing into her strong personality.

Their home was pleasant, almost the picture-perfect American dream house in Naperville. They had four bedrooms. A two-car garage. A white-picket fence. A vegetable patch. Space for a pool, if needed.

She loved the city of Naperville, only forty-five minutes' drive from the hustle of Chicago. One of the safest and highly educated small cities in the country, it was the perfect place to raise her children. Best of all, it felt a million miles away from the stress of life as a divorce lawyer in the depths of Chicago's skyscrapers.

"I need to see the kids." Stacey said as she stepped through the waist high gate and started to walk up the path to the front door. "Have they had dinner?"

"Aren't you going to tell me what's going on first?" Carl approached her, but Stacey folded her arms and looked away. Carl hesitated and stopped before embracing her. "Noah and Zoe are watching television. They've been fed. They can't hear us."

She gripped her arms tight across her chest, and avoided eye contact. "They've charged me with first degree murder. I'm out on bail." She lifted up the leg of her trousers to reveal an ankle monitor. "I've got to wear this."

Carl's mouth dropped open. "I thought you said it was a mistake. That it'll be sorted out by the morning. That the bail hearing was just a formality before the charges were dropped. You said this was a mistake."

"What do you want me to say, Carl?" She snapped. "It isn't sorted out. The cops have charged me with murder one. They think I did it. They think I stabbed a man named Joe Fielding."

He moved away slightly. There was fear in his eyes. But worse than that, worse than the fear, was the doubt he showed.

"I didn't do it." Stacey whispered. "I didn't kill anyone. I didn't stab the guy."

Carl nodded his response. He went to hug her, but she stepped back again.

"I need a shower first. I need to wash the feeling of prison off me." She stepped past him. "What did you tell the kids?"

"I told them you were called away for work and

you had to travel for a case." He murmured. "Is Tex Hunter the right guy to defend you? You have a past with him."

"We had a past a long time ago."

"He's too personally involved. You said it many times—if you're personally involved in law, then you'll miss things. He'll miss the important pieces because he's too close."

"There's someone else I'll meet with. John C. Clarke. If he's the right fit, then I'll ask him to take over the case." Stacey took another step towards the door. "I'll talk to him tomorrow."

"Stacey." Carl called out.

She waited on the step, staring at the front door. There had been a growing distance between them, and it seemed to be widening every month. She wanted to go to him, to hug him, but she couldn't remember how. "What is it?"

"There's something you should know."

She turned. "What? What could possibly be that important?"

Carl hesitated. "There was a man at the school today."

"What do you mean 'a man'?"

"When I went to baseball practice with Noah, there was someone past the outfield, in a suit. He wasn't a parent."

"And you think it's connected to this?"

"He was watching Noah. The whole time." Carl ran his hand over his black, short-cropped hair. It was graying at the sides. "I'm worried, Stacey. What have you got caught up in? Is this one of your divorce cases seeking revenge? What if they come after the kids? You defend women who have been the victims of domestic abuse. What if one of those men have changed their target to you?"

"This is just a big mistake. That's all." She whispered. "It'll be over soon. I'm sure of it."

"What if it's not? What if you were set-up? What if this is some lunatic that's taken things too far?"

Stacey stared at him for a long period of time, her mouth hanging open. Tears filled her eyes again. She blinked them back.

"Mom!" Noah opened the front door. "Are you back already? Dad said you'd be gone for a few days."

"Hi, sweetie." She wiped her eyes with her sleeve before turning to Noah. She hugged him tightly. "Mom is back now."

"Do you have to go back to work? Dad made us eat the worst spaghetti and meatballs ever. He said he followed your recipe, but it was terrible. Like, yuck! I don't even think it could be considered food. You won't travel away again, will you? You won't make us eat Dad's spaghetti and meatballs again?"

Stacey smiled. "I hope not, sweetie."

But she wasn't sure if her statement was true. From that day forward, life was about to change dramatically.

# CHAPTER 4

TEX HUNTER and Esther Wright rode in the back of the black sedan. Dressed in a dinner suit, Hunter looked across to Esther. She looked dazzling in her red dress. He'd only given her five hours' notice of the dinner function, and somehow, she'd managed to look like she had five weeks to prepare. The dress ran down to her knees, highlighting her long slim legs, her blonde hair draped over her shoulders, and she smelled like a light bouquet of a thousand flowers.

"Don't be a pervert." Esther teased when she caught Hunter staring. "Stop ogling my legs."

"You look amazing tonight, Esther. Not that you don't look amazing at other times, I mean. You always look amazing." Hunter stumbled over his words. "It's just you don't usually wear a dinner dress to work, and I mean, that, well, um, you look amazing."

"For a man that has a way with words, you're hopeless at compliments." She squirmed a little, happy to have impressed him. She pulled a strand of blonde hair over her ear, and the grin on her face broadened. They sat in awkward silence for a few long moments as they approached their destination.

"Your brother Patrick left a message earlier today. He said he had a lead with finding your sister Natalie." Esther broke the silence. "Are you sure she wants to see you now? Three and a half decades is a long time not to talk to someone."

"I spoke to Patrick. He found an address in Mexico, in a tourist town named Puerto Vallarta on the Pacific coast. She's been working as a waitress in a family run café for the past few years. We think she's got a family, perhaps two teenage boys. She's covered her tracks really well. No social media, no internet information, no data on her name. She completely wiped our family name from her history. There really isn't a lot of information out there."

"But what says she'll actually talk to you even if you find her? There's a reason she left Chicago all those years ago and hasn't returned."

"We're family. If she knows the truth about my father's case, like I think she does, then she'll want to talk." Hunter looked out the window as the car slowed. "My big fear is that I won't recognize her. She's my sister, but I haven't seen her in thirty-five years. Ever since she got on a plane and fled Chicago, I haven't seen her. Haven't even talked to her. Not even a letter between us. And back in those days, photos weren't taken very often. They were a special occasion type of thing. I barely have any photos of her now. I don't even know what she looks like."

"Did you ever think that maybe she doesn't want to be found?"

"Often." Hunter looked out the window as the car stopped outside the event center, a dinner function with a number of guest speakers, headlined by Christoph King, a republican advocate. "But I need answers. And she has them."

Hunter thanked the driver, left him a healthy tip, then exited the car, holding the door open for Esther. She stepped out, dazzling in her red dress and red heels. She smiled as she caught his eyes staring again.

"You hate these things, Tex. A room full of lawyers, raising funds for a conservative political group? Why come now?" Esther asked as she stood on the sidewalk.

"This political fundraiser is organized by Michael Vandenberg, of Vandenberg and Wolfe Family Law Offices, and Christoph King is due to give a speech here."

"A room full of lawyers and business men expressing political view-points? It sounds like a nightmare to me."

"Our goal is to find the connections between Vandenberg and King. We'll ask around and see what these people can feed us. If we get to talk directly to either Vandenberg or King, it's a bonus." Hunter looked up to the grand building. "Christoph King is the man who's offering to buy out Dr. Mackie's company. After Vandenberg approached me the other day, I'm willing to bet King and Vandenberg have very close ties."

"Right. Christoph King wants to buy Dr. Mackie's company." Esther responded, disappointed it was all work and no play. "It's good to hear you're focusing on the Mackie case."

"The people at this function are mostly lawyers. Chicago Law School alumni."

"Of course. They all know Stacey Fulbright, don't they?" Esther drew a deep breath when Hunter didn't answer. "I know Stacey's case is going to take a lot of your focus but don't forget you've still got Dr. Mackie's case on the table. He's a nice guy. I like him. He's sweet. Just an honest, respectful man. The sort of family man that good girls dream about."

"Dr. Mackie is a lovely man." Hunter responded. "Stacey is an old friend—"

"Ex-lover."

Hunter stopped before they walked up the stairs to the entrance. "Is this going to be a problem for you?"

"Of course not." She lied. "Just don't lose sight of what's important. Dr. Mackie has to be your top priority as we head towards the trial. Stacey Fulbright is… well, she's a divorce lawyer who represents victims of domestic abuse. It's admirable, but it's also dangerous. Family and finances are emotionally charged fields, and you're not even going to be the lead on the case. She said she's going to bring in someone else, remember?"

"I need to do what I can to help." Hunter waited a moment, and then walked forward, opening the door for Esther to step through into the building. The lady at the reception desk took their names, checked them off a list, and welcomed them into the conference.

Nestled within the Downtown district, the ballroom in the historic Beaux Arts building had a sophisticated Art Deco interior with a sense of modern style. The function hall felt spacious. It had high ceilings, dotted by five chandeliers, and at the front of the room, there were fifteen round tables, covered by white tablecloths. The stage was set up for speeches, with a large banner displaying the organization they were supporting, and a wide display screen sat to the side of the stage. At the rear of the room, the attendees were mingling, standing around and grabbing any drink that went past. The attendees were well dressed, and mostly an older crowd.

"Our goal is to gather information about Michael Vandenberg and Christoph King. Vandenberg dropped a hint last time I saw him, and I want to know what it's about. But we've only got until the speeches start, because I don't want to listen to these guys talk. I want to slip out the side door before they invite us to sit down." Hunter looked at his watch. "We've got an hour to mingle. Try and find out anything about Vandenberg and King that's not publicly available—where they meet for lunch, where they drink, where they play golf. We're looking for any link we can investigate further, and perhaps later exploit."

As they began to mingle, Esther moved around a

pregnant woman.

"Do you know who you should never argue with?" Esther whispered as she leaned close to Hunter. Hunter shook his head. "A pregnant woman." Esther continued. "They have two brains and you only have one."

"Now is not the time for jokes." Hunter grinned as he took two glasses of champagne from the waitress. He handed one to Esther. "Although, by the look on your face, I can tell you're going to say another one."

"What do you call a cheap circumcision?" Esther's smile was broad as she looked at him. "A rip-off."

Hunter shook his head, his dimples showing as he stepped away from her. They mingled amongst the well-dressed crowd of lawyers for the next hour, listening to well-worn stories of past courtroom battles. Most people knew Vandenberg and King, if only by association, but solid leads weren't forthcoming. As the clock ticked closer to the hour, Hunter directly caught the eye of Michael Vandenberg.

"You got Stacey Fulbright out on bond?" Vandenberg approached Hunter when he caught him looking in his direction. "That woman is a raving lunatic. I read about her case after I saw you. She probably did it to poor Joe Fielding just to prove that men aren't the stronger sex. All those left-wing yuppies are the same. Everything's ok as long as you agree with them. If not, they throw a tantrum and begin a riot."

"She's messed up this time. She's in too deep." Fellow law partner Joanne Wolfe followed Vandenberg into the conversation. Together, they had built Vandenberg and Wolfe Family Law Offices from the ground up, making it one of the city's powerhouse divorce firms with more than fifty lawyers working in their Downtown office. "It's no surprise though. A young girl like that stepped into a dangerous world, and she couldn't handle it. No surprise at all. When you're out there representing divorced couples, emotions run at an all-time high. I'm surprised she made it this long without snapping. There's so much emotional drama in a divorce case. That's why you need thick-skinned people like me, not little girls like Stacey Fulbright. She played with fire, and she got burned."

If she was in a children's movie, Joanne Wolfe would be cast as the witch. It wasn't hard to imagine her on a broomstick, cackling as she spread disharmony to everyone. She had a long nose, weathered skin, and dry, thin hair, with a bad dye job. Some gray hairs were still visible. Her fingers were long, and she often pointed at people when she talked to them.

"You both worked with Joe Fielding, didn't you?" Hunter questioned.

"At our firm, we all did. It's sad, but he's easily replaced," Vandenberg stated without a hint of emotion. "Stacey Fulbright, the murderer. Who would've thought? I guess it's always the ones you don't expect. Just look at your father. Nobody thought a quiet accountant from the suburbs could murder eight girls. It was eight girls, wasn't it? Or was it nine?"

Vandenberg couldn't hide his smile. He thrived on pushing people's buttons. He loved to turn the emotional screws tight, pressuring a person until they snapped.

"I think it was eight. That's what I remember from the media reports." Wolfe replied when Hunter didn't. "His legacy has followed you around like a bad smell, hasn't it? A father's son."

Again, Hunter didn't respond. His focus was on trying to resist crushing the champagne glass in his hand. He was there for information, not a verbal duel with other lawyers.

As partners in a high-valued divorce firm, Michael Vandenberg and Joanne Wolfe had money, power, connections, and an arrogance that outweighed everything else. Wealthy clients meant large payouts, and their firm attracted the best of them.

"But I'm surprised you're here, Tex." Joanne Wolfe added as she sipped on her champagne. "I've never known you to be supportive of these causes. I haven't seen you at a political fundraiser for a long time."

"I vote for policies, not parties. Political parties shouldn't be treated like football teams— you don't choose one and support them for the rest of your life.

Political parties are there to make our country strong—both parties have times where they get it right, and they both have times where they get it wrong. I vote for policy, not party."

"Passionate. I like that." Wolfe said, but the joy didn't reach her face. "But I don't think it's the real reason you're here. I think you're here to gather information about your case with Dr. Mackie. I'll save you the trouble. He was getting divorced, and he saw an opportunity to exploit a young woman. He sexually assaulted her when his wife wouldn't touch him. The problem was that Dr. Mackie chose the wrong woman to try and exploit. Katherine Jennings is a fighter, and she'll take the case all the way."

"And I'm sure your law firm will find a way to profit out of his predicament."

"We're opportunists, Hunter. If we see a chance, we take it." Vandenberg added. "And the opportunity has presented itself. Dr. Mackie can sell his business to Christoph King, and then we can split the proceeds as marital funds. I'm sure if Dr. Mackie chooses to sell, then we can settle the sexual assault case with the girl. He gets to keep his medical license, and everyone is happy. It's that simple."

"Simple." Wolfe smiled. "Just convince Mackie to sell the business."

"You're always talking work, Joanne." Christoph King quipped as he greeted Joanne Wolfe with a small hug, and a kiss on the cheek. "It's good to see you. Thank you for coming."

31

She smiled uncomfortably, before turning to introduce King to Hunter.

"You're the man who's defending that left-wing crazy airhead? That woman cost me a lot of money in my first divorce. Millions, in fact." Christoph King was short and round, and his suit jacket struggled to reach around his waist. He had thin ginger colored hair, and his face was an unhealthy shade of red. Of German descent, his facial features were hard, and his green eyes never settled in one place for long. "I never liked Stacey Fulbright. Nasty left-wing piece of work."

"That doesn't sound like an unbiased opinion." Hunter stepped forward, his height dwarfing Christoph King.

"Didn't say it was." King stepped back. "But I'm not here to argue. As long as you bought a ticket to be here, that's all I care about. The money goes to good causes; you know? More Republicans on the City Council. That's about the best cause a person can have. Chicago is so one sided that it's unhealthy. Balance is needed. I'm not saying our goal is to make it a red state, but everything needs balance. Yin and Yang."

"How did you know Joe Fielding?"

"What is this? A police interview? We're out for a fun night, but there's always one guy who's all work and no play, isn't there?" King laughed with fake charm. "I knew Joe. Our paths had crossed many times, and we go way back. And as much as I'd love to stay and chat about it, I have to take Mr. Vandenberg up to the podium so we can deliver our speeches."

"I'll take any excuse to get away from talking about work," Vandenberg joked.

King laughed as he turned away, followed by a chuckling Vandenberg. People started to take their seats at the tables in preparation for the upcoming speeches.

Hunter looked across to the other side of the room, and caught Esther's eye. He nodded towards the main doors, indicating it was time to make an escape. As Esther stepped through the crowd, Hunter turned back to Wolfe. "And what are you doing here? Have your political opinions changed since last time I saw you?"

"I'm just trying to keep my clients happy. We've all got to play the game. It's not what you know, it's who you know that can pay you the most. And this is my target audience—rich middle-aged men going through a mid-life crisis." Wolfe finished her drink and began to walk towards the tables. After five steps, she stopped and turned back to Hunter. "Enjoy the night, Tex… and be careful on your drive home."

# CHAPTER 5

TEX HUNTER leaned against the wall by the main window in his office, hands in his pockets, staring at the jagged skyline. The view of Chicago's Downtown buildings provided him an anchor, a sense of calmness in his chaotic world. Every week, he ensured he took a moment to turn around and look out the window, and remember how lucky he was. All it took was a moment, a grateful second, to reset.

His hefty mahogany desk had two files laid out in the middle, a computer monitor to one side, and a laptop to the other. Two of his favorite pens rested next to the files, a notepad next to them. His office was spacious, enough room for a couch, a bookshelf, and an area to pace the floor over and over.

"Your twelve o'clock, Dr. Mackie, is here." Esther Wright popped her head in the door, distracting Hunter from his moment of calm.

Hunter nodded his thanks to Esther and turned back to the file on the table. He opened the file, refreshed his memory, and ran his hand through his thick black hair. There was always more than one case, always more than one place to focus his attention.

He hadn't been able to sleep the night before. His mind had been rumbling with the thoughts of Stacey Fulbright's murder charge, and the thought of her ten-year-old son, Noah, sitting through the agony of a felony trial. Noah Fulbright was the same age as Hunter when he watched his father dragged off to prison. Even at that age, even before he was a teenager, Hunter was certain his father was innocent. In the thirty-five years since the conviction for the murders of eight girls, Hunter's opinion hadn't changed. It had only grown stronger.

"Mr. Hunter." Dr. Mackie walked through the office door, closing it softly behind him. "Thank you for seeing me today."

"Dr. Mackie." Hunter shook hands with his client. "Always a pleasure."

Dr. David Mackie's grip was firm. He was well-groomed, mid-forties, and had the look of a man that could run a sub-three-hour marathon. His pressed white shirt sleeves were rolled up to his elbows, exposing his toned forearms, and his black slacks were creaseless. His light brown hair was receding, but his skin was glowing with good health.

"I need this case over with, Mr. Hunter. People are starting to ask questions. Some of my patients have even gone to other clinics. Even though it's all lies, this mud is starting to stick." With graceful movements, he sat down on the chair opposite Hunter's desk. "It shouldn't be this easy to destroy someone's reputation. All this girl has is her word, and she's destroying everything that I've spent my life building."

"That's what I wanted to talk to you about." Hunter sat down in his leather office chair. "We're getting closer to the trial date and the prosecution is beginning to present better deals. They've already spent a lot more time on this case than they would've liked. They want to be out there nailing violent offenders, not dealing with these smaller cases of assault. The closer the trial gets, the better the offer."

Dr. Mackie looked away. "You know how I feel about a deal."

"Hear me out." Hunter turned a file towards Dr. Mackie. "They've put a suspended sentence of two years on the table. You'll still be charged with Criminal Sexual Assault under Illinois Statute Chapter 720, Criminal Offenses 1.20. If you take the deal, your accuser, Miss Katherine Jennings, has also requested a charitable donation to a female crisis center."

"And my doctor's license?"

"That would be up to the medical board, but their history of forgiving sexual assault cases isn't good. It's likely that you would lose your license to practice medicine, at least for a period of time."

"So I'd be forced to retire? All because some girl made up a story to get some money? This is ridiculous. I'm forty-five, and I've dedicated my life to helping others. I don't do this for the pay. I do this because I want to help people." Dr. Mackie stood and began to walk around the room, unable to sit still. "You know where you can put that deal. In more than two decades as a doctor, there hasn't been one other complaint. Not one. You really think at this age, with everything I have, I would risk it all to sexually assault a girl I've never met?"

"This isn't about what I think."

"It is to me. It's about what you think, it's about what my family thinks, what my patients think, and what the community thinks. This is about my reputation. This is twenty-five years of hard work gone. Just like that. Just because of one liar. It shouldn't be like that, Mr. Hunter. That's not how the justice system is supposed to work."

"We're not done yet. We can still take this to trial and prove your innocence."

"And further destroy my reputation? Have my name in the media? I've spent twenty-five years helping people. I've built my reputation from nothing. I had nothing as a kid. I didn't even know my parents, and I lived in foster homes for my entire childhood. But I still made it through medical school, where I worked hard, and I've worked hard every day since. All that work, gone in an instant." Dr. Mackie scoffed as he stopped pacing the floor. He leaned his weight on the back of the chair. "I'm sure the witnesses all know each other. It's too much of a coincidence. Did she refuse another polygraph test?"

"She did." Hunter nodded. "But she's well within her rights to do that. She's claimed the recounting of the day will only add to her trauma."

"If she just took a polygraph test, this would all be over. Can we force her to do it?"

"Unfortunately not."

"The polygraph test would prove she's lying." The frustration was eating at him. Over the past five months, his hair had become grayer, the bags under his eyes larger, and the headaches were now a constant in his life. "I've gone over that day so many times. None of it makes sense. This girl comes into my clinic, says that she has a rash on her inner thigh, and then accuses me of touching her inappropriately. Says I fondled her breasts, and digitally raped her. I didn't do it. I couldn't have. I don't have it in me to do that. You believe me, don't you?"

"I wouldn't have taken the case otherwise." Hunter said. "There are too many coincidences in the circumstances. The accuser was a new client, the first witness was also a new client, and the second witness was a delivery driver, who was also delivering products for the first time. They're all new to your clinic. There's no evidence, there's no video footage, and there's no other claims. It's all too clean and all too rehearsed. I believe you, Dr. Mackie, but this is a court case. This is about what we can make the jury believe."

"Then what do we do?"

"We have to prove your innocence in court. That's the challenge. I have no doubt you're telling the truth when you say you didn't sexually assault the girl, but we have to prove that you're being set up by the accuser and the witnesses."

"I can't believe my wife would do this." He mumbled. "I loved that woman, and now she wants to destroy me. She set me up. All for the mighty dollar."

"We can't prove that yet."

He blinked back the tears in his eyes as he tilted his head back. He'd thought Sarah was the one to stand by his side forever. He didn't worry about the ten-year age gap between them. Age was only a number to him. He dreamed of having a family. Four kids. Two boys, two girls. When Sarah found out she couldn't have children, she was devastated. It destroyed her, and in turn, tore their relationship apart. He did all he could to support her, but she pushed him away. Every time she looked at her husband, she saw her own failures. He did everything he could, offering to adopt instead, being her shoulder to cry on, always being there for her, but she couldn't move past it.

"My divorce lawyer said she set this up, but he's not very good at explaining things to me. He starts talking on one subject and then changes to another and then another and then another, and never gets back to the original topic."

"Then I'll explain it clearly for you." Hunter leaned forward. "Under Illinois divorce law, the medical clinic and the company you own are a 'separate property' or 'non-marital property,' because you started the company before the marriage began. Because she didn't work in the company, or assist in any way, it means the company isn't included in the divorce settlement. It belongs solely to you. The company, which includes ownership of the building and land, is worth more than $10 million. Your ex-wife can't touch this company as part of the divorce settlement. However, if the business is sold during the marriage, then the money becomes 'marital property,' which means she has claim to the funds."

"Which is why her divorce lawyers are so desperate to force me to sell, isn't it?"

"If Vandenberg and Wolfe Family Law Offices make an extra $5 million in a divorce settlement, then their bonus fee structure rises to $250,000. It may sound like a lot to pay the lawyers, but they're proving their worth."

"By setting me up."

"By pressuring you to sell the business. They could be opportunistic, and have seen the chance to force the sale when you were charged with sexual assault. We don't have any evidence about who has set you up."

Dr. Mackie's fists gripped together. The frustration was clear. He moved to Hunter's bookshelf, looking at the photos on the middle shelf. There was a hand full of pictures, snapshots of Hunter on international vacations and at famous locations, but only one family photo—a photo of his convicted serial killer father, laughing as he hugged his three children. The photo was taken a year before his father was sent to prison.

"I've worked my entire life serving others." Dr. Mackie stared at Hunter's family photo. "I treat older veterans for free and I treat the elderly at a reduced rate. I thought I was doing the right thing by working hard and helping my community, but while I was helping others, my wife was more interested in getting with a twenty-five-year-old kid. I don't understand why she's fighting this divorce so hard—she's the one who cheated. She's the one who wants the divorce so she can be with her twenty-five-year-old boy-toy." His face strained with pain. "And now I've got lawyers coming out of my ears. I've already had a meeting with my divorce lawyer this morning, and now I'm meeting with a criminal lawyer. I'm going to have to work until I'm a hundred and five to pay you guys off."

Hunter nodded, unsure of how to respond. When he was at Law School, his advisor recommended Hunter take a course in improving his 'bedside manner.' Show more care, his advisor said. Let the client know you're committed to the case. Don't be cold and aloof. In his first years as a criminal defense lawyer, Hunter tried to show more emotion in his client meetings, but it felt uncomfortable and forced. As he became older, he left that side of things to others. He was a lawyer, he reasoned, not a psychologist.

"We've looked for any connection between the

witnesses and Vandenberg and Wolfe Family Law Offices, but at this point, we haven't found anything." Hunter moved the focus back to the case. "The witnesses also don't know each other and have never crossed paths. If the witnesses all knew each other, or they all had interactions with Vandenberg and Wolfe Family Law Offices, then yes, perhaps we would have a case to argue. But right now, we have two witnesses, one male and one female, claiming they saw you grab the defendant's breasts, whisper in her ear, and then fondle her privates. And Miss Jennings appears to be a solid witness herself. She appears credible."

"I didn't do it." Dr. Mackie sat down and put his head in his hands. "I didn't touch her in that way. Why doesn't anyone understand that? All the witnesses are lying through their teeth. The delivery guy said he looked into the room from outside, and the blinds were open, but if I'm with a client, I never leave my blinds open. Never. The courtyard looks into my office, so I just wouldn't do that. In my five years treating patients in that room, I've never once had the blinds open."

"If we can prove the blinds were closed, then we can discount his witness statement. We'll look into it." Hunter made a note on his pad. "Apart from the first witness, Ms. Perkins, were there any other new patients that day?"

"One more. Booked in twenty minutes after Miss Jennings. I've never had three new patients in one day before. Never."

"I didn't see the third new girl on the appointment list?"

"Her appointment was cancelled at the start of the day. She didn't show up."

"And the other patient's name?"

"Becky Bennett." Dr. Mackie said. "I'll have my secretary forward her details to you."

Hunter made notes on his legal pad. "We'll look into it. See if she's the link that connects all these new patients together. We'll do our best to find something."

Hunter paused for a moment. He hated taking on sexual assault cases, he hated the idea of pressuring the victim on the stand, but Dr. Mackie had presented a good argument when he asked Hunter to defend him. Something didn't add up in the case. Over the last five months, after reviewing all the evidence, Hunter was sure Dr. Mackie was innocent. "If we had evidence that it was a set-up, then we could build a solid defense. Apart from your soon-to-be ex-wife, is there anyone out there who would want to see your doctor's license revoked?"

"Christoph King."

"Because he's trying to buy the business?"

"Not just that. We've had some loud arguments, and he hates me. He's the owner of the medical clinics which are popping up everywhere. GP Extra, the business calls themselves. He wanted to buy my clinic a year ago, and I refused. He put a lot of money on the table for me to sell, fifteen percent more than the value price, but I told him I wasn't interested, because if he gets my clinic, then he gets a monopoly on the local area and can raise the prices through the roof. I have some elderly patients who won't be able to afford it, and they'll have to travel an hour for their regular care. That's why I didn't sell to him. He thinks being a doctor is all about money. That's all these clinics are to the businessmen—money makers. They don't care about the patients."

Hunter picked up his pen, ready to write. "It might be the start of something to build upon. It could be something we use in court."

"But be careful." Dr. Mackie said. "I've had some blow ups with him. He's not a nice guy, and he's known to be merciless with anyone that dares to challenge him."

# CHAPTER 6

EVEN ON the sunniest of days, the office of criminal psychiatrist Patrick Hunter had little natural light. The blinds were rarely opened, and along with the dark colors of the wooden walls and the leather couch, it created a cave-like atmosphere. The room smelled like a vintage furniture store—a combination of aged mahogany, used leather, and old books. This wasn't a place to party, Patrick would say, it was a place to work, to focus, and meet with clients. The bookshelf on the left wall was packed with books on criminal psychiatry, from the floor to the ceiling, all except for the middle row. That row was reserved for his prized possession—a signed 1985 Chicago Bears football. Patrick loved his Bears. The toughest team, the grit, the determination, the defense. He didn't care if they weren't winning all the time, as long as they were playing with a tough defensive attitude.

He looked at his watch: 5:55pm. It was unlike his younger brother, Tex, to be late, and he was twenty-five minutes past their arranged time. When Tex hustled into the office, Patrick was sitting at his desk, feet up on the table, reading a well-worn and dog-eared copy of Catch-22 by Joseph Heller.

"What's your excuse?" Patrick greeted his brother, not raising his eyes from the book.

"Traffic." Hunter replied as he closed the door behind him. "I don't know which cars to trust."

Patrick squinted at the reference, unsure what it meant. He placed his book down, stood, walked to the back of the room, and removed two whiskey glasses from the cabinet. He poured a healthy amount in each and handed his brother one.

Hunter smiled, sat down, and then looked around the office. "How's work?"

"Today, I had a potential serial killer sitting just where you are now." Patrick said. "She was one of the few people to genuinely scare me."

"She?"

"And only twenty-one. She's been having re-occurring urges to kill many people. She's never done anything wrong, never anything violent, but she's having murderous delusions as the result of heightened anxiety." Patrick sat down and kicked his feet back up on the desk again. "I feel sorry for kids these days. Their anxiety is heightened everywhere they turn. They're constantly told the world is burning, political rivals have to be their enemies, and everyone else seems to have a perfect life, thanks to the wonders of social media. This generation of kids is going to have a meltdown in a few years, and it's not going to be pretty."

"Looks like you won't be out of a job anytime

soon." Hunter said. "How's my nephew?"

"Max is good." Patrick smiled. "He's worked his way up from being a cleaner on one of the tourist boats that cruise up the river, to a tour guide. And now he's studying for his boat license. Thinks he'll even be a captain one day soon. He's got that good Hunter work ethic."

"Maybe Natalie does as well."

Patrick paused and stared at his whiskey. It never took his younger brother long to turn the conversation to their dysfunctional family. Patrick would rather bury those references, forget his father ever existed, leave the past for the history books, but his brother never let it go. After a while of staring at his glass, Patrick took a long sip of whiskey. "I know how much this is your life goal, Tex, and it's the only reason I'm helping you find her. I'm only doing this to help you, not that old criminal behind bars."

"That old criminal is your father."

"And a convicted serial killer." Patrick took his feet off his desk and leaned forward. "You tell me what you have first and then I'll let you know where I'm at with Natalie."

"Our lead on the Cinco Casino appears to be correct. It was an underground casino in Wicker Park during the eighties. It was run by the mob, but South Americans reportedly came in and took it over in '88. Things got violent, a turf war, so the South Americans shut it down. And when I say it was violent, I mean, very violent. Twenty-five people went missing in the area over a fifteen-month period. People got scared, rumors of beheadings, and bodies being dumped in the Chicago river in slabs of concrete. That fifteen-month period of violence was the fifteen months before our father was arrested for murdering eight girls. It's not a coincidence. There was talk that the gangs moved in when people started to refuse to pay their debts. People were being killed, knocked off for owing money."

"Any official record of this?"

"Nothing in the police files."

"And?" Patrick pressed.

"And this could be it. Don't you see the connection? Our father is innocent, and he was set up by the South Americans. This is the lead we've waited thirty-five years for."

"What are you suggesting? He was set-up because of his gambling debts?"

"Maybe our father owed money to the casino. Maybe they set him up to take the fall for the killings. We need to find Natalie and find out what she knows. We know she wants to help—that's why she sent all the evidence back to Chicago."

"But it's been years since she sent anything." Patrick sighed and stared into his whiskey again. He drew a long breath and then leaned back in his chair. "I spoke to Alfred yesterday."

"Alfred? You're not even going to call him 'Dad?'"

"I haven't called him 'Dad' in many years." Patrick shrugged. "You can call him that if you like, but he stopped being my father a long time ago. He's old, Tex. He's aging very quickly, and the cancer is eating him away. He's barely a shell of a man anymore."

"Even more reason why we need the truth now." Hunter held his eyes on his brother. "You haven't been in to see him at Cook County Prison in more than half a decade. Why now? Why the trip to see him?"

"I wanted to see his reaction when I told him I'd found Natalie. And I watched him very carefully, Tex. That's what I do. I read people's reactions, and their responses, and the way they hold themselves. That's my job and that's what I study."

"And?"

"And he was scared, Tex. I'd never seen him scared. Even when they convicted him, even when they denied his appeals, I never saw fear. Disappointment, yes, but never fear. When I mentioned Natalie's name, he looked anxious. And when I told him we had found her, and we were going to talk to her, it was pure fear I saw in his eyes." Patrick looked away. "And then the old man pleaded with me to leave it alone. He was begging me not to go and see her. He begged me to never mention her name again."

"Why?"

"He didn't answer another question from me. Told me to leave it all alone."

"Why do you think he did that? As a psychiatrist, why do you think he was telling you that?"

"I don't know." Patrick drew a long breath. "But I know he doesn't want us to question her."

Hunter stood and walked over to the only family photo in Patrick's office—a photo of Patrick with his arm around his son, Max. They looked happy—smiling, and carefree. Happiness wasn't a word Hunter associated with family. "Natalie knows something about what happened to those murdered girls. She sent information that said she saw someone near the site where the girls were buried. Her voice wasn't heard in court. If we can get her to talk, then we have a chance at proving his innocence."

"Tex, there's something else. I think you'll need to sit down for this one."

"What is it?"

Patrick moved to the filing cabinet on the left-hand side of the room. He picked out the first file and flung it onto the table towards Hunter. It landed facing him. Hunter walked to the table, opened the file, leaning forward as he read the first page of a transcript. "What is this?" he whispered.

"It's our sister's criminal record." Patrick said without a hint of emotion. "Five charges laid against her, five trips to prison as a Mexican citizen. The reports show she applied for citizenship the second she landed as an eighteen-year-old, and then spent the next ten years in and out of some of Mexico's worst prisons. These aren't minor criminal charges against her. This is serious violent crime."

"All these charges are more than twenty years

old." Hunter started to process the information. "Come on, Patrick. We were all angry after our father's trial. I got into a lot of fights at school, and even you got into fights at college. You, the pacifist of the family, were getting into fights. It was hard not to be angry after what we went through."

"I agree there would've been a lot of confusion for her, especially as she fled the country. The transition to another country would've only added to her bewilderment. New culture, new foods, not knowing the local customs. It would've been hard, but it was hard for all of us. We were all confused. We were all scared. We went from a peaceful and average life, to one full of hate and turmoil. And maybe that confusion manifested itself as violence. However, these charges are more than just little scuffles. These violent assaults are bad enough to land her in a Mexican prison, and I doubt these were the only times she was violent. These were just the times she was caught."

Hunter sat down and read the reports again. "Her last trip to prison is more than fifteen years ago. That's a lifetime ago. I'm sure she's a different person now."

"Can't you see it, Tex? It's right in front of you. Our father was protecting someone when they charged him with killing eight girls. You said it yourself. You said Alfred was innocent, and you were sure he was protecting someone else. Natalie was sending evidence back to Chicago because she knew the truth. She was trying to get her father out of prison because she knew he was innocent. She disappeared off the face of the planet, and nobody could find her."

"What are you saying?" Hunter shook his head.

"Alfred has spent his life in prison for someone else's crimes. After talking to him, I finally agree with you. There's a possibility Alfred may be innocent. I can see that now. He's told you so many times to leave this alone, and you know he's holding something back from you. Why would he do that, Tex?"

Hunter didn't respond as he stared at the files in front of him.

"Natalie has been to prison five times for violent assault. Five times. All five occasions were in Mexico City. Badly beating up people in bars, in homes, or on the street. Really badly. Two of the attacks are on men who are noted as being larger than her and she still managed to put them both in the hospital. She's broken jaws, broken bones, and crushed a woman's hand with a hammer. This is a woman full of rage, fury and anger. And perhaps, just perhaps…" Patrick stared at his brother.

"Don't say it." Hunter shook his head.

"You have to see it, Tex. It's right in front of you."

"Don't say it, Patrick."

"You have to acknowledge the evidence. It's there. It's all there on the page. Look at it. It's the explanation we all missed. This is it."

"No. It can't be true."

"Tex." Patrick took a deep breath and walked around the table. He leaned on the table next to his younger brother. "There's a chance that Natalie Hunter is the killer our father was trying to protect."

# CHAPTER 7

IT TOOK Hunter more than an hour to roll out of bed the next morning. Five aspirin, along with five glasses of water, followed. Even after half a bottle of whiskey had disappeared the night before, Hunter found it hard to sleep. He needed to forget his feelings, forget the thunderous thoughts rolling around in his head, forget the theory that his sister could be a serial killer. He wanted to move away from the ideas his brother presented, but the theory fit.

And what if Patrick was right? As a criminal psychiatrist, could he be correct in his assessment of their sister? And where did that leave Hunter's fight for justice? Where did it leave everything he'd fought so hard for?

Hunter had spent most of his adult life fighting for his father's freedom. Fighting for the truth. He knew his father was innocent. He always knew it. His father had refused to plead guilty to the crimes, but also refused to answer questions about the events that took place over those days. In hindsight, Hunter remembered that he also refused to talk about Natalie. Was his father doing it to protect his daughter? And what if he was? Could Hunter expose his sister? He didn't know the answer to the question, and there was only one avenue to the truth.

He had to speak to Natalie.

Despite his reluctance, Patrick agreed with the idea. They knew she was working in a café in the coastal Mexican town of Puerto Vallarta. The woman had spent her life away from Chicago, and Hunter doubted whether she'd be open about discussing the case with them over the phone. In fact, he was sure she'd disappear the second she heard they were looking for her. The brothers needed to travel to Mexico and surprise her. It was the only way.

After a slow morning, Hunter parked his car on the side of the road, took another aspirin and rubbed his temples, before he picked up his briefcase and exited the car. The grass was freshly cut next door, and the smell wafted down the street. Hunter took a moment to take it in before he sneezed.

Stacey Fulbright's family home in Naperville hadn't changed in the five years since he was last there. Nice suburb, nice lawn, nice trees. They had nice neighbors and a nice community. The local school was nice. The shopkeepers were nice. The police were nice. The roads were nice, the gardens were nice, the smells were nice. Everything around him was the same, safe, comfortable living. It was a formula sold to the masses as a suburban dream, but it was also Hunter's idea of a nightmare. He needed the drama of the city. The energy created by millions of people crammed together. The rush. The fear. The heightened awareness. It fueled him. Perhaps one day, he reasoned, when it was time to slow down and smell the roses, the suburbs would appeal to him.

He knocked twice on the door, careful not to make too much noise for his aching head. It wasn't long before Carl answered.

"Thanks for coming out here, Mr. Hunter." Carl looked up to Hunter's tall figure and then offered his hand to shake. "Please, come in, Stacey's waiting in the kitchen. She's refusing to leave the house. She's even refusing to go into the garden. Perhaps you can talk some sense into her? Tell her it's not that bad? I'm going to take the kids out while you guys discuss the case."

Carl turned and called out for the children, before leading Hunter into the dining room. On the hardwood dining room table, piles of papers were spread across the surface. Stacey sat at one end, still in her dressing gown, hair disheveled, and looking even paler than she had been days before. She barely looked up as Hunter entered the room.

"Can I make you a cup of coffee?" Carl offered as the kids hurried down the stairs. Hunter accepted.

"Thank you for coming out." Stacey stared at the table; her arms folded across her chest. "I'm sorry I couldn't make it into the office. I'm... I don't want to leave the house."

"I understand." Hunter said as he took a warm cup of coffee from Carl. "Thank you for the coffee."

Carl kissed his wife on the side of the head, and then called out for the kids again. Noah and Zoe ran into the room, hugged their mother, and then raced out of the door to buy ice-cream with their father.

"Noah and Zoe don't know yet." Stacey said after the front door slammed closed. "Although I'm sure Noah is aware that things are different. He's a smart boy and I'm sure he knows something is happening. The secret must've gotten out in the community by now. People talk out here. Everyone is in everyone's business."

"That's human nature." Hunter placed his briefcase on the table, then sat down. "I was the same age as Noah when my father's trial began. It was hard for me to avoid it, almost impossible. Even without the internet, I was aware of everything that was happening around that time. Ten-year olds are smart, and you won't be able to hide it from him much longer. It's time to talk to him."

Stacey looked up. "And you turned out alright, I guess."

"Maybe." Hunter replied. "Noah needs to hear it from you, rather than his friends at school. People will be talking in the community and it's better you tell him what's happening. You don't want him coming home and asking strange questions, and you don't want him to start believing the rumors."

She nodded. As much as she wanted to protect her children from the drama, she knew she couldn't. She couldn't keep them locked up until the trial. But telling the children, telling them that she was about to go through a criminal trial, would make it all seem so real.

"The prosecution has made a new allegation—Joe Fielding attacked you in the same parking lot a number of weeks ago, and you made a complaint to the police, however you later withdrew the allegation, perhaps when he tried to bribe you."

She looked up in shock. "What? They think that was the same guy? How do they know that? The police asked me to withdraw the statement, but I refused. I didn't withdraw the complaint."

"The form is signed by you stating that you wished for your complaint to be withdrawn."

"I knew the cop who took the report was dodgy. I knew it because he didn't want to take the report in the first place. He said there was nothing they could do because there was no evidence. He refused to even fill in a form. I forced him to take the complaint, but he protested and said that it would ruin his arrest figures. He knew they couldn't solve it." She shook her head. She then looked at Hunter. "How did they know it was Joe Fielding?"

"They don't, but that's the theory they've put on the table. You claimed that an unknown assailant grabbed your behind in the parking lot five weeks earlier, and you then carried the letter opener in your bag after work every night to protect yourself."

"That's not true, but if that's their theory, then it's self-defense. The case is closed."

"We could run with that, but they're going for excessive force. There were no marks on you when they arrested you, no signs of a struggle, and given there were five stab wounds in Fielding's neck, you're possibly looking at murder two. If they successfully argue that you approached him first, or arranged to meet him, then you could still be looking at murder one."

"This is ridiculous." She turned to the window. "I didn't touch him."

"Joe Fielding worked as a private investigator, and he was sniffing around another case of mine before his death. His name came up in a sexual assault case I'm dealing with. I already had a file on him, and it appears he wasn't a nice man." Hunter opened his briefcase, withdrew a file, and placed it on the table. "The police tech team have pulled apart Fielding's phone, and looked at the files stored on it. There's evidence he took photos inside your office."

"What?" She turned back to Hunter.

Hunter removed a photo from the file and slid it across to Stacey. Her face was white with shock.

"That's my office. When was he in there?"

"The timestamp on the photo suggests he was in your office a week before his death. In the early hours of the morning."

She bit her lip. "What were the other photos of?"

"The police tech team is trying to find that out. Their timeframe for finding the deleted files could be as long as months, and it might delay the trial. Do you have any idea what he wanted to talk to you about?"

Stacey shook her head as she moved to the kitchen counter. She removed a knife from the top drawer and took an onion from the fridge. With fine precision, she started slicing the onion, sliding the knife through the vegetable with ease. Her focus was impressive. "The kids still need to eat," she explained. "I'm trying my best to go on with life, even with this murder charge hanging over my head. I haven't left the house in days, but I'm doing what I can." She put the sliced onion into a slow cooker and removed another one from the fridge. "I have no idea why Joe Fielding was in my office. All I know is that he contacted me two weeks ago and said he had information to sell me. I wasn't interested in it, but he was persistent."

The kitchen was expansive, sterile, and filled with every gadget imaginable. The butler's pantry to the side of the room only added to the sense of suburban bliss. The smell of cut onions started to fill the room, and Hunter could feel an itch in the back of his throat. He watched the knife as Stacey moved it. It was sharp. "Why did Joe Fielding come to you to sell information? Why not someone else?"

"I've been trying to think about that. The only reason I could come up with is that it was related to one of my cases. He was working in Vandenberg and Wolfe Family Law Offices. I've dealt with them so many times on divorce cases."

"Including Christoph King's first divorce."

She stopped slicing the onion, staring into the distance. She drew a long breath before she continued. "King's second divorce was represented by Joanne Wolfe, not his first. His first divorce cost him five million and the divorces since have barely cost him a cent. I represented King's first ex-wife, Cassandra Mills, and he hired some young kid fresh out of law school, looking to save money, but I tore the kid apart. The poor guy didn't stand a chance. King used to beat his first wife badly, and we had police reports and lots of photos. He even beat her in public. The brutality of his attacks were quite confronting, and the female judge sided with us. We got way more from the judge than we should've, and even I thought it was unreasonable. But that was my job. I had to do what I was employed to do. And King... well, King never let it go. I got death threats, people crashing into my car 'accidently,'" she made air quotes with her fingers to strengthen her point, "and I was mugged in broad daylight. I'm sure it was all organized by King. He was so vindictive. I went to the police over and over, but I couldn't prove anything."

"I've got my investigator looking into King."

Stacey blinked back a tear, looking away from Hunter. She wiped her eyes with the back of her sleeve. "It's the onions."

"Of course."

"Tex," She paused and composed herself. "John C. Clarke has agreed to take the case over. I think

61

you're too close to this to defend me. John's a great criminal lawyer, and this is more up his alley. You're amazing, Tex, but I don't think you're the right lawyer for this case."

Hunter nodded, unable to hide his disappointment.

"Thank you for everything." She continued. "But this is my life, and it's too much of a gamble for you to work this. You're too close. I have to do what's best for my family."

"I understand." The stoic look on his face returned. "I can help your new lawyer. Get him to call my office and come in for a chat. I'm happy to help in any way possible. I'll sit second chair and support him."

"Thanks, Tex. Thanks for everything. Send me the invoice for your work so far, and we'll settle up."

"You're not paying a cent to me. I always said I would help you if you needed it, and I'm a man of my word. If you need me, I'm here."

She offered a smile. "John's first suggestion was to drag this case out as long as possible to put pressure on the prosecution. He wants them to make a mistake, slip up, and then he'll push for self-defense. He thinks the longer we drag this out, the longer we have to build our defense case. The State may even get to the point where they drop the charges." She looked around the kitchen. "But I don't know how long I can do this. I'm trying to pretend that everything is normal, but I can't even leave the house.

I've already had suicidal thoughts. I don't want to put my family through any of this, Tex. I don't want to put Noah through what you went through—years and years of turmoil. I saw the effect it had on you when we dated. You might be good now, but that damage marks a child for life."

"I got through it, and so will Noah. He's got a good family around him." Hunter said. "I'll help John research the case and I'll get my best investigator on this. We'll get this sorted out, Stacey. Trust me."

# CHAPTER 8

INVESTIGATOR RAY Jones grunted as he reached into the engine of his truck and moved the wrench with great force. His shoulders tensed, his face squeezed tight, and his butt cheeks clenched. Sweat dripped off his brow, his teeth ground together, and his muscles strained. Once he had moved the nut to its tightest point, he squirmed out from under the engine and saw Tex Hunter standing near him.

"Why don't you let yourself in?" Jones smiled. He stood and brushed his thick forearm across his brow.

"I rang the doorbell." Hunter replied. "But nobody answered."

"I was under the car, changing the oil and giving my baby some new parts. I could do with a hand, but you're a bit overdressed to work on an engine."

"As Mark Twain said—clothes make the man. Naked people have little or no influence in society."

Jones laughed as he grabbed a towel off the back of a chair and cleaned the grease off his hands. The house in South Kenwood was pleasant, and although small, it was a source of pride for Jones. The two-bedroom home had a narrow yard, a one-car garage, and a patio just large enough to shelter his outdoor equipment—a barbeque, a plastic table, five plastic chairs, an exercise bike, and a set of weights. Jones had parked his truck over the grassed area in the yard, which was bathed in sunlight, to replace a number of parts.

"How's the new girlfriend?" Hunter asked.

"She dumped me."

"This one didn't even last a month. What happened?"

"She said I ruined her birthday. I don't know how I did that. I mean, I didn't even know it was her birthday." Jones laughed and shrugged. "And she kept complaining. She said that I had two major faults—I don't listen and... something else."

The six-foot-four African-American private investigator spent a lot of time in bars, gyms, and barber shops. He was a scholar of the streets. He spent time on the corners, walking the blocks, hanging out in parking lots. He knew where trouble was and he knew how to stop it. A huge man, his reputation preceded him most places he went.

"How did it go with finding your sister?" Jones asked as he moved a box of tools into the back corner of the patio. "Any luck?"

"Patrick got a lead in Mexico, and we're going to fly down and talk to her but it's complicated. She's spent a lot of years in prison and we're not sure of the person she is today. She hasn't been to prison in fifteen years, but we don't know what we're walking into. I don't even know if she'll talk to us."

"What'd she go to prison for?"

"Violent assault."

Jones froze as he closed the hood of the truck.

"I can see what you're thinking." Hunter responded. "But we don't know anything yet. Before we make any assumptions, we need to talk to her. We have to find out what she knows."

"And if it isn't good news? What do you do then?"

"I don't know." Hunter shook his head. There weren't many times when the expectation of the future overwhelmed him, but he'd barely been able to turn his thoughts off. Work was his only escape. Any hint of emotional turmoil in his life was usually met with a change in focus. "I need to talk to you about Dr. Mackie's assault case. Any luck on a connection between the witnesses and the other new patient, Becky Bennett?"

"Do you know what people say about cases like this? It's mission impossible. These witnesses have zero connections between them. I've looked at their phone records, their internet search history, their jobs, their families, their friends, their family's friends, their friends' friends... and I've got nothing. Not a thing. Nothing on social media, no overlapping locations, no jobs at the same times, no places near each other's addresses. Not even a restaurant in the same neighborhood. Nothing at all. It looks like the lives of these witnesses have never even crossed the same path."

Hunter took off his jacket, rolled up his sleeves and loosened his tie, before picking up one of the plastic chairs, and placing it in the sunshine. He loved the February sun in Chicago. There was a romantic glow to it. In his vacations further south, he found the sun had more burn, leaving a sting on the skin, but the further north he went, the softer it felt.

"Dr. Mackie is determined to fight this sexual assault charge." Hunter squinted as he looked skyward. "In terms of the charge, it's on the lower end of the spectrum and he could even escape prison time, but he doesn't want to admit to something he didn't do, and the prosecution isn't going easy on him, given the current political environment. They have a defendant who's willing to testify and two witnesses. It's a strong case, but they've got nothing other than the word of these people. No physical evidence and no video footage. No history of abuse. No other accusations. Nothing. If we can discredit these witnesses, or find a connection that links them together, then they don't have a case."

"You've got an alleged victim testifying, and two people who claim to have seen exactly the same thing. Without a connection between the alleged victim and the witnesses, it'll be hard to win."

"And that's the issue. It's exactly the same thing. Their reports are almost word for word the same, and their description is almost textbook. There are some sentences that are identical in the reports. When two people witness something, they see it through different eyes and different angles. There would naturally be discrepancies in what they saw, but in this case, there aren't any."

"So you really think that someone set this up? It's quite the scheme, if they have."

"It's hard to defend against, isn't it?" Hunter said as he leaned back in the chair, almost forcing it to buckle. "There's no proof other than what was said, and what was said seems to be well-rehearsed. What we know is that the accuser was a new patient, as was one of the witnesses, and the second witness, a delivery driver, was also making his first delivery to the clinic. None of them had interacted with Dr. Mackie before."

"And you think it's because of the divorce case?"

"It has to be. That makes the most sense. A large settlement for this case would force Dr. Mackie to sell the clinic. If Dr. Mackie doesn't sell the clinic, then it can't be included in the divorce settlement. But if he's forced to sell it, if he's forced to offload the company, then there's an extra ten million in the pot for the divorce. And you can be guaranteed the wife would want more than half of that."

"And the buyer?"

"Christoph King, a former corporate lawyer turned businessman. Owns a lot of medical clinics across the country. I need you to look into his previous investments, and see if anything similar has ever happened elsewhere. King acquired a lot of medical clinics quickly, more than fifty in the last five years. I want you to look into them and see if there's any element of foul play or undue pressure in any of the sales." Hunter leaned back and closed his eyes, letting the vitamin D wash into his skin. "I have another case, not one that I'm working on directly, but I'm going to ask for your help on it. Have you ever heard of a guy named Joe Fielding?"

"Sure have. I've known Joe Fielding for decades, but I can't say we're friends. He's a fellow private investigator but not one that I would recommend. Sleazy type. Has a lot of gang connections. And he's well known as a very paranoid man. He's perhaps the most paranoid guy I've ever met." Jones picked up his cell phone from the table. "I've got his phone number somewhere."

"You won't be able to contact him."

Jones squinted his response.

"He was murdered last week." Hunter was blunt. "He was the victim in the Stacey Fulbright murder case that I'm working on. Stabbed in the neck five times."

"Joe Fielding is dead?" Jones looked around his yard. "Well, I know you shouldn't speak ill of the deceased, but that man was a racist, sleazy, slob who had no sense of morals."

"What do you know about his personal life?"

"Not much." Jones walked through the glass sliding door into his home, leaving it open as he stepped into his kitchen. He took a pre-mixed protein shake out of the fridge, and walked back out the door, shaking it up and down. "Want one?"

Hunter shook his head.

"Joe Fielding worked for a lot of different people. A freelancer private investigator. A lot of things were rumored to be off the books so he didn't have to pay tax." Jones knocked back the protein shake in large gulps. "He had a small office out in Logan Square but most of his clients were businesses like insurance companies, family law firms, and business investment firms. He was married to one of the lawyers once, but they weren't married for long. He used her connections to make contacts, and build his business profile."

"Do you remember who the lawyer was?"

"Sure do. I remember her because the marriage was such a mismatch—he was a dirty PI, and she was a high-flying lawyer." Jones sat down next to Hunter. "Her name was Joanne Wolfe."

# CHAPTER 9

THE OFFICES on the fifty-first floor of a skyscraper on North Wacker Drive in The Loop, Chicago, were a testament to the success of Vandenberg and Wolfe Family Law Firm. The moment a potential client stepped out of the elevator, it was hard not to be in awe of the smooth-running machine. The reception area was humming with activity, well-dressed lawyers coming and going, and phones ringing off the hook. Behind the reception were the offices and meeting rooms, all with views down the Chicago River or over the nearby city. The views were impressive enough to be a tourist attraction. But the fifty first floor was a front— holding only the spotless reception area, the offices of the senior lawyers, and the conference rooms where all client meetings were held. Well below them, on floors five to nine, the machine churned. It was where the majority of work was done—where the blinds were closed, papers were prepared and filed, the calls made and answered, and junior lawyers sweated deadlines.

Tex Hunter strode past the reception area on the

fifty-first floor without stopping. His determined laser focus forced people to step out of his way.

"You didn't tell me everything." Hunter swung open the door to the private office of Joanne Wolfe. "You lied to me."

Joanne Wolfe was sitting behind her desk in her office and looked up from the file she was working on, pen in hand. Floor to ceiling windows were behind her, framing the stunning views to the west of the city. Expensive artwork lined the left and right walls, and the office had enough space for two couches, a coffee table, and a whiteboard. Her office was spacious, well-lit, and modern, but it felt soulless and empty.

"Tex Hunter." She said. "I don't remember seeing you on my appointment list today."

Wolfe's secretary trailed behind, panting. "Sorry, Ms. Wolfe." She said at the door. "He just walked through here. I asked him to stop, but he didn't listen."

Hunter kept his stare directed at Wolfe. "You were married to Joe Fielding."

Wolfe raised her eyebrows, scoffed, and looked at her secretary. She waved her secretary away, who then kept her head down and closed the door as she left.

"Why don't you have a seat?" Wolfe pointed to the chair opposite her desk. "Coffee?"

"Joe Fielding." Hunter grunted as he walked up to her desk. "How long were you married?"

"Not long." Wolfe responded. "He was my second

husband, but it was more of a fling than a marriage. It was more than a decade ago. We rushed into it, and it only lasted five months. I didn't love him, he was a charming sleaze that promised the world, and I fell for the act. He love-bombed me, and as soon as we were married, he ignored me. We divorced amicably, and I knew he was a good private investigator, so I recommended him to some of the lawyers who worked here. I had no problem with him working for other lawyers in the firm. Vandenberg did a lot of work with him, as did East, one of the junior lawyers. Once we divorced, I had no feelings for the man."

"You hated Fielding enough to murder him." Hunter baited her.

"Settle down. Let's not jump to any ridiculous conclusions without evidence." She held her hands out. "I'll tell you what you want to know, but first, I want to know why you're not taking self-defense on this. Claim it was excessive use of force?"

"Stacey says she's innocent. That's her right to dispute it."

"And you? Why aren't you convincing her to negotiate a deal for self-defense? Say Fielding attacked her first? He was a violent guy, and I'm sure you'll find a lot of witnesses who would be willing to testify to that. With the strength of their testimonies, it would be hard to argue Stacey acted in any other manner than self-defense. Even with excessive force, it's manslaughter and perhaps a year, maybe two, with a suspended sentence."

"We know Fielding broke into Stacey's office a week before he died. He took photos in her office. That wasn't a coincidence. And if we find out your family law firm instructed him to do that, you'll feel the full force of the law. Firms like this don't recover from charges like that."

She looked away, towards the photo of her daughter, who was the result of a one-night stand. Her daughter had seen her through three marriages, many shallow relationships, and years of heartache. Looking back, she often wished she treated her daughter better, spent more time at home, but everyone has a degree in hindsight.

"You didn't get along with Stacey, did you?" Hunter stood in front of Wolfe's desk. "You hated each other."

"Ah." She mocked. "Now you're digging too deep and clutching at straws. Stacey's a rival, someone I have to hate. We're on opposite sides of the fence. That's how divorce law works. She wants the best for her clients, and I want the best for mine. Do I like her? No. Not even close. She's nasty to me, and has said some horrible, personal things."

"Where were you the night that Fielding was murdered?"

"No, no, no." Wolfe stood and walked around her desk. "The truth is that Stacey Fulbright murdered Joe Fielding and was stupid enough to leave the murder weapon there. Personally, I hope she goes down for it. Not for Joe, but for every divorcee that

she's screwed. And I'll be happy to see her go down."
She spent a moment in Hunter's shadow, before
moving to the office door. She opened it and waited
with her hand on the door handle. "I have an
appointment. It's time you left."

Hunter walked to the door. He glared at Wolfe,
and walked through the hall, passing a number of
junior lawyers. Most had their heads down, avoiding
eye contact, too frightened to look in any other
direction. They were scared of their boss, and they
had every right to be. Joanne Wolfe's reputation
wasn't a nice one.

And Hunter had to find out just how nasty she
could be.

# CHAPTER 10

STACEY FULBRIGHT'S paranoia was debilitating. Every movement in the shadows was met with hesitation, every sound met with sudden looks over her shoulder. Her eyes darted all over the shopping mall as she walked from the parking lot to the children's clothing shop. It was the first time she'd been to the shopping mall in weeks, and the fear was overwhelming. She could feel the anxiety grip her stomach and taste a metallic tang in her mouth.

When one man walked too close to her son, she almost screamed in fear, but she was doing her best to hold it together. She had to appear normal for her children. Her husband had been insistent that she leave the house. He'd been saying that for days. It was good for her mental health, he said. As she walked through the mall, she was starting to dispute the advice.

The multi-level mall was busy for midday Thursday, many people pushing past to get where they were going. It smelled new, clean, and the noise of chatter made the walkways seem hectic. Her goal was simple—a new sweater for Noah and a new dress for Zoe. A quick in and out trip to the mall. This was no time to linger. Their targeted shop was on the second level. She parked her car in the multi-level lot, checked for any vehicles following, and then dragged her children into the shop. Their calls to stop for a snack at the doughnut store were refused. Noah asked to use the bathroom, but he was met with rejection. Despite his plea, she didn't want him in the bathroom without an adult. She couldn't leave him alone.

They hurried through the shop, not even trying on the clothes. She asked them to choose the clothes they wanted, and then purchased them without a second look. When she stepped out of the shop, she saw the man in the suit. He was staring at them. She grabbed Noah and Zoe by the hand. She turned and started striding to the parking lot.

The man followed.

She quickened their pace. Tears began to fill her eyes. Her heart was pounding against her chest.

Not her children. Not her offspring.

The man followed and continued staring at them. He wasn't even trying to hide it.

She turned and glared at him, but he didn't flinch. He was tall, broad, and she could see tattoos across his knuckles. She didn't want to get close enough to read what the tattoos said.

The dolls on display at the toy store caught Zoe's eye and she tried to step towards them. Stacey pulled her back, hurrying to the car. The man continued to follow them. She looked at the help desk, located near the entrance. It was empty.

Her suspicion was overwhelming. Was he a threat? Or just a man at the mall? Her doubt was sickening. She could feel it in her stomach, taste it in her mouth.

"Mom, why are you sweating?" Noah asked as they hurried into the parking lot. "It's not hot."

"Just…" She wiped her brow. "I'm just in a hurry to get home."

"Why?"

"I have to… get back for your father. We have to get dinner ready." Her excuses were lame, and she could tell that Noah didn't believe her. "Come on. Keep up." Noah looked over his shoulder. Stacey grabbed him by the hand, picked up Zoe, and broke into a jog. "Noah, keep up."

She dashed towards the car.

She unlocked the car, and helped Zoe into her car seat. Noah jumped into the back seat and buckled up faster than she'd ever seen before. He didn't complain once. She shut the back door of her car and looked around the lot.

No one.

The man hadn't followed her out of the mall.

She took a breath and the tears welled up in her eyes. She wiped her eyes with the back of her sleeve, sniffed back another tear, and entered the car. She started the car and locked the doors. Taking a large breath, she stared into nothing, trying to compose herself. She was being paranoid, she told herself.

There's nothing to worry about.

She began to reverse, satisfied they were out of danger. It was paranoia, she repeated to herself. It was distrust.

But as she drove to the exit of the parking lot, she saw a figure she knew well.

Standing by the exit gate, staring at her car, was a rival lawyer, watching her closely. Stacey stared at the figure, who didn't move from her position, standing next to a pole.

Was it a coincidence? More paranoia?

But when Joanne Wolfe made a pistol symbol with her hand, and then pretended to shoot at her car, there was no mistaking it.

Her children were in danger.

# CHAPTER 11

TEX HUNTER walked into the Green Mill Jazz Club, part of Chicago's history, a bar that had been graced by the likes of Charlie Chaplin, Al Capone, and Billie Holiday. It took more than a few moments for his eyes to adjust after stepping inside the doors. The bar was dark in the right places, barely lit in the wrong ones. The floor was sticky, and the place smelled of cigar smoke, even though it hadn't been legal to smoke inside for more than a decade. The booths were full of people talking quietly, but the seats around the bar were mostly empty, except for a few men hunched over their drinks. Hunter sat on one of the empty stools and ordered a whiskey.

Michael Vandenberg looked twice at the man next to him and then sighed. Hunter waited for Vandenberg to open the conversation. It wasn't long before he did.

"I come here because this place reminds me of traveling to Louisiana before they changed the drinking age. You're too young to remember those days, but in the early eighties, when I was 18, we'd travel south because the legal drinking age was still eighteen in New Orleans, and not only could you go to a bar, but the place was a party haven. Any time of day, any day of the week. That place was a constant festival of drinking. We'd travel for a week, in a beaten-up van that was bound to die on us, and party hard for days and days on end." Vandenberg smiled as he looked longingly towards the stage at the end of the bar where the jazz band were setting up. "They were good memories. Innocent times."

"You were never the innocent sort."

"True." Vandenberg chuckled. "I used to load up the van and bring the whiskey back by the carton load to sell to other students. Even in times of fun, I was still looking to exploit the law. I should've known that I'd be a lawyer one day."

The band started playing. The music was gentle, not too loud, with a smooth swing to it, but they were just getting started. The horns, representing the bright and bursting syncopation of New Orleans-style jazz, were soon coming. After the bartender handed Hunter his drink, he poured two large cocktails for the young women standing next to Hunter.

"That's a big drink." Vandenberg leaned close to Hunter and nodded to the girls. "Quite the leg-opener."

Unimpressed by the comment, Hunter held his gaze on Vandenberg.

"You know what I mean, Hunter. Two more of those drinks and their legs will be open." Vandenberg made the action with his hands. "You get what I mean, right? Us red-blooded males have to stick together."

"You're a disgrace." Hunter grunted, almost ready to punch him. "Those girls are young enough to be your granddaughters."

"Hey, don't judge me. I'm just doing what God intended. I might be almost sixty, but my gun still fires." Vandenberg leaned backwards from the bar and shouted over to the girls with the drinks. "Hey pretty ladies. I have money. Lots of it."

The ladies turned their backs to Vandenberg, intimidated by his aggressive overtone.

"Don't talk to them again." Hunter said. "Or I'll break your jaw."

"Alright, big guy. Settle down. You don't have to be everyone's protector; you know?" Vandenberg put his hands up. He paused for a few moments before turning back to Hunter. "So Stacey Fulbright, the murderous lawyer. Has she taken the deal yet?"

"You'd like that, wouldn't you?"

"I had nothing to do with Joe Fielding's death, if that's what you're asking."

"I'm not."

"Well, I'll tell you this—Stacey Fulbright made a lot of men angry. There are a lot of divorced men out there that would love revenge on her. She's taken money away from men that didn't have it to lose. If you want to take the set-up defense to court, I'd be looking into the ex-husbands of her clients before you start looking anywhere else. You'll find plenty of violent men angry with her." Vandenberg turned back to the band as the beat picked up. "And I hear that you're not even leading this case? Who'd Stacey give it to?"

"John C. Clarke is leading this one. I'm sitting second chair."

"John C. Clarke?" Vandenberg let out a small whistle sound. "Tex Hunter and John C. Clarke—the all-star criminal defense team. That's going to be quite the look in court. Quite expensive too, I imagine. Your fees alone would break most people."

"I'm doing it as a favor."

"Free?" Vandenberg scoffed. "You should remember the words of Benjamin H. Brewster— 'A lawyer starts a career giving $500 worth of advice for $5, and ends giving $5 worth for $500.' I'm in the latter group these days, and you'll never catch me being stupid enough to give my advice away for free." Vandenberg paused for a long moment as the saxophone broke into a solo performance. He closed his eyes and swayed side to side. It was hard not to smile. The up-tempo music soaked into the soul, uplifting even the coldest of hearts. After the solo had finished, followed by a number of cheers, Vandenberg turned back to Hunter. "What are you even doing here, Hunter? Did you come past to listen to some jazz?"

"I'm giving you a heads up that your firm's dodgy practices are about to be exposed in court. When Stacey Fulbright's case makes it to court, Joe

Fielding's business dealings are going to be discussed in an open environment and it's not going to reflect nicely on you."

Vandenberg stopped drinking mid-swig. He paused before finishing the drink and looking back at Hunter. "What good would that do?"

"It would expose bad practice."

"And? I mean, what are you trying to prove? Our firm had nothing to do with his death. Stacey got angry and lashed out, it's nothing more than that. It's not worth it, is it?"

"It'd expose the lengths you go to increase the value of the divorce cases. Like the sexual assault charges you made up against Dr. Mackie to gain extra money for his settlement."

"Oh…" A moment of realization hit Vandenberg. "I get it. I get what you're trying to do. You're trying to blackmail me into letting Dr. Mackie's divorce settle before he's forced to sell the practice."

Hunter didn't respond.

"Clever, Hunter. Very clever." Vandenberg raised his finger in the air. "With Dr. Mackie's case, we saw an opportunity, and exposed it. Nothing more. We wouldn't be doing our jobs if we didn't pressure him to sell the company. We have to do what's best for our client and that means getting the most money for her."

"Setting him up for sexual assault charges is a dirty tactic."

"We had nothing to do with the sexual assault

case, however we do have the connections to make it go away. I heard Christoph King has offered ten million dollars for the sale of the company. When we're talking about that amount of money in a divorce case, we can make things happen. And Dr. Mackie's wife isn't my client anyway. She belongs to one of the junior lawyers."

"A junior lawyer that you manage."

"Right." Vandenberg grinned and turned back to the musicians as the trumpet player began. It was hard not to tap a foot to the performance. When the band finished their song, an original, everyone in the bar clapped in unison, some even standing and whistling their appreciation. "We're not easing back on Dr. Mackie's divorce case. There's ten million on the line there." Vandenberg turned to Hunter and finished his drink in one last gulp. "As a fellow lawyer, I'll give you this advice—be careful were you dig. Our divorce firm is not the type of place that you should try and blackmail. We don't take kindly to people who want to ruin us, and we've got a history of getting revenge on people that do."

"I'm going to dig until I find the truth."

"Of course you are, but you're stepping into dangerous territory. You need to convince Dr. Mackie to sell his company, and you need to convince Stacey Fulbright to take a deal for manslaughter. That would be the best outcome for everyone…" Vandenberg placed the glass back on the bar. "Including Stacey's children."

# CHAPTER 12

AFTER ANOTHER seventy-five-hour work week, Hunter stepped out of his office, rubbing his temples, and stood on the sidewalk, waiting for his ride home. The app on his phone said the car was five minutes away, but the timing was never accurate. The traffic made sure of that. The one-way traffic streamed down West Jackson Boulevard, in the Loop, a chorus of horns and engine roars. The sidewalk was wide, but busy, filled with a rush of workers looking to escape for a weekend away from the city. The last moments of sunset were sheltered by the high-rise buildings on either side of the street, and a chill in the air was setting in.

The witness list for Dr. Mackie's sexual assault case had been updated by the prosecution and Hunter was surprised by one of the new names—Christoph King. He had come forward and made a report to the police about what he saw that day. He stated he saw the alleged victim, Miss Katherine Jennings, just after the assault occurred. Hunter didn't believe a word of the statement. It was all too neat, and all too clean.

Waiting on the sidewalk, Hunter watched a black

Mercedes sedan, with windows tinted too dark to be legal, pull over and stop in the bus only lane. Behind it was a black SUV, similar to the one that stalked Hunter's car only days earlier. The door of the Mercedes sedan opened and Christoph King stepped out.

"Mr. Hunter." King called out as he approached. He was dressed in a blue suit, and held himself well. He lifted his aviator sunglasses off his head and swirled them in his hand. "What a pleasant surprise on a lovely Friday evening. What a fortuitous coincidence."

"This doesn't look like a coincidence to me." Hunter stood tall, towering over King. "You're going to testify in the case against Dr. Mackie?"

"I saw what I saw. I saw Miss Jennings sobbing as she left the medical clinic." He smiled, but it was forced. "And that's what I wanted to talk about. I'm a man who knows how to negotiate, and I'm sure you're also a reasonable listener. I wanted to talk about Dr. Mackie and his unfortunate situation. He seems to be in a bit of trouble, but I can assist him. I'm a helpful guy." He laughed. His stomach shifted up and down as he did. "I have connections that can make things disappear, if you get what I mean."

"Out of the goodness of your heart?"

"Not likely. I'm not a charity." King looked around the street, studying the passing crowd for any prying ears. "Maybe we should go inside your office to talk?"

"No."

"Somewhere to be?" King questioned.

"Anywhere but here with you."

"Now, now, Hunter, I'm not here to argue with you, and I can tell you that I'm very helpful to people that help me. If you could have a quiet word with Dr. Mackie and encourage him to sell the clinic to a worthy buyer, perhaps present my name and offer, then I can make things disappear. Dr. Mackie would feel a lot less stressed if he just sold the clinic."

"Did you set this up?"

King's mouth hung open for a moment. "Nothing like that. I'm merely an opportunist. All I'm saying is if you help me, then I help you. A mutual acquaintance of ours has found himself in a predicament. That's all. I'm sure there would be financial compensation worthy of your effort. But if you don't help me, I can persuade you in other ways."

Hunter leaned closer to King, bringing his mouth close to King's ear. "You can't threaten me. If you want to know how tough an opponent I can be, then you should keep pushing my buttons."

"A tough negotiator. I respect that." King stepped back. "I'm doing the right thing and letting you know the opportunity is there, if you desire a pleasant outcome for everyone involved. The sale of Dr. Mackie's medical clinic would make things go away. I'm sure of it."

Hunter looked at King's raised hand. "Where's your wedding ring? You were wearing it last week at the function."

"Ah… you're observant." King rubbed his fingers as he put his hands down. "Well, that's a touchy subject."

"Going through another divorce?"

"Maybe."

"And let me guess, Vandenberg and Wolfe Family Law Offices are handling your case."

"That's none of your business."

"As soon as you became a witness in Dr. Mackie's case, your whole world became my business. I'd imagine any divorce is worth a lot of money."

"That depends on how good Joanne Wolfe is." King turned and began to walk away. "All I'm saying is there's an opportunity for Dr. Mackie to make things disappear. If you can convince the good doctor to change his mind about the clinic, you know where to reach me. I expect to hear from you soon, Hunter."

King raised his hand in the air and rubbed his thumb and index finger together, indicating cash, as he walked back to his car.

Hunter's ride pulled up to the curb. Hunter waited until King had stepped back into his car, staring at the car as it passed. When King's car drove past on West Jackson, Hunter entered the waiting Uber, greeted the driver, and then checked over his shoulder. The dark SUV was waiting behind them, allowing their car to pull out into traffic. Hunter watched the car out of the rearview mirror, watching as it stayed on his tail.

The Uber driver made small talk as he drove through traffic. He was Polish, and had been in Chicago for five years. Hunter admired the Polish. They were strong, hard-working, with a no-nonsense attitude.

After a number of turns, they pulled into Lower Wacker Drive, a complicated subterranean roadway. A shortcut for local drivers, the underground artery was almost impossible for tourists to navigate. The sunlight was blocked by the road above, causing the area to be constantly damp. In some sections, the low ceiling echoed the noise of the passing traffic, leaving most drivers unable to hear the music in their own car. Dim orange lights guided the way around the forest of concrete pillars, and the signs were minimal, as were the lines on the road.

Homeless camps dotted the edges of the underground lanes. Out of the rain, wind, and snow, the concealed passageways were a popular place to stay. Most had addictions and mental health issues. This was not a place for a passing driver to stop and ask for directions.

Lower Wacker was busy, but flowing. The driver knew to pay attention—tourists lost in the underground roads were known to make sudden and stupid decisions about where to turn. Hunter looked over his shoulder and watched as the SUV pulled closer. He couldn't see the driver.

As the sedan picked up speed, they approached another turn. Hunter buckled his seatbelt.

The SUV came at them fast. Hard. It clipped the back corner of the Uber. The jolt jerked Hunter forward.

The sedan spun around, the lights flashing past. Hunter gripped the door, waiting for an impact. After the second spin on the greasy road, the car bumped into the wall. No major impact, and only a slight jolt.

When he realized he was ok, Hunter leaped out of the car, looking through the traffic.

The SUV waited nearby.

With adrenaline surging through him, Hunter ran towards the SUV. A car skidded next to him. Another blew their horn.

As soon as Hunter was within striking distance, the SUV squealed it's tires and sped off. It weaved its way through the narrow streets. Hunter stood in the middle of the road, watching it disappear into the distance.

There were no license plates.

# CHAPTER 13

AFTER THE weekend, Hunter sat at his desk and called the Uber driver about the accident. There were no cameras on Lower Wacker Drive, and no sign of an SUV hitting another car, the driver said. The cops couldn't do anything, and there was nothing more to follow up. Just an unfortunate accident on the notorious road, the cops told the driver. Hunter knew they wouldn't get an outcome. Hunter offered to help the driver, but the driver said he was covered by insurance.

For most of Saturday and Sunday, Hunter's thoughts were focused on Noah Fulbright. How could he help the boy avoid his mother's trial? His mother was doing everything she could to shield her children from the trauma of a murder trial, but the reality was about to hit her family in the face.

Stacey Fulbright had barely left the house in a week. She was scared to use the phone in case it was tapped. She barely let the children leave the house either. Carl was doing his best to hold their family together. He was trying to keep things normal around the kids, but the pressure of the justice system was tearing them apart. The tension was palpable every time Hunter called to check on them.

The more Hunter thought about Noah, the more he thought about his own upbringing. His aunt Rebecca, his father's sister, took him in after his father's conviction. She was emotionless, cold, and hatred filled most of her movements. She had no interest in raising Hunter, but did so out of obligation. Her own children had already left home, and she showed no interest in going around again. She barely spoke to him, never offered a hug or a healing touch, and only spoke words of hate for Alfred Hunter.

When Hunter was fifteen, as the school was cracking down on his aggressive behavior, his aunt Rebecca tried to slap him, but she could barely reach up to his jaw, and he easily dodged her attempt. She hated Alfred for the pain he brought to the Hunter family name, and it showed as she took out her frustrations on Tex. His older cousins never came to visit, trying to distance themselves from such a horrific experience. Two cousins even legally changed their surname to 'Punter.' The conviction destroyed his family, and any sense of belonging that he hoped for. His older brother Patrick was the only one who ever had his back, but he was at college, trying to work through his own emotions.

While his teenage years were filled with coldness, Hunter appreciated everything his aunt did for him, and often thanked her. She wasn't interested in his praise. On the day he turned eighteen, she told him to move out. He stayed another month before moving to a college dorm. He tried to show his appreciation for her sacrifice, but she wanted to leave the past behind her. He sent flowers to his Aunt every birthday, and cards at Christmas, but he never received a response. Never even a phone call. Once her duty to her family was done, that side of the family tree was dead to her.

He hated that Noah Fulbright might have to suffer the same pain.

"Thinking?" Esther Wright entered the office with a file pressed against her chest. "That must hurt this early on a Monday morning. You haven't even had your second coffee yet."

"I'm always thinking."

"You never switch off, do you?" She placed the paper files on the desk. "You know; you shouldn't print so many paper files. The world is heating up, and chopping down all these trees is not good for the environment. And computers are a thing these days."

"Can't use them. They hurt my fingers." Hunter grinned.

"You're exaggerating."

"115% of people exaggerate."

"Quoting percentages now?" Esther said. "Well, you should know that I always give 100% at work. 98% from Monday to Thursday, and 2% on Fridays."

Hunter smiled. He reached forward and took one of the files.

"We've got the depositions this week for Dr.

Mackie's case." Esther sat down. "It all starts tomorrow. There may be a chance that one of the witnesses slips up."

"The prosecution will have prepared them well, and I don't expect any surprises, but this is still important. It'll give us an insight into how they're going to present the case and provide the groundwork for us to move forward. If we get nothing, then Dr. Mackie has to start to seriously consider a deal."

A knock at the door caught their attention.

"Mr. Hunter?" A man leaned in the door. "The name's John C. Clarke, Clarke with an 'e.'"

"John. Welcome." Hunter looked at his watch. "We weren't expecting you for another twenty-five minutes."

"I'm an early type of guy." John C. Clarke stepped into the office, and offered his hand to Hunter, before turning to Esther and shaking her hand. "And you must be Esther. We spoke on the phone earlier. You're as beautiful as you sound."

"Lovely to meet you." Esther smiled at his easy charm.

"Please, sit down." Hunter pointed to the chair opposite the desk. "Esther and I were just discussing another case, but we'll switch gears to this one. You don't mind if Esther stays during the meeting?"

"Not at all." Clarke smiled. "I would love that."

John C. Clarke's posture was perfect—straight back, relaxed shoulders, head held high. He was well groomed, and a strong smell of woody cologne followed him. His hair was gray, eyes were blue, and his smile was broad.

"I've got the forms over here for the transfer of the case." Hunter picked up the forms from the side of his desk. "Everything has been prepared. All you have to do is sign the forms and take it to the court."

"Thank you." Clarke looked at the forms. "And, as we discussed on the phone, I'm happy for you to continue as second chair. I have no ego in regards to this. The best thing for the client is the best outcome, and I could use your expertise. You'll see things that I won't."

"Agreed." Hunter nodded. "It's been years since I've been second chair, but I'm determined to see Stacey get off this charge. Whatever you need to push this case forward, let me know. I have a few other cases going, but I'll make the time for Stacey."

"What are your first thoughts then? Do you think she killed Joe Fielding?" Clarke crossed one leg over the other. "It all seems a bit strange to me."

"Stabbed a private investigator in a parking lot late at night? No. I don't think so." Hunter shook his head. "My first reaction was no, and the further the case has gone, the more that notion has been strengthened. I can't see her losing control and killing this guy. And if she did it, she wouldn't have left the murder weapon next to his body."

"Although she does have an angry streak. That's well known." Esther added. "The prosecution is going to play on that and tell the jury about her past."

"No doubt. I read about the man she shoved when she was in a divorce settlement meeting. She said the man approached her and then threatened her, but he still tried to press charges. A report was filed but nothing became of it. I'm sure he'll testify against her." Clarke said. "It was interesting that the cops found codeine and Valium in her office. She'd admitted previously to having blackouts while taking those medicines to control her stress levels. She could've lost control and not remembered murdering Joe Fielding. And if that's true, the prosecution is going to throw that at us during the trial."

Hunter agreed. "The prosecution's going to state she was stressed, took her medications, left the office, and walked into the parking lot in a daze. She found Joe Fielding in the parking lot, perhaps trying to blackmail her, and then she lost control and stabbed him five times. Nobody would've heard anything and there's no cameras. She gets into a panic, and drives away pretending nothing happened. They have her walking into the parking lot at 11:15pm and leaving ten minutes later. No footage inside the lot."

"The placement of cameras is convenient, isn't it?" Clarke rested his hands on his thigh. "If there was a camera inside the parking lot, we could solve this case today. Have we looked into any dash-cams from other cars in the lot?"

"We've looked and there's nothing. Stacey's been using the same parking lot for five years and was well aware of the location of the surveillance cameras.

That's what the prosecution will say, and it's a strong argument." Hunter said. "They can place her there, make the connection to Fielding, present a motive, and then the jury will be easily won over by the murder weapon. It has her fingerprints on it." Hunter opened one of the files. "If we can figure out what Fielding was working on; we can figure out what he was doing near her office."

"That's the key, isn't it? What was Joe Fielding doing there?" Clarke stated. "Do you have anything on that?"

"We do." Esther said, reaching for another file off Hunter's desk to hand over to Clarke. "Although Fielding was a freelance private investigator, he was doing a lot of work for Vandenberg and Wolfe Family Law Firm. His name has come up in a lot of their investigations, and he's clearly connected to them."

"And what does he do there?" Clarke ran his eyes over the files.

"Investigates divorce cases, by either digging up evidence on the estranged partner or…" Esther paused. "Digging up dirt on the opposition's lawyer. There's some unsavory practices happening in that firm."

"Whoa." Clarke raised his eyebrows. "This is looking tricky. So, I guess you know what my next question is then?"

"Five cases." Esther said. "Either recently resolved or currently ongoing divorce cases between Vandenberg and Wolfe's office and Stacey Fulbright's clients. We're looking into them now, but there's one previous case which stands out. It's an older case. Years old. Christoph King and his divorce from Cassandra Mills. Stacey represented Mills and took Christoph King to the cleaners for millions more than she should have. And he's held a grudge ever since."

"I know of Christoph King. Round guy. Loud voice. Ginger hair. He does some interviews for Fox News when they need a one-sided opinion on Chicago politics. A Republican man." Clarke nodded. "Legally, what's the approach?"

"There's no witness to the event, nor any direct evidence that shows she did it." Hunter said. "If we can find another potential suspect, someone with ties to the case and a motive, then we have a chance of convincing the jury that there's not enough evidence to convict Stacey."

The trio talked for the next hour, exchanging notes and information. Clarke was easy to talk with, unassuming, and had minimal ego. He had enough money to retire to the Bahamas and play golf for the rest of his life, but slowing down didn't interest him. After more than an hour of discussion, Clarke collected the files, and thanked Hunter and Esther for their help.

"Stacey said you were good at your job, Mr. Hunter, and I'm very happy for you to continue as part of this case." Clarke said as he stood. "Because with the names that you've suggested, I think danger isn't going to be far away."

# CHAPTER 14

RAY JONES was waiting in Burnham Park, on the shores of Lake Michigan, relaxing on a wooden bench, taking a long drag on a joint. The sun was glistening off the dew on the grass, a breeze blew off the lake, and joggers hurried past on the track that hugged the edges of the water. There was a couple nearby, lounging on a picnic rug, enjoying a hamper for lunch. The horizon seemed to stretch on forever under the reflection of the sun, and Jones had his gaze locked onto it.

"Ray." Hunter greeted Jones. "You looked relaxed."

"Tex." Jones took another long drag of the green tobacco, held the smoke in his mouth for a moment, and then blew it out. He moved the joint towards Hunter. "Want some?"

"No, thanks." Hunter shook his head. "Not my thing."

"I've been thinking..." Jones began, "about dinosaurs."

"Okay..."

"Did you know that dinosaurs were only

discovered two hundred years ago?"

"I didn't."

"Think about that for a moment, Tex—these creatures roamed our earth for millions and millions of years, and we only found out about them two hundred years ago. That's crazy, right?"

"Right."

"These giant creatures literally owned this planet for millions of years and we didn't even know they existed. George Washington, Benjamin Franklin, Christopher Columbus, Isaac Newton, Napoleon, Beethoven, Shakespeare, Da Vinci, even Jesus' disciples... none these people even knew dinosaurs existed. None of them. They'd never even heard of a T-Rex. These things were on our planet for millions of years, literally millions of years, and no one even know they existed." Jones' eyebrows creased together. "So I've been thinking—what else don't we know? What will we discover in the next two hundred years? What will the people of 2200 look back on and say? Will they say, 'Imagine living in a time where you didn't know the spiritual world existed?'"

"Whoa. Ease up on the wacky tabacky there, pal." Hunter smiled.

"But think about it, Tex. Really think about it." Jones looked at the end of his joint. It was almost finished. "As humans, we think our knowledge is complete. We assume we know everything that's happened in the past, or everything around us, or what's likely to happen next, but it's not true. It's just not true. Just because we can't prove something doesn't mean it doesn't exist. Nobody could prove the existence of dinosaurs until 1820. If you had said dinosaurs existed before that, you would've been laughed at and told you were mad, probably even shipped off to an asylum."

Hunter stared out into the lake as the thoughts processed through his head. "You're talking about religion? Just because we don't have proof but have faith?"

"I'm talking about everything. Religion. Spiritual healers. The power of the universe. There could be so many things we don't know. There could even be more dimensions—a magnetic dimension, a spiritual dimension, a paranormal dimension, and a… well, whatever dimension. Possibly something we haven't even thought of yet." Jones didn't take his eyes off the horizon. "And then our great, great, great grandchildren will be sitting here in two hundred years' time saying—can you imagine the fifth dimension, the spiritual world, was only discovered two hundred years ago? Crazy."

"Mind-blowing." Hunter patted Jones on the shoulder. "Now, I'm too scared to even ask what you've found in Stacey Fulbright's murder case. Evidence the murderer traveled from a different dimension, perhaps? That could prove she's innocent."

The joke broke Jones' gaze, and he laughed heartily, before standing and moving towards his truck, parked in the lot behind them. He was a hulking giant of a man, and as he got older, his movements were followed by a loud grunt and moan. He walked over to his truck, opened the passenger door, and pulled out a file.

"Report on who Stacey Fulbright was representing in the divorce cases. Here's a list of names. Nothing too much that I can find on the information databases. She was representing fifteen wives in various stages of divorce at the time of the murder, and they've all been handed over to her associate. She wasn't representing any males at the time of the murder, but she's represented many in the past. She was also talking to a number of women, her assistant said another five to ten women, but nothing official. I've got some of their names, but not all of them."

"And the other side? The husbands?"

"All accused of domestic violence, so all of them have the ability to snap. The listed ones are mostly run-of-the-mill white-collar type guys. Successful, angry, but nothing that says they're a killer. I've got a few more names to check, but at first glance, it doesn't look like much." Jones placed the file on the hood of his truck and opened it. "Do you really think a husband would take out revenge on a lawyer?"

"Who knows?" Hunter shrugged. "Maybe Stacey was empowering the women, and the husbands saw her as the reason the marriage was falling apart. Maybe they saw Stacey as a target."

"Or maybe Joe Fielding had information for

Stacey on one of the divorces?"

"And was trying to blackmail her? That's possible." Hunter drew a breath. "Any luck finding Joe Fielding's assistant?"

"No trace of anyone named Rebecca White that matches her description. Nothing. It's like she vanished into thin air."

"We need to find her. Maybe she changed her name? She'll have something to add to the case." Hunter turned, placed his hands in his pockets and looked out to the distance. "Stacey has officially given the case to John C. Clarke, a very competent lawyer, so I won't be the lead on this anymore. We'll still do everything in our power to help, but it's no longer our case."

"How do you feel about that?"

"It's the right decision. I don't like it, but it's the right decision. I'm too close to it. Too personally invested in getting her off. And that might mean I miss a really good chance to deal out, or take a manslaughter charge."

Jones nodded. "How about Dr. Mackie's case? How'd the depositions go?"

"Nothing of substance. The first witness was solid, the second questionable, but they stuck to their guns. I need something to connect all the witnesses together. That's what we need to win. Something. Anything. Dr. Mackie's determined to take this to trial, and at this point, it's clear he's going to lose. Jury selection is within a week, and I don't like our chances of even getting a hung jury."

Hunter watched a car circle past in the distance. It was the third time the car had slowly driven past the entrance to the parking lot.

"Well, you might be in luck. I had to do some digging, and I mean really deep, but in Wisconsin, in one of the earliest medical clinics that Christoph King opened, I might've found something." Jones moved back to the passenger seat of his truck and took out another file. "He bought this medical clinic after some jostling, and it's gone on to be one of his most profitable clinics."

"And what swung the sale in favor of King?"

"Sexual harassment allegations against the previous managing director."

"That's good. That's something we can work with."

"What makes it even better is that the allegation was from a new patient."

Hunter's mouth hung open for a moment. "A set-up? If it's worked before, then King could try it again. Do you have a name for the patient?"

"I'm working on it, but everything was signed with non-disclosure agreements and locked away. Her name has been wiped from just about everything."

"Find me the name. We need to talk to her." Hunter watched the dark car drive past again. It was too far away for Hunter to see the plates. He stepped forward, and the car soon drove away under Hunter's stare. He turned back to Jones. "I have to go back to the office, but promise me you're not going to drive in your current state. You're so high that you're a danger to everyone on the road. I don't want to be defending you in court for vehicle manslaughter."

"Too true. And I don't feel like going anywhere right now." Jones' head drifted to the side a little, and then he looked over at the park bench. "Looks like a good place to sit for a few hours."

Hunter smiled. "Just don't go slipping off into another dimension. I need you in the real world."

# CHAPTER 15

STACEY FULBRIGHT peered out the window of her living room. Like a nosy neighbor, she stared from behind the blinds, pulling them back just enough to look outside with one eye. The van was still there. It had been there all morning. It was a new white van, clean, but she hadn't seen anyone drive it. Her husband suggested that the neighbors had bought it, but she didn't believe him. She was starting to doubt everything he told her.

She was once so proud of her home, but as the days went past, she couldn't find the energy to maintain it. The floor was dirty. The indoor plants were dry. The dust was beginning to gather in the corners. All she wanted to do was curl up in a ball and lay on the couch. Carl was doing his best to maintain the house, maintain some sense of normalcy, but he was juggling work, the children, and her sanity. He'd already taken all his vacation days. He'd already used up all his energy.

"Stacey," Carl said as he approached her. He knew not to sneak up on her. There were enough broken plates and glasses in the house already.

As she leaned against the window, Stacey kept her eyes on the van.

"Stacey?" Her husband remained at the entrance to the living room, a safe distance away from his wife.

She turned.

"Stacey, this has to stop. You can't spend all day at the window. You're beginning to scare the kids."

"Scare the kids?" She let go of the blind. "They should be scared. Someone set me up. There are killers out there who have targeted me. And I think they're in the van."

"They're not in the van." He sighed, and rubbed his brow. "Stacey, I need you to stop this. We can't keep going on like this."

"And what else am I going to do? I've been charged with murder, Carl. I'm looking at twenty-five years in prison. Did you hear that? Twenty-five years in prison. What else am I supposed to do? Play happy family and pretend like none of this has happened? Forget about it all until my court date?"

He looked away. "I don't know what you're going to do. But I've been thinking… it's best for the kids and I to go away for a while. We're going to stay with my parents in Florida. They've got enough room down there to put us up. It would be nice—"

"Nice? I'm facing a murder charge and you're talking about 'nice?'"

"It's starting to affect the kids, Stacey." His voice was firm. "They're scared. They know something isn't right. But if I go down to Orlando with them, then we can have fun at a theme park, let them forget all this for a while. It's like Tex Hunter said, this trial is going to have a profound effect on them, just as his father's had an effect on him. I don't... I don't think that's healthy for them. I've got to take them away from this. My work has an office in Orlando, and I can work remotely from there for a few months until the trial's over. Mom and Dad will look after the kids while I go into the office. They can do online learning down there. The school said they can send through all the work. It's better than... it's better than staying here with you."

Stacey stared at the floor. At the time she needed him the most, he was walking away.

But he'd been walking away for years. Where had the excitement of their twenties gone? Where had the passion gone? Where was the desperate love they once had for each other? She looked at the photo of their wedding day sitting on the hallway cabinet. Her chest heaved up and down. They looked so happy. So in love. Where was that love now?

She knew she'd put their marriage on the back burner for years. She'd been just as guilty of ignoring the growing distance between them. Work, family, kids, responsibility—it all added up to the demise of their relationship. Life was hard, busy, and their marriage was the first thing to suffer.

"We're leaving in the morning. Flight is at 10:05. I'll get the kids packed now. They'll miss you, but I've told them you need to stay here for work. You should read them a book tonight before they go."

"You want me to face the trial alone?" She whispered.

"I've spoken to Mr. Clarke, your lawyer, and he agreed it's the best thing for the kids. He'll help you through this. He's a good man. And your mother can help you. She's only thirty-five minutes away by car. I've already talked to her—she said she'll stay with you during the trial, if you want. She'll be here every day." He leaned against the wall. "I just don't think that keeping the kids in Chicago will be healthy for them. The other kids at school are already teasing Noah about the charges, saying things like he's the son of a murderer. That's only going to become worse once the trial starts. I've got to take them out of this city, to a place where they can forget it all. The teachers have given them work to do. They'll still be learning."

"Don't I even get a say in this?" She murmured.

He shook his head. His eyes lingered on her for a long moment before he turned and began to walk away down the dark hallway.

"Wait. Carl."

He stopped and turned, leaning his closed fist against the wall.

"If this…" She folded her arms. "If this doesn't work out the way it should, and I'm sent to prison, I want you to promise me you'll look after our kids."

"Of course."

"Promise me, that if something happens to me,

you'll do everything you can for our children."

Her husband stared at her, nodded his response, and then walked away.

# CHAPTER 16

RAY JONES came through on his investigation into the purchase of a medical clinic in Wisconsin by Christoph King. He found the name of the woman who accused the practicing doctor of sexual assault, forcing the sale of the clinic, but she refused to talk via phone. When Jones offered to drive Hunter to Milwaukee, two hours north, to interview her face-to-face, he was happy to accept and leave the office for the day. Hunter loved the city known for its beer and baseball, and he had great memories of heading north to Milwaukee in his twenties—especially the summer German festivals full of beer, cheese and Bratwursts.

After an easy drive on the I-94, Jones parked on the street in Downtown Milwaukee, and removed his jacket from the trunk of the car, still feeling the chill in the February air.

"What did she say when you talked to her on the phone?" Hunter asked, turning the collar of his coat up.

"Not much. She shut her mouth the second I asked about her previous appointments at the medical clinic. She said she couldn't talk about it, and she was busy. After that, she hung up the phone."

The two tall men approached the Hyatt Regency Milwaukee, strolling past the valets, and through the double-glass doors. The foyer of the four-star hotel was impressive. The building was hollowed out in the middle, with an atrium that stretched to the top floor of the eighteen-story building. Glass elevators ran up and down the inside, providing a wide view over the internal courtyard.

"Welcome to the Hyatt Regency. Are you checking in?" The smile across the woman's face was broad. She was tanned, brunette, and her smile was easy, full of genuine affection and care.

"Not quite." Hunter stepped forward to the reception desk of the hotel. "We would like to talk to you, Miss Heather Monroe."

"And who are you?" She raised one eyebrow.

"My name is Tex Hunter. I'm a criminal attorney. And I'm investigating your previous sexual assault claims against Dr. Lighten."

She jolted back in shock. "Um..." Her eyes darted around the room, looking behind Hunter. She lowered her voice, and leaned closer to him. "I don't know what you're talking about."

"We can talk about it now, or we can subpoena you to appear in court in Chicago to discuss your association with Dr. Lighten. We're happy to do it either way."

"I can't." She stared at Hunter with a blank expression. "I'm not allowed to say anything."

"We understand you signed a non-disclosure statement, however if criminal activity is involved, we can force you to talk about it under subpoena." Hunter said. "At this point, we only want to talk. Nothing more."

She stared at him, mouth open and face blank. She looked to her colleague next to her behind the front desk.

"I can cover for you." Her colleague whispered, pretending to look at her computer and avoiding eye contact with Hunter. "You should take your lunch break now. Take an hour. We're not busy. I can cover for you."

"Not here." Heather said. "Be in the bar across the road, Major Goolsby's, in five minutes. I'll talk to you there."

Hunter and Jones agreed and then walked out the front sliding doors. They crossed the road to the bar. On the front window were large stickers promoting the Milwaukee Bucks, the Green Bay Packers, the Brewers and the Admirals, Milwaukee's second tier ice-hockey team. Major Goolsby himself appeared above the door as a cartoon with a cowboy hat drinking a pint of ale. Inside the sports bar was dark, featuring brown wooden furniture and black floors. The row of red lights along the ceiling did little to brighten the place. There were too many television screens to count, each with a replay of a recent sporting match, and many posters and flags representing pride in the sporting success of the area.

This was clearly the bar that warmed up fans before games for the nearby stadiums, and then handled the aftermath of wins or losses.

The jovial barman greeted them with a large smile. "What'll it be fellas?"

"Two pints of pale ale." Jones held his fingers up to confirm the number. "And a plate of your spiciest wings."

Hunter and Jones sat away from the service area in the furthest corner of the room, sitting at a small round table in the almost empty bar. It was before lunch, and the quietest time of the day for the staff. Still, the smell of beer and body odor filled the air. They sat near the window, looking across the road at the Hyatt Regency. They watched as Heather Monroe exited the hotel and jogged across the four lanes of traffic to the bar. She took off her coat as she walked inside.

"I don't know what I can say, or even if I'm allowed to talk about it." She kept her voice low as she sat down. "Can you really make me go to court?"

"We don't want to, Miss Monroe, but we can." Hunter said. "Or we can avoid all that if you're just honest with us. We don't want to expose you; all we want is information."

"There you go fellas." The barman carried the plate of buffalo wings in a plastic basket, along with a small bowl of celery sticks, and two beers to the table. "Anything for this beautiful lady?"

She smiled politely but waved him away. She

waited until the barman reached the serving area before she continued. "I signed a non-disclosure agreement about my appointment with Dr. Lighten, and I thought that was it. I thought I'd never have to deal with it again."

Jones picked up one of the wings, bit into it, and his eyes almost popped out of his head. "Wow. That's got some kick."

"It gets cold up here, you know?" Heather smiled. "Gotta keep the food hot to warm up the insides."

Jones wiped his mouth with a napkin and shook his head. "Whew. These wings are on fire."

Hunter took a sip of his beer, and then turned back to Heather. "We want to talk about your time with Dr. Lighten. We'll ask you a few questions and you can tell us if we're infringing on the details of the non-disclosure agreement or not. We'll start with general questions that you'll be allowed to discuss, and then we'll see if there's anything else we need to talk about."

"I was a patient there." She brushed a strand of brunette hair over her ear. "I know I can say that."

"And what happened when you were a patient there?"

She hesitated.

"We don't want to get you into trouble." Jones wiped his brow with a napkin as the sweat started to build. "We just want to talk about it."

"Off the record?" She asked.

Hunter nodded. "If you want."

"I need you to say it. I need you to say that this is off the record and nothing's going to come back to me. I've spoken to my cousin in Chicago. She's a cop—Detective Regina Heart—and she told me, if anyone asks, I have to make sure it's off the record. I asked her advice about the non-disclosure agreement, and she told me to sign it. Going through the courts to charge Dr. Lighten would've been a long, hard process. And she would know. She works in the sexual assault unit."

"I know Detective Heart. She's a good person." Hunter said. "For now, this is off the record."

"Ok. Off the record." She drew in a deep breath, and looked around the room. It was still empty. "I was sexually assaulted by Dr. Lighten, but before the case made it to court, he sold the business and retired from his medical clinic, so I dropped the charges against him. The prosecution team decided not to pursue the case once I withdrew my testimony."

"And what did you receive for signing the non-disclosure agreement?" Hunter pressed.

"What do you mean?"

"I'm sure you didn't just sign an agreement without any benefit to you."

She looked around the bar again, then out the window to her workplace. She was edgy, nervous. Her breathing had increased, and her face was starting to turn red.

"I don't know what I can say." She whispered. "I don't want any trouble, ok? I just want to do my job and go home to my family at night."

"We know Dr. Lighten denied the charges you presented." Hunter said. "What we want to know was who convinced you to make a complaint to the police in the first place. Did you know the woman who claimed to witness the event?"

"Becky Bennett. She was a patient in the waiting room. I'd never met her before, and the doctor's clinic denied she was even there. They said she was lying, and they didn't have any record of her at the clinic."

Hunter nodded. The name meant something to him, yet he couldn't place it. "How much were you paid to make the claims?"

She shook her head slowly. There was no shock on her face, only fear.

"This is still off the record." Hunter reassured her. "Nothing is coming back to you yet."

"I was paid enough money to put a deposit on a house." She whispered. "My family is in that house. My kids, my husband, my mom. We're hard workers, and this was a chance to get ahead. This was like winning the lottery for us."

"Okay." Hunter said. "Who paid you the money to make the sexual harassment claim? Did it come straight from Christoph King, the man who purchased the medical clinic?"

She bit her lip again and shook her head.

"Then where did it come from?"

"A guy paid it to me."

"Which guy?"

She looked over her shoulder and leaned forward. "If I tell you, will you please leave me alone?"

"For now, yes."

She stood up and grabbed her coat. She put it on, and looked at the door, before turning and leaning down to the men.

"I'll tell you this now, but I won't testify about anything. If you put me in court, I'll deny everything."

Hunter and Jones provided her a small nod.

"The doctor was a sleaze and was getting divorced for the fifth time. He assaulted me in an appointment and I made the report to the police. I wasn't going to go through with the charges but then someone approached me. His name was Joe." She whispered. "He was from the doctor's wife's law firm. He encouraged me to pursue the complaint, and he even said that I should make up extra charges against the doctor. I refused to do that, but I saw no harm in chasing a conviction on what actually happened. The law firm wanted to force him to sell the clinic so they could take the cash. I wasn't sure how it worked but they said the divorce settlement couldn't benefit from the medical clinic otherwise. The charges were real, but I wasn't going to follow through with it until Joe paid me. Two weeks later, the doctor settled. He presented the non-disclosure agreement."

It fell into place for Hunter. "And the name of the law firm?"

"Vandenberg and Wolfe Family Law Office."

# CHAPTER 17

AS HUNTER came back from Milwaukee, Patrick called to say he'd booked a flight to Puerto Vallarta. The next available flight was Friday morning. It was four-hours direct. Hunter agreed. Before he knew it, he was flying out of Chicago's O'Hare International Airport, traveling to question his estranged sister.

The Mexican town of Puerto Vallarta sat on the coast line of the Pacific Ocean, along the same latitude as Hawaii, in the Bay of Banderas. The tourist town was nestled beneath the stunning backdrop of the Sierra Madre mountains, with large hotel chains rising off the beaches and more water activities than a person could dream of. The sun was blaring, the sky was drenched in clear blue, and a fresh sea breeze blew through the streets. "It's like being back in the womb." Patrick said as they walked off the plane. "It's 98 degrees and there's enough humidity to make it feel like we're wrapped up in a cozy blanket."

They checked into a seaside hotel, unloaded their luggage, and walked to the restaurant strip, a block away from the beach. They chose to sit across the road from where Natalie worked, resting on two metal chairs outside a restaurant. They ordered coffees and waited, and it wasn't long before Hunter's breath caught in his throat. He saw her. There was no mistake. Natalie Hunter was working the tables across the street, a smile on her face as she joked with tourists.

Natalie had aged gracefully. Her once straight blonde hair was wiry and free, her skin was tanned, and she held herself well. She looked fit for her early fifties, and she moved with a vibrant hustle. She was taller than Hunter remembered, and her ripped forearms made it look like she could crush a coconut with her bare hands. Hunter could spot a number of tattoos under her shirt sleeve, mostly covered to avoid attention.

"That's her, alright. No doubt about it." Patrick said after they'd watched her for five minutes. He ran his hand along the rim of his small, white sombrero hat, which he'd bought at the airport. "That's our sister, Natalie Hunter. It seems strange to say, but she looks so different, yet so familiar. Even after not seeing her for thirty-five years, it's still so easy to recognize her."

"Are you sure you want to wear that hat while you meet her? It looks ridiculous." Hunter said. "You scream tourist from a mile away."

Patrick took the hat off, looked at it and shrugged. "Can't be too careful down here. The sun can be harmful in the south. Skin cancer is a big killer in these parts."

Hunter threw a number of bills on the table, leaving the waitress a sizable tip, and began to walk to the café across the street. Patrick followed. Hunter's heart pounded in his chest as he waited for a car to pass. He didn't know what he was walking into. Natalie had a violent past. She had a nasty streak. But was she a killer?

Hunter and Patrick walked onto the patio of the café and sat at the table in the corner, under the overhanging mesh cover that blew in the gentle breeze. It was quiet and they were five tables away from the other tourists. In the middle of summer break, Hunter could imagine the café overflowing with people, lined up for a seat, eager to enjoy the local cuisine, but at this time of year, the place was tranquil and quiet.

Hunter sat on the metal chair and Patrick followed, sitting across from him. Natalie was distracted as she walked out of the café and into the bright sun. Pen and notepad in hand, she expected to see a couple of tourists sitting at the table, asking for the most American meal they had.

When she laid eyes on the men, she gasped. Dropped her pen. Time seemed to slow as she stared at her brothers, and it took her a moment to compose herself. Although time had changed their bodies, although time had aged them, they were still the people she remembered. She knew them the second she laid eyes on them.

"Hello Natalie." Patrick took off his hat. "It's been

a while."

Natalie looked over her left shoulder and then her right one. She turned to check the stairs. Her gaze ran up and down the street.

"Patrick." She whispered. There were no smiles, no heartfelt hugs. She turned to her youngest brother. "And Tex? Is that really you?"

Hunter stood. "Hello, Natalie."

"No. No. Not here." She stepped back from his towering figure. "Please, not here." She turned and looked back at the doors of the café. Her breathing was short. She gripped her chest. "I knew this day would come, but not now."

"We need to talk." Hunter said. "It's been a long time and we have some questions."

She backed away further. "I can't talk to you. That's... no-one is supposed to know I'm here. I left for a reason."

"That's what we want to talk to you about, Natalie." Patrick remained seated and composed, one leg crossed over the other. "And we're not going anywhere until we talk."

She shook her head. "I can't talk to you."

"As nice as the beach looks, we didn't come here for the holiday." Patrick said. "We're not leaving until we talk."

She looked at Patrick, then to Tex, then back to Patrick. The concern was painted on her face. "I can't talk to you here." She whispered. "Over there. In the laneway between those two buildings, behind the dumpsters. Be there in ten minutes."

Natalie pointed across the road, towards a small access lane between the main road and the walkway. It was between two hotels, secluded from view. She didn't wait for a response. She turned and rushed back into the café.

Patrick looked at Hunter and raised his eyebrows. "It looks like she wasn't expecting us today," Patrick joked. "She seemed a little surprised by our family reunion."

Hunter didn't respond.

"Tex, wait." Patrick jumped up and grabbed his brother's arm before he walked away. "What if it's a trap? What if she's sending us over there to be beaten up? I'm sure she knows some dangerous people, and she didn't seem welcoming." He looked around. "This is a foreign country. People go missing here. If we go into that alley, we might not walk out."

"That's a risk I'm willing to take." Hunter pulled his arm away from his brother, stepped off the patio, and crossed the street. Patrick followed, jogging to keep up with his long striding brother. They squeezed between two dumpsters, and the smell in the alley was overwhelming. One of the nearby restaurants cooked seafood, and the dumpster was full of it's off-cuts. The rest of the alley didn't smell much better. Although a sea breeze blew through, it didn't drown out the smell from the dumpsters.

"If it's a trap, we're screwed." Patrick said. There was a metal gate at the beach end of the alley, locked by a large chain and a dead bolt. He picked up a metal bar lying near the dumpster and leaned it against the wall. "Just in case."

After five minutes, Natalie held good on her promise. She walked towards them, alone. She squeezed between the dumpsters, checked over her shoulder again, and came closer.

"Is he dead?" She asked. Her arms were folded, and she remained a distance away from her brothers. "Is that why you're here?"

"Our father's not dead yet, but he doesn't have long left. He has cancer." Hunter responded. "We want to know the truth about what happened thirty-five years ago. We know he didn't murder those eight teenage girls. And we know that you know what happened. We know that you were sending information to Rick Cowan for years."

She gasped again, held her hand against her chest, and then looked over her shoulder. "I can't help you with that. I don't know anything."

"Yes, you do, Natalie." Patrick replied. "We know you were sending information back to Chicago. You know what happened, and we want to know what you know."

"You never should've come here. It's too dangerous. I can't help you. People will die if someone sees you here."

"Why?" Hunter stepped closer. "What happens if someone sees us here?"

"It's... it's complicated. I can't talk about it."

"Can't or won't?"

She hesitated. "I won't talk to you about it. I'll never talk about it. Ever. I didn't want our father to go to prison, but I can't risk what I've built here in Mexico. I have a family. I have sons to protect. I'm sorry, but you've wasted your time coming here. You'll find no help here." She turned and began to walk away. Before she passed by the dumpsters, she stopped, turned and looked back at them. "My brothers. It's good to see you. You both look amazing."

And then she walked out of the alley.

# CHAPTER 18

ESTHER WRIGHT waited at the entrance to the Garfield Park Conservatory, five miles west of Downtown Chicago and home to one of the countries largest greenhouse conservatories. Behind the gates she could hear the happy voices of children on the bright Sunday afternoon. There was freedom in their yells, joy in their screams of delight. The 10-acre site, both indoor and outdoor, was a delight to anyone who needed to escape the turmoil of the city close by. When Hunter called to say he'd arrived back from Puerto Vallarta that morning, Esther insisted that he needed to stretch his legs before they started another trial.

When Hunter stepped out of his car, he was rubbing his eyes. He looked like he hadn't slept in days. Esther greeted him with a gentle hello, and they wandered next to each other through the large conservatory. Hunter talked little about his two-day trip to Mexico, but she could tell he was hurting. She could see it in his face. He talked more about the soft sands on the beach than the encounter with his sister. When she tried to ask about Natalie directly, he shut down. Talking about his family was the only time she ever saw cracks in his armor, and all she wanted to do was grab him and hold him tight. Tell him it was going to be ok. But she couldn't. Not yet.

"I've been thinking about kids a lot lately." Esther said, after they'd been walking through the green space for twenty minutes.

"Any kids in particular?"

"Funny." Esther smiled. "No, I've been thinking about whether I want kids."

"And the answer?"

"I do." Her voice was quiet. "And then I got around to thinking about kid's birthday parties. Balloons are so weird. It's like saying, 'Hey, happy anniversary of your birth, here's a plastic bag full of my hot breath.'"

Hunter laughed. "That's one way to look at it."

"Talking of family, I found out my grandfather is addicted to Viagra."

"Really?" Hunter took a sip from his water bottle.

"Yeah. It's sad news, but nobody is taking it harder than my grandmother."

Hunter spat out his drink, and turned away, shaking his head. "That's terrible."

"You think that's bad?" Esther grinned. "Well, my father was born a co-joined twin, but they separated them at birth, no problems. But it means I have an uncle, once removed."

Hunter chuckled, shaking his head as he stepped away from Esther. He walked for a while, a broad smile stretched across his face, before he stopped next to a small pond, leaning against the metal railing.

"Family is a weird thing. It's a bond you share, no matter what." Hunter's head dropped. "Natalie didn't talk to us at all. She wanted to run away the second she saw us. She said we shouldn't have come."

"She didn't give you anything? No hints or clues?"

"Nothing, and I'm not sure she'll ever talk. Maybe she'll talk after our father has passed away." Hunter stared at the pond, lost in the calm reflection. "But what good is the truth then? Our father will have died in prison as an innocent man."

Hunter didn't say another word as he walked outside into the sunshine. Esther waited until the anger had left his face before she started talking again. They continued to walk outside, and their conversation drifted onto many topics. The weather. The traffic. The news. Politics. Sport. Movies. Esther talked about her dreams of traveling to France and seeing the Eiffel Tower. She talked about how she studied the French language at school, and how she longed to taste the local cuisine. Hunter talked about his love of French wine, and they both laughed about the idea of eating snails.

They stopped for a cold drink, sitting on a rock under the shade of a large Oak tree, and spent a quiet moment reflecting on life. They watched families walk past, happy and cheerful, and Esther felt a pang of jealousy. When the feeling became too much, she stood and lead them through the nearby gardens.

Their conversation turned to gardening, before they joked about their city, but eventually, as always, their conversation drifted back to work.

"You're saying it looked like Vandenberg and Wolfe Family Law Offices have paid accusers before to make accusations against doctors?" Esther asked. "That's insane. What else could they have done?"

"Who knows? But Dr. Lighten's case appears to be exactly the same set-up that's been used for Dr. Mackie's sexual assault case." Hunter said. "Dr. Mackie's wife, Sarah Mackie, is being represented by one of the junior lawyers at Vandenberg and Wolfe. A lawyer named Jake East, but I'm sure the case is big enough to have Joanne Wolfe or Michael Vandenberg look into it over his shoulder."

"So you think…" Esther ran her hand along the leaf of a large green plant. "I mean; you think that this doctor's wife is trying to get him for a big settlement? Force him to sell the medical clinic so she can take the funds? That's what all this is about?"

"Legally, they can't touch the medical clinic through the divorce, at the moment. Under Illinois law, even though the business is worth millions, because he started the business before the marriage, it can't be included in the divorce settlement. But if he sold it, and took cash before the divorce is settled, then it's part of the settlement. His ex-wife would get her hands on an extra few million dollars, and I have no doubt the firm would benefit financially as well."

"So the more she makes, the more they make."

"And here's the thing. There's someone we know who worked for Vandenberg and Wolfe Family Law Offices."

"Joe Fielding." It clicked in Esther's head.

"Exactly."

"If it worked the first time," Esther added, "then they've repeated what they did in Wisconsin. Contact King, ask him if he'd like to buy the business, and then add pressure to the sale."

"It's a simple set up." Hunter drew a long breath as they walked through the exit of the gardens. "It means they all walk away winners. But this time, it looks like they planted the accuser."

"So I guess we've got to expose it in the trial?" Esther said as they approached the parking lot. "That's going to be hard to prove."

"It is." Hunter said as he stood near Esther's car. His car was in the other direction. "Esther." Hunter drew a deep breath. "Would you like to have dinner? A French restaurant, perhaps?"

"With you?"

"Yes."

"As a date?"

Hunter nodded.

"Oh…" Esther brushed her blonde hair over her ears. "Maybe after the case ends."

"Dr. Mackie's case?" Hunter squinted. "It'll be over soon."

"No. I mean… your father's case."

"My father's case?"

"It takes up your whole life, Tex. It's your whole world."

"What are you saying?"

"This crusade that you're on to save your father." She folded her arms across her chest and looked away. "This drive to find the truth about your family is honorable and it's noble and it's amazing, but it leaves room for nothing else in your life. That's what you've been married to for the past three and a half decades. I know that's why you haven't dated anyone in years—you're married to your father's case."

"I..." He drew a long breath. "I'm close, Esther. Very close. I'm so close to finding the truth. But I need to know what Natalie knows."

"And if you don't? What if she never talks?"

"If she doesn't talk... then the case is over."

Esther nodded, before she stepped towards her car. "Then that's when we should have dinner."

# CHAPTER 19

THE GEORGE N. Leighton Criminal Courthouse was the big league, a triumph of law and justice in Chicago. It was a massive hulking presence in the neighborhood of Little Village, five miles west of Downtown. Despite its prestige amongst the law community, many Chicagoans had never passed the building, unless they'd been charged with a felony or called for their civic duty to serve on a jury. Unlike the slicker, newer Downtown court buildings—the Daley Center and the Dirksen U.S. Courthouse—the courthouse on 26th and California Ave was a testament to a time past. The daily parade of felons, mobsters, politicians and celebrities had been happening for more than seven decades, and the line of potential criminals showed no signs of stopping. Crime was big business in Chicago, and the courthouse was often one of the final stops for the people who didn't succeed. While the courthouse was labeled by some as outdated, those who worked there opted to call it 'old school.'

Inside the building, in a courtroom that had heard thousands of criminal charges, Tex Hunter waited at the defense table, reviewing the notes he'd made for his opening statement. There wasn't much that compared to the first day of a trial. The nerves. The anticipation. The heightened awareness. Some people ran marathons, some drove fast cars, but Tex Hunter got his thrills by having someone's future in his hands.

Supporters, spectators, and media had filled the seats of the courtroom behind him. Bailiffs stood at the front of the room. The prosecution table was filled with three lawyers, and two assistants sitting behind them. They typed fast on their laptops and whispered their conversations. The atmosphere of the courtroom was hectic and intense. Full of racing murmur. Sexual assault by men in positions of authority was the public's current moral panic, and the media were latching onto any case that seemed half-interesting.

Dr. Mackie, dressed in a black suit, waited next to Hunter, leaning forward, his shoulders almost touching the edge of the table, fighting back the feeling that he was about to be sick. He was edgy, not because of his guilt, but because of his fear of the system. He looked at Hunter. "Tell me we've got a chance to win this."

"Now is not the time for doubt." Hunter turned to him, speaking in a slow, calm tone. "We've got an angle to push for the defense of this case. If we can ask the right questions, then we can smoke out a detective who will help us. That's our major play."

"Which detective?"

"Detective Regina Heart. She's not part of our case yet, but I'm going to force her hand. She may be able to convince a reluctant witness to help us." Hunter drew a breath. "We've also got information on some of the witnesses that will make them crack, and it'll make the entire trial look like a fraud, but we need them to give us something. If not, then our only hope will be to put you on the stand. But like I told you before, that has to be a last resort."

"I'm willing to do it. I'm willing to stand up there and talk about these lies. I've said it over and over— Katherine Jennings is lying. I can convince the jury." He blinked back the tears in his eyes. "I can tell them the truth."

Hunter nodded, and tried to focus his attention on the notes in front of him. He believed Dr. Mackie. He had no doubt. The doctor had lived his life with integrity and honor, and he couldn't imagine him giving that honor away to fondle a young lady. But his belief wasn't going to win a court case. Miss Jennings' testimony would be key, and Hunter was willing to push the envelope to expose her lies.

When the lead bailiff walked into the room, and called the court to stand for Judge Reed, Hunter drew a long breath. He stood, calmed his thoughts, and focused. The court rose to its feet and Judge Reed plodded into the room. The judge rested in his leather chair, read the file in front of him, and called the court to session. After his first statement to the court,

Judge Reed called the jury members into the room. They stepped through the side door, led by the bailiff, and all looked to Dr. Mackie first. There was confusion on some of their faces. A squint here, a look of surprise there. That was good. But it was the firm upper lip on one lady, and a snarl by another woman, that concerned Hunter. They had already decided he was guilty.

From his raised position, Judge Reed talked to the jurors about their responsibilities, and the fact they had to leave any preconceived ideas behind. Judge Reed talked to the jury at length about the court process. Once they all agreed to their responsibilities, he explained the purpose of the opening statement—a roadmap for the case. A projection of what the evidence may show. When the jury nodded their agreement, Judge Reed invited lead prosecutor Dawn Rollins to make her opening statement.

She moved to the lectern, and placed her notepad on the wooden platform in front of her. She adjusted the microphone, and smiled at the jury. Rollins was dressed in soft colors, a deliberate choice to appear welcoming and friendly. She was a petite woman, and her smile was disarming.

*****

"May it please the court. Ladies and gentlemen of the jury, thank you for your service to the court. We welcome you with open arms and remind you that you must bring no preconceived ideas or feelings into the court case. You must listen to the case, listen to the evidence that's presented to you, and listen to the facts.

My name is Dawn Rollins, and with my colleagues here, Mr. Trent Lovell and Miss Paula Hornsby, we are going to present the case of criminal sexual assault against Dr. David Mackie.

In this climate, we, the citizens of Cook County, have to acknowledge that people in a position of power have an undue influence over vulnerable people. Our duty as citizens of this community is to protect the vulnerable. We cannot allow the strong to take advantage of the weak. We cannot allow those in power to prey on the defenseless.

Make no mistake, Dr. Mackie is not a harmless man. He's a person in authority. A person that people trust.

And he took advantage of that trust.

Miss Katherine Jennings is a brave woman. She has stepped up and done what many haven't, and she's made a criminal report. She reported Dr. Mackie for taking advantage of her. In this case, in this court, you will hear direct testimony from Miss Jennings. She has made the courageous decision to tell us what happened on that day. And make no mistake, it is a very valiant decision. We are asking her to talk about a traumatic sexual event in front of a room full of people she doesn't know. She will be nervous. She will be scared. But don't think that means she isn't telling the truth. Making an allegation of sexual assault is not the type of attention most women want to bring on themselves.

Miss Jennings will explain that she went to the doctor with complaints of a rash on her upper leg and lower back—later determined to be the result of poison ivy, which had accidently rubbed against her skin. Her testimony may be very hard to hear, perhaps uncomfortable, but I implore you to listen to everything she has to say.

When in Dr. Mackie's office, the doctor provided her two Valium pills to ingest. He said it was to calm her down. Then, she was asked to remove her dress for the doctor to check the rash. Dr. Mackie asked her to be completely naked. She felt uncomfortable; however, she trusted the doctor. She undressed.

Once naked, Dr. Mackie groped her breasts and digitally raped her. It's as horrible as it sounds.

Another patient, Miss Daisy Perkins, was looking for the bathroom and accidently entered the doctor's room and saw this happening. You will hear from this witness and she will tell you the shock she experienced when she opened the door to Dr. Mackie's office.

You will also hear from delivery driver, Mr. David Denison, who walked past the patient's room and saw her through the side window. He will explain that, through the window, he saw Dr. Mackie groping Miss Jennings.

You will hear from a witness who saw Miss Jennings after the assault. Christoph King was entering the building as Miss Jennings was leaving. He will explain that he saw Miss Jennings crying after she left the doctor's office.

You will hear from other witnesses who will advise how Miss Jennings reacted after the event.

During this trial, you will also hear from expert witnesses who will explain the events in more detail.

Detective Jessica Nam, from the Chicago Police Department, will explain the report that she took from Miss Jennings. Detective Nam will explain the evidence that was collected with the Chicago Police Department's Sexual Assault Evidence Kit. You will hear that Miss Jennings submitted to a blood test, and was found to have Valium in her system. This is a drug that Dr. Mackie had at his office, and is commonly used to calm people's nerves.

You will hear from expert witnesses who will describe the embarrassment, pain and trauma that a sexual assault victim will go through after such a traumatic event. Dr. Mary Wellings, a respected psychologist, will explain the victim impact assessment that she wrote after interviewing Miss Jennings.

This trial isn't a matter of 'he said, she said.' This is a case where we have witnesses who are willing to testify about what they saw.

Make no mistake, this is a crime.

A horrific one.

And in perhaps no other crime is a victim scrutinized so vigorously, nor so intensely. Most victims of sexual assault fear being judged for what happened to them, which leads to many victims withdrawing their cases, or not reporting them at all. It takes a lot of bravery to stand up.

That's what our victim is doing. She's making the brave decision to confront the system.

Victims of sexual assault may suffer harassment, retaliation, and unfair treatment in their community or workplace, and the pain and discomfort of being questioned is one of the worst things that ever happens to most people. A person doesn't make the decision to take a case to trial lightly.

This case will be hard, it will be tough, but I implore you to listen to the evidence.

I thank you for your service to this courtroom. Thank you for acknowledging the truth."

\*\*\*\*\*

As Rollins delivered her opening statement, juror number five sneered. The youngest person on the panel at thirty-five, she was already angry with Dr. Mackie, and the case hadn't even begun. It was hard for the general public to ignore the current media coverage about the abuse of women by men in positions of trust, influence, and power. The media had begun to apply the same guilty notion to all males in positions of authority, but in a court of law, every case had to be judged on its merits, and its merits alone.

A trial is told through two storytellers, the prosecution and the defense, and selecting the right audience to listen to the tale is an important part of the process. The voir dire, the jury selection process which happened before the case began, had been a battle for the defense, however, there was no way to tell how a person would react to the evidence. Consultants were paid in the hundreds of thousands to assess a juror's suitability, but Hunter preferred to rely on his instinct and experience to predict their choices. When asked the right questions, the potential juror would point to their preferences—what websites did they read on a regular basis? Where did they source their news? Which social media platforms did they use?

Questioning the jurors was part of the subtle psychological process of figuring out which way a person might lean. Hunter had planned for a more mature jury—they would be more likely to believe a doctor and doubt a young woman—and he'd gotten his wish. There wasn't one person under thirty-five, and five people over sixty. Seven men, five women.

Juror ten, an older male mechanic who had worked hard his whole life, appeared to have contempt for any person under twenty-five. Juror twelve, in her late sixties, looked like she would doubt every word that came out of Miss Jennings' mouth. She was a complainer, a conspiracy theorist, and a person who questioned everything.

Those two jurors would be Hunter's focus as he delivered his case.

Hunter stood, made eye contact with juror ten, and nodded. Juror ten automatically returned the nod. Standing behind the podium, Hunter began his opening statement.

\*\*\*\*\*

"It's important that right now, at the start of this case, you understand that Dr. Mackie is innocent. Right here and now, that should be your opinion. Sitting there in that jury box, you must presume that Dr. Mackie is innocent.

The presumption of innocence is what our great court system is based on. That's what our justice system relies upon—the presumption of innocence. At this moment, there should be no doubt, nor any question, in your mind. You must look at Dr. Mackie sitting at that table and see an innocent man.

Dr. Mackie is a respected medical practitioner, with more than twenty years of service to his community. During that time, he has not had one complaint. Not one.

Dr. Mackie did not assault Miss Jennings.

That will become obvious to you as we progress through this case. In this era of attack, Dr. Mackie is an easy target.

My name is Tex Hunter and I'm a criminal defense attorney. Along with my team, I represent Dr. David Mackie.

We will present expert witnesses who will state that false claims of sexual assault can happen. It's a sad occurrence when people wish to take advantage of the system, but the truth is that it does occur. According to the research studies, false claims of sexual assault happen in 10 percent of cases. That means one in ten allegations of sexual assault are made up. They are made up for a variety of reasons, however, the strongest reason is money.

A widely respected 2009 study, authored in part by a University of Massachusetts professor, concludes that while most sexual assaults go unreported, of those that are reported, between 2 to 8% are falsely made. That's a lot. You will hear from expert witnesses who will explain this to you in more detail.

During this trial, you will hear that Miss Jennings instructed her lawyers to present an offer to withdraw her accusation for a one-million-dollar payment. That's a lot of money. Enough money to motivate someone to make a false allegation.

You will hear from the receptionist of Dr. Mackie's medical clinic, Larissa Smith, who will testify that in five years of working for the medical clinic, no other person has accidently walked into the wrong room. Not one person in five years.

She will also testify that no other delivery driver has ever seen into a doctor's room, because in the five years that she worked for Dr. Mackie, she never saw the blinds to his office open. Not once. We will present photos to you that will show that Dr. Mackie's blinds are always closed.

You will hear from expert witness, Dr. Amelia Lofty, who will state that factors such as stress, alcohol or drugs can affect a person's memory. She will explain that leading questions by investigators and extensive media coverage on the subject of sexual assault can cause a contamination and alteration in memory. She will explain that some people 'want to try to remember more,' and that could lead to filling in the gaps of an ambiguous or weakened memory with details that then start to feel like memories.

We must remember this is a court of law. This is not a court of opinion. This is not a court where we guess an answer. We must abide by the law.

Finding Dr. Mackie not guilty does not mean you find him innocent or that you don't believe the witnesses. What it means is there isn't enough evidence to make a decision beyond a reasonable doubt.

I want you to remember that. If you find Dr. Mackie not guilty, it doesn't mean that you don't believe Miss Jennings. It means there isn't enough evidence to charge the defendant.

This is a court of law, where we listen to evidence, and only, the evidence. This isn't where you decide an outcome based on assumptions.

You require evidence to make a decision. You will not have enough evidence to make a decision in this case. Your only choice is to find Dr. Mackie not guilty.

Thank you for your service to this court."

# CHAPTER 20

WHEN MISS Katherine Jennings first stepped through the courtroom doors, all the eyes of the attendees were focused on her. She didn't look up. She looked at the ground, head leaning forward, shoulders hunched. She dragged her feet, and refused to look in the jury's direction. Dressed in black, almost like she was attending a funeral, her arms were crossed against her chest, and her black hair was tightly drawn back. Her entrance deserved an Oscar nomination.

Every step she took was under the stare and judgment of the jury members. Her actions, more than her words, were on trial. No other crime demanded the attention and pressure on the victim like a sexual assault case.

For most of his career, Hunter had refused to take on sexual assault or rape cases. He felt the justice system, the system he held so dear, was balanced in favor of the attacker, not the victim. He hated the way the victim was essentially on trial. He couldn't bear to put a victim through the trauma of speaking about those personal experiences not only in the same room as their attacker, but in front of a room full of people they didn't know.

But when Dr. Mackie came to him, protesting that he didn't touch the young woman, he saw truth in his eyes. Dr. Mackie presented the evidence, and it made sense to Hunter. Hunter considered the case for a week, investigated Dr. Mackie's claims, and when he was satisfied the doctor was telling the truth, he took the case. With every week that passed, that truth became consolidated in Hunter's eyes.

Dawn Rollins stood, walked to the lectern, and started questioning with a gentle tone.

"Miss Jennings, I understand how hard it is for you to be here today. Thank you for having the courage and bravery to step forward. Not just for yourself, but for every victim of sexual assault. May I get you anything, perhaps a glass of water?"

"Yes, please." Her voice was meek, quiet. "A glass of water."

One of the bailiffs moved to pour her a glass of water. The packed courtroom was awkwardly silent until after Jennings had taken a sip.

"Miss Jennings," Rollins continued. "Can you please tell the court what you were doing on the date of November 5th?"

"I attended a medical clinic in the Gold Coast and saw a doctor for a problem I had."

"And is the doctor you saw on that day in this courtroom today?"

"He is."

"And can you please identify him for the court?"

"It's that man sitting there at the defense table." She pointed at the defendant. "Dr. David Mackie."

"And can you please tell the court why you went to see Dr. Mackie that day?"

"I had a rash on my upper-thigh that didn't go away. I'd had the rash for about five days and it was getting worse, so I thought I'd better go to the doctor to check that it wasn't anything serious. I'd checked the internet and most websites said this sort of rash was best to get checked out by a doctor."

"And why not see your usual doctor?"

"I don't have a usual doctor in Chicago. I grew up here, but I've only just moved back from New York. I've spent the last five years living in Brooklyn, so I had to find a new doctor. Dr. Mackie's clinic had the soonest available appointment."

"When you arrived at Dr. Mackie's office, can you please explain what happened?"

"I checked in with reception, and sat in the waiting room. There were a few people waiting, because the clinic also has other doctors working there. Five or six, I think. Dr. Mackie was on time, which I thought was good. He introduced himself, and then led me to his room. He seemed nice. He said that I seemed nervous and that I should take the two pills he had in his hands to relax."

"Did you know what the pills were?"

"I didn't know exactly, but he said they were relaxants. He asked me to tell him when I started to feel the effects of the pills. While I waited for drugs to take effect, we had a general chat. We talked about what I had been doing earlier that day, about the weather and about my life. Nothing important. After about ten minutes, I told him I was feeling the effects, and that's when he asked me to lie down on the examination bed."

"What happened then?"

"I was uncomfortable about having a man look at the area around my upper thigh, but the drugs made me feel relaxed. And I thought he was a professional, so it would be fine. I..." Her lip began to tremble, and the tears welled up in her eyes. "I just didn't expect him to do that."

"Take your time, Miss Jennings." Rollins said. "When you're ready, can you please continue and tell the court what happened next."

"He asked me to undress so he could look at the area better. I took off my dress, so I was just in my underwear, and lied down. He looked at the rash, but then he asked me to continue to undress and take off my underwear." Her lip quivered again. "He even asked me to take off my bra."

"Did you?"

She nodded, paused, and wiped her eyes. "Yes."

"Then what happened?"

"He began to feel the area around my thigh..." Jennings covered her face with her hands and began to sob. The jury were captivated. "He began to..."

"Take as much time as you need." Judge Reed

showed his softer side. "The court will allow you all the time you need to talk about what happened."

"Thank you," Jennings dabbed her eyes with a tissue and composed herself. "Dr. Mackie said he was checking the rash. He said... he needed to look closer. He began to feel the area around my upper thigh and then he touched my private parts."

"Did you have a rash there?"

"No. It was only on my thighs."

"What happened next?" Rollins' voice was soft.

"He..." She drew a deep breath. "He inserted his fingers inside me."

A jury member gasped. Rollins allowed the silence to sit in the room for a moment before she continued. "Did he say anything about this?"

"He said I shouldn't worry and that it was part of the medical examination. He told me to stay calm and to be quiet."

"Can you please tell the court what happened next?"

The questioning continued for another two hours. Jennings spent the time describing the event in detail, almost word for word what was written in the victim statement. She broke down a few times to let out the tears, and Rollins offered a tissue each time. There was barely a noise in the courtroom. The crowd were mesmerized by her presentation. She was well-spoken, pretty, and vulnerable. It was hard for the jury to draw their eyes away. As the day drew to a close, Rollins finished her questioning.

"When you went and saw Dr. Mackie, did you trust him?"

"Yes. He was a doctor. He was supposed to be the person I turned to in need. He was supposed to protect me. I went to his office for medical advice about a rash, and I never expected this to happen. I just didn't think it could happen to me. I'm a strong woman. My parents raised me to be strong, but I couldn't stop him. I don't know why I didn't stop him."

"Did you protest at any time?"

"No, I was frozen with fear. I didn't understand what was happening."

"Have you been back to a doctor since?"

"No," Jennings shook her head. "I'm not sure I will ever feel comfortable around a doctor again. I fear them. I fear being in a room alone with an older man."

"Thank you, Miss Jennings. I cannot imagine how difficult that was for you." Rollins turned to the judge. "I have no further questions."

When Rollins finished her questioning, Judge Reed called for a close to the day's proceedings. Hunter had hoped to begin his cross-examination on day one, however Rollins dragged the testimony out as long as possible. It was a deliberate ploy from the prosecution. The jury left after day one with only one side of the story in their mind, and that initial impression was given time to brew in their minds overnight.

The courtroom was full and buzzing at the start of day two, but as Judge Reed walked into the room, the crowd hushed. It became dead quiet. A nervous anticipation filled Hunter's stomach. The Chicago Tribune ran a story about Jennings' testimony, and it was clear which side of the fence they sat on. Although they used the word, 'alleged attacker,' it was hard not to read into the story. Dr. Mackie's public reputation had taken a hit.

When called by Judge Reed, Hunter moved to the lectern. His cross-examination had to be performed with surgical precision—he had to question the witness' statements, but not destroy her as a person or take advantage of her vulnerability. The jury had sympathy for Miss Jennings, and any attack on her would be seen as callous and insensitive. Hunter had to be gentle and soft in his approach, and not attack the seemingly defenseless girl on the stand. His tone was calm, and his demeanor was open. "Miss Jennings, thank you for coming to the court again today. Can you please tell the court where you're currently employed?"

"I'm employed as a barista in a coffee shop in River North."

"Part-time?"

"Yes."

"Do you make much money from that? Perhaps you make a lot in tips?"

"Objection. Relevance." Rollins said.

"Your Honor, I'm trying to establish the witness's

credentials." Hunter argued. "This is important in establishing the background of the witness."

"Go on." Judge Reed snipped. "But make it brief."

"Miss Jennings, do you make a lot of money in tips from your employment?"

"No, not much money at all."

"Before November 5th last year, did you have much savings?"

"None."

"So would it be fair to say that your financial position was dire?"

She nodded.

"Miss Jennings? Please answer verbally."

"Yes. That would be a fair assessment."

"And how is your financial position now?"

"Better."

Hunter could feel Judge Reed's eyes bore into him. He was stepping as close to the line as he could while asking about her savings. "Being a barista isn't what you always wanted to do in life, is it? What other career choices have you wanted to make?"

"An actor."

"An actor." Hunter repeated. "Did you ever act on Broadway in New York City?"

"I was in five different shows that were off-Broadway, yes."

"And what was the last show about?"

She didn't answer.

"Miss Jennings, what was the last show that you performed in about?" Hunter pressed.

"It was about a woman who accused someone of sexual assault."

"Did the woman that you played falsely accuse someone of sexual assault?"

"Yes."

"And what happened at the end of the play?"

"Even though she was lying, the woman received a large payout from the person she accused of assault." She felt the pressure to explain herself further. "The play was about a girl who was being bullied and physically abused by her boss. It was fictional."

Hunter nodded, as did one of the older men in the back row of the jury. The uncomfortable pause hung over the room for a while. "Miss Jennings, do you plan to sue Dr. Mackie in civil proceedings after this trial?"

"I have no plans for that."

"But it's possible you could?"

"I suppose."

"Are you aware of the payouts that go to victims of sexual assault cases?"

"Not really."

Hunter walked to his desk, removed a file, and walked back to the lectern. "Miss Jennings, yesterday the prosecution submitted your phone records to the court as Exhibit 5. They presented evidence that your first call after the appointment was to your mother, who you spoke to for fifteen minutes. After that conversation, you called two friends. The fourth call was to a victim support line for just under five minutes. All these calls were made one after the other. The next call you made was two hours later. Can you please tell the court who your fifth call was to? Was it the police?"

Jennings stared at the prosecution table.

"Miss Jennings?" Hunter pressed. "Was your fifth call to the police?"

"No."

"And who did you call?" Hunter raised his eyebrows. "And I'll remind you that your telephone records have been entered as evidence into the court by the prosecution."

"I called my friend, Thomas Lane."

"Your friend?" Hunter raised his eyebrows. "When was the last time you talked to this friend before this date? Perhaps you talk regularly on the phone?"

She paused for a long moment. "It had been a while."

"More than a month?"

"Yes."

"More than two months?"

"Probably."

"More than a year?"

"I think so." She shrugged.

"How old is this friend?"

"He's in his late fifties."

"And this friend, a person you hadn't talked to in more than a year, what's their occupation?"

She stared at Hunter.

"Miss Jennings, please answer the question."

"He's a senior high school teacher."

"What sort of teacher?"

"A good one."

"That's not what I was referring to, Miss Jennings." Hunter paused. "What subject does Mr. Lane teach?"

"Drama."

"You called a drama teacher before you called the police?"

"Objection." Rollins stood. "Asked and answered."

"Withdrawn." Hunter was quick to respond. "Were you taught drama at school by Mr. Lane?"

"In the past, yes."

"How many years?"

"I can't remember exactly."

"One year?"

"No. It was more like two or three years."

"Was he the person you turned to when you wanted acting advice in your career?"

"I guess so."

"In fact, Mr. Lane set up the audition for your latest play, didn't he?"

"That's right."

"So after the alleged incident occurred, your instinct was to call an acting coach that you hadn't called in over a year. Why do you think that is?"

"He's a friend. I was attacked and I'm allowed to

call my friends. He was the person I thought I could talk to. I didn't know what else to do."

"What did you talk about to your acting coach?"

"I don't remember our exact conversation."

"So when did you call the police?"

"After I talked to Thomas."

"Directly after?"

"No."

"How long after did you call the police?"

"Two days."

Hunter shook his head and looked to the jury. The eldest man on the jury shook his head as well. Hunter had researched the drama teacher, and asked him to testify, however Thomas Lane stated he couldn't remember their conversation. Hunter was sure Lane was lying, but without a transcript or recording of the phone call, there was little Hunter could prove.

"Miss Jennings, do you know a man named Joe Fielding?" Hunter stepped around the lectern and rested one elbow on it.

Jennings' eyes shot to the prosecution table. Rollins looked back at the witness, confused.

"The name doesn't ring a bell," she responded.

"Doesn't it?" Hunter walked back to the defense table and removed a photo of Fielding from one of the files. "Have you ever seen this man?"

"He looks familiar." She rubbed her cheek. Her breathing rate had increased. Her skin started to appear clammy. "Maybe I've met him before."

"Do you know where you met Mr. Fielding?"

"No, I don't remember that."

Hunter nodded. The prosecution team whispered to each other, unsure of where Hunter was going with the line of questioning. Hunter held his gaze on Miss Jennings for a long moment, before closing the file in front of him.

"Thank you for your time, Miss Jennings. No further questions."

# CHAPTER 21

AT FIVE-PAST-ELEVEN on day two, psychologist Dr. Mary Wellings walked to the stand full of confidence. She swore her oath without emotion, and sat in the witness box without even the slightest of smiles. Her hands were folded. Her black hair tied back without flair. Her jewelry was nice, but not expensive. To this audience, she presented herself as a woman without feelings. She was an expert, an unaffected observer of the facts. Despite her lack of flair, she had an undeniable presence. Her natural arrogance translated to confidence in front of the jury.

Prosecutor Rollins began by confirming Dr. Wellings' credentials, which only added to the weight of her expertise. Her qualifications were impressive. She was a Harvard Graduate. Well-published. Presented speeches all over the world. She'd testified hundreds of times in sexual assault cases. The statement of her credentials was essential to establishing her ability to discuss the case as an expert witness. Unlike an eyewitness, who is limited to only discussing what they saw or did, Wellings was charged with assessing the available forensic psychological evidence and rendering an opinion for the court. After a lengthy introduction, Rollins began her questioning.

"Is this the assessment you made about Miss Jennings here?" Rollins held a five-page document in the air.

"It is. I interviewed Miss Jennings about the impact that the sexual assault had on her, and compiled the findings into the report. The report you have in your hand is the result of many hours of interviews and many hours of assessments. We recorded the interviews, and I was able to watch those interviews after the initial consultation."

"How many times did you interview Miss Jennings?"

"Five times."

"How long were those interviews?"

"The longest was over two hours, but each time we talked for at least an hour. In all, we talked for more than seven hours."

"And can you please read the court the opening paragraph of the victim impact statement?"

"'Miss Katherine Jennings has displayed significant mental harm from the sexual assault that occurred in the Mackie Gold Coast medical clinic on November 5th. Miss Jennings went to a person of trust and authority, and had that trust broken. She has displayed textbook trauma behaviors after the event.'"

"And what are some of those textbook

behaviors?"

"Fear is the most common behavior. Victims who have been assaulted typically avoid anything that reminds them of the assault. In this instance, Miss Jennings displayed a lot of fear in her behavior after the assault. She avoided all medical practitioners, even female ones, and has avoided men around Dr. Mackie's age."

"Has Miss Jennings' displayed any other behaviors?"

"Flashbacks, guilty feelings, depression, anxiety. Of most concern were the flashbacks she described. These are worrying because when this happens, it is almost as though the assault is occurring again. These flashbacks woke her up during the night."

"In addition to these behaviors, how else did Miss Jennings react to the trauma?"

"A person reacts to trauma at three levels. These are physical, mental, and behavioral responses. These reactions can occur separately or simultaneously. For instance, a flashback can trigger a physical response, such as increased heart rates, or a feeling of being ill."

"Interesting. Can you please tell us how you assessed Miss Jennings' reaction in more detail?"

Over the next hour, lead prosecutor Rollins took Wellings through line after line of the five-page report, elaborating on the important points. The witness talked in depth about Miss Jennings' appearance, her feelings, and her thoughts. They talked about her actions. They talked about the terms in the report. And finally, they talked about the alleged assault itself, and the words Miss Jennings used to describe it.

When Rollins had finished questioning the witness, Hunter read through his notes on the legal pad in front of him. "Dr. Wellings." Hunter began sitting behind his desk. "You've done a lot of talking about this report. Obviously, you've observed a lot of behaviors from Miss Jennings. Can you please tell the court where those interviews took place?"

"In my office." Her answer was blunt, and as soon as she finished answering, she folded her arms across her chest.

"Nowhere else but your office?"

"That's correct."

"You state that Miss Jennings is now afraid of public spaces?"

"Yes."

"Have you observed her in a public space?"

"She told me she was afraid of public spaces after the assault."

"You've stated in your report that Miss Jennings is now afraid of men in authority. Did you ever witness Miss Jennings avoiding men in authority?"

"That's not my job. My job, as an expert in this field, was to talk to Miss Jennings about her traumatic experience."

"Are you avoiding answering the question, Dr. Wellings? I asked whether you've witnessed these behaviors in person, or whether you were merely told about these behaviors?"

"Objection, Your Honor," Prosecutor Rollins interrupted before the witness could answer. "The court can see where Mr. Hunter is taking this line of questioning. However, the witness has already conceded that the information she has presented in the Victim Impact Report is the result of talking to the victim, not witnessing it in person. Dr. Wellings is an expert witness and her expertise is well established."

"Agreed." Judge Reed responded. "Dr. Wellings, are you willing to state that you have not witnessed Miss Jennings in any other environment than your office?"

"That's correct." Wellings responded.

"Then the objection is sustained. Mr. Hunter, we've established the environment in which the interviews took place, so please move on with your questioning."

Hunter nodded and turned a page on his legal pad. "Dr. Wellings, in all your assessments of sexual assault victims, have you ever found a person to be lying?"

"No," she shook her head.

"And how many assessments have you performed?"

"More than five hundred."

"More than five hundred." Hunter repeated. "And not one of those reports have stated the person is lying?"

"That's correct."

"Do you remember Mrs. Jane Longley?"

"I do." She slowed her speech pattern, not aware of where Hunter was taking the questioning.

"Were you aware that after you presented the Victim Impact Report to the court, and you testified about that Victim Impact Report, just as you're doing now, that the person Mrs. Longley accused of sexual assault was found guilty?"

"I am."

"And were you aware that the person she accused has since been released from prison?"

"Objection. Relevance." Rollins called out.

"Your Honor," Hunter said. "The prosecution has presented the witness as a reliable and creditable source. We have every right to enquire about her creditability."

"Overruled." Judge Reed turned to the witness. "You may answer the question."

"No, I wasn't aware that her attacker had been released from prison. I don't keep tabs on all my past cases."

"Mr. Joshua Mamet, the accused attacker, spent five months in prison before evidence was found that proved he wasn't even in the same neighborhood at the time of the alleged attack. Were you aware of that?"

She shook her head. "This is news to me. Like I said, I don't keep tabs on all of my past cases."

"Mr. Mamet pleaded not guilty and said that Mrs.

Longley was lying to exact revenge on him because he had rejected the married woman's advances at a bar. Did your Victim Impact Report, the one that you presented to the court, the one that you talked about to the jury, state anything about the fact that you thought she was lying?"

"I don't think so."

"Are you aware that since the evidence came out that Mr. Mamet was innocent, that Mrs. Longley admitted she was lying about the assault because she wanted to 'punish' Mr. Mamet for rejecting her?"

The witness shook her head.

"Dr. Wellings?"

"No, I wasn't aware of that, but that case is more than five years old. I've written more than a hundred reports since then. However, I do remember that Mrs. Longley had a history of mental health issues before she made the report to the police."

"Were you aware that Mrs. Longley had been charged with perjury in relation to lying to the police, the court, and the jury?"

"Like I said, I don't keep track of all my cases."

"Please answer the question. Were you aware that Mrs. Longley had been charged with perjury for making up an allegation of sexual assault?"

"No." She snapped. "I wasn't aware of that."

Hunter paused for a long moment, allowing the new information to sink into the minds of the jurors. "So if a client presented their story to you and lied to your face, lied directly to you in an interview in your office, would it be fair to say that you'd believe them anyway?"

The witness looked to the prosecution. The shock was written on their faces as well.

"Dr. Wellings?" Hunter pressed.

"No, I can tell if a person is lying."

"Could you tell that Mrs. Longley was lying?"

"There were…" Her heart rate increased. Her reputation was on the line. "She had a history of mental health issues. There were elements that did set off alarm bells with her statements."

"Really?" Hunter raised his voice. "Where were those elements stated in the Victim Impact Report that you presented to the court? Did you talk about those elements when you presented your findings to the jurors?"

"I chose not to include them."

"You chose not to include them?!" Hunter slapped his hand on the table. "You're telling this court, this jury, that even if you think a person is lying, even if you think they're not telling the truth, you withhold that information from the jury?"

"Well, yes and no. I mean—"

"Dr. Wellings." Hunter's voice boomed. "You're here, in this court, to tell the whole truth. You've admitted that you've previously presented information to the court that's not the whole truth. You deliberately withheld information. Your statements and your reports are so false that they've previously caused an innocent man, an innocent man, to be convicted of a crime he did not commit. Do you expect this court, or this jury, to believe a single word that you say?"

"I…" Wellings looked like a deer caught in headlights, shocked at the sudden turn of events. "I don't understand the question."

"Did you suspect Ms. Jennings was lying or are you withholding that information as well?!"

"I… Listen, that case—"

"Motion to Strike this witness' testimony and the Victim Impact Report from the record." Hunter interrupted the answer and turned to Judge Reed. "This witness has admitted that she previously presented information to a court that was not the whole truth. She has admitted that she knowingly, and deliberately, withheld information that may have proved a man's innocence. Her testimony, nor her report, can be taken in good faith and is extremely prejudicial against the defendant."

Hunter had to strike the report from the court. Without the Victim Impact Report, the prosecution's case weakened. If the report was left in, the prosecution could regain the lost ground on re-direct.

"Prosecutor Rollins?" Judge Reed looked to the prosecution for a response.

Rollins turned and talked amongst the junior lawyers, before standing. "We strongly object to the motion on the basis that Dr. Wellings' expertise is well established in this field and a mistake in one in five hundred cases is not significant."

"The truth is significant in this court." Hunter retorted.

"Your Honor—"

Judge Reed held up his hand to stop Rollins protesting any further. "Dr. Wellings, do you admit that you previously withheld information from a court that could've influenced the jury's decision?"

"Not deliberately. I chose not to include the information because…" She paused to consider her answer. "Because I didn't think it was relevant at the time. I didn't talk about it in court because… well, it would've weakened the case against the attacker."

Judge Reed stroked his thumb over his chin. "The Motion to Strike the witness testimony is granted. Dr. Wellings, you may step down."

"But I haven't—"

"Dr. Wellings, I would suggest that you don't make this any worse for yourself than it already is." Judge Reed stated, before turning to the jury and explaining they could not use the report, or any statement made by the witness, to form their decision about the case.

Hunter sat down. It was a clear win for the defense.

And he wasn't done yet.

# CHAPTER 22

THE FOLLOWING morning, Hunter filed a motion for a mistrial with prejudice, due to the damaging and highly improper statements made by the expert witness. Judge Reed read the motion, asked the jury a number of questions about their understanding of how to disregard Dr. Wellings' testimony, and then promptly rejected the defense's motion.

Following the motion deliberations, the atmosphere in the courtroom was tense. For Hunter, the adrenaline charged excitement of the previous day had become a droning headache. He hoped the five cups of water, three coffees and two aspirins would help, but they were having little effect. He sat at the defense table, reviewing his notes, distracted by the constant movement of Dr. Mackie next to him. Dr. Mackie's leg bounced up and down under the table, unable to control his nerves. He rocked back and forth a little. Even the newspaper reporters mentioned how nervous he looked in the courtroom.

"When the jury walks back in after lunch, you need to be calm. Take some deep breaths, and calm your mind." Hunter advised his client. "The more nervous you look, the guiltier they'll think you are. You need to look composed and confident. Every second of this trial, someone in that jury box is judging you."

"But I am nervous." Mackie responded. "I've never been more nervous in my life. I feel like I could vomit any second. I wasn't even this nervous when I skydived last year. I jumped out of a plane, and I wasn't this nervous. This is my livelihood on the line. Everything I've worked so hard to build could be gone in a week. Maybe I should negotiate with the girl?"

"Is that what you want?"

"How much does she want?" Mackie whispered.

"They said a million in compensation would make this go away."

"A million? I'd have to sell the company to raise that sort of money."

"That's their plan." Hunter nodded. "The only way for you to save your career and hold onto the clinic is win in court, but the choice is yours. The prosecution has left the deal on the table. All we have to do is talk to them."

Mackie looked around and then knocked his foot against the wastebasket next to him. "Not yet. Not just yet. Not when I'm innocent."

The bailiff called everyone to rise for the arrival of Judge Reed. Once the jury was welcomed back into the courtroom, Rollins called the next prosecution witness.

Daisy Perkins entered the courtroom and looked to the jury. She offered them a large smile before being sworn in. Born to a swimsuit model and multimillionaire father, Daisy Perkins won the genetic bingo—athletic, blonde, tanned, blue eyes, straight teeth, and perfect skin. Her upbringing was charmed until her fifteenth birthday, when her father was sent to prison for fraud. Her luxurious lifestyle was stripped away overnight, and now at twenty-one, she was employed as a server in a burger restaurant.

After Rollins spent ten minutes asking preliminary questions of the witness, she turned the focus to the events of the day in question. "Miss Perkins, what were you doing on November 5th?"

"I had an appointment with Dr. David Mackie at 1pm. The appointment was in the Gold Coast Medical Clinic on Elm St." Perkins's voice was high-pitched and shaky. "I called the office and made the appointment about one month before I arrived."

"Did you attend the appointment?"

"Yes." She ran her fingers through her ponytail. "I arrived early and then waited for the appointment."

"And what time did you arrive at the Gold Coast Medical Clinic on Elm St?"

"I arrived at around 12:15. I was early, but I was feeling ill, so I sat in the doctor's waiting room. I didn't want to walk around before the appointment. After a while, I asked the receptionist where the restroom was, and she directed me down the hall."

"When you walked down the hall, did you walk

into the restroom?"

"I was attempting to walk into the restroom, but I took a wrong turn and I accidently walked into another doctor's office. I was feeling so sick, and I was, like, confused. I just didn't have my bearings about me and I accidently walked through the wrong door."

"Do you know whose office you walked into?"

"At the time, no, but I recognize the man now. It's the man sitting at the defense table. Dr. Mackie."

"And when you walked into the office, what did you see?"

The witness rubbed her neck as she prepared to speak about what she saw. "I opened the door, thinking it was the restroom, but it wasn't. I was shocked when I opened the door. It was Dr. Mackie's office, and when I walked in…" She paused for effect and bit her lip. "There was a woman on the bed in his office. The patient was naked, like literally naked, and he had one hand on the woman's groin, and the other on her breast. She didn't have any clothes on, not even her bra. I couldn't believe it. I didn't… I didn't understand what was happening."

"What did you do?"

"I was shaken, embarrassed, and confused. If I knew then what I know now, I would've said something. But I just apologized for going through the wrong door, and left to find the restroom. I didn't know what was happening. I didn't understand it. If I had known he was abusing her—"

"Objection. Calls for speculation." Hunter called out.

"Sustained." Judge Reed replied. "Miss Perkins, please stick to what you saw, and not your interpretation of what you saw."

Perkins nodded and then brushed the tip of her nose with her index finger. "Yes, sir."

"Can you please tell the court how the doctor reacted when you entered the room?"

"He was angry I came into the room." She pulled on her earlobe. "He said it was a private room and I was violating his patient's privacy. He was shocked at first, but then he was angry."

"Did you leave right away?"

"I did. I apologized and closed the door."

"What did you do next?"

"I went to the restroom, and went back to the waiting room. Then I attended the appointment with Dr. Mackie, and left. It wasn't until I received a call from the police that I knew…" She looked up to the judge. "That I became aware there had been a complaint about the doctor."

"When you went into your appointment with Dr. Mackie at 1pm, was it on time?"

"No, he was about fifteen minutes late."

"And when you started the appointment, did Dr. Mackie say anything about the incident you saw?"

"He laughed. Like, literally laughed. He thought it was so funny that I walked into his doctor's office instead of the restroom."

"Did you spend long in his office for your appointment?"

"No. He was rushed and distracted. I told him what my problems were. I was suffering a lot of anxiety, a lot of nerves, and I couldn't sleep. I told Dr. Mackie that I needed something to ease my insomnia, and my previous doctor had prescribed pills to help me, but that was years ago. Dr. Mackie then wrote a prescription, and gave me a small box of pills for my symptoms and told me to go home and rest."

"Do you know what those pills were?"

"Valium."

"Thank you, Miss Perkins. No further questions."

Hunter accepted the offer to cross-examine the witness, but took his time reviewing his notes, before opening his laptop and typing in a number of comments.

"Miss Perkins," Hunter began with a firm tone, "while looking for the restroom, how many wrong turns did you make from the reception area before you arrived at Dr. Mackie's office?"

"I'm not sure." She avoided eye contact with Hunter.

"As introduced by the prosecution earlier on day one, this is the floor plan of the Gold Coast Medical Clinic, Exhibit 25." Hunter entered more details into his laptop, before he turned to the courtroom monitor at the side of the room. "Miss Perkins, as you can see, the waiting room is marked with an X, and Dr. Mackie's office is marked with a Y. The restroom that you wished to use is marked with an O." Hunter paused while the jury looked at the floor-plan of the building. "As is marked on this floor plan, the restroom is in a straight line from the reception area. In fact, there's even a sign next to the reception desk pointing straight down the hall. However, you made two wrong turns before you settled on a door to choose. Why was that?"

"I was sick and confused. I didn't really know what was happening."

"As you can see on the floor-plan, you also passed another five doors on the hallway before you entered Dr. Mackie's office. Can you please explain that?"

"I thought it was the restroom at the end of the hallway. That's what the receptionist said—she said I would find the restroom at the end of the hallway. But I was so sick and confused. I must've taken a wrong turn."

Hunter typed more commands into his computer and presented a photo of Dr. Mackie's door. He introduced the picture as evidence to the court. The door was plain white, with the clearly marked name of Dr. Mackie at eye level in bold writing. "What is it about this door that said restroom, more than the other five similar doors that you passed?"

"I don't know why I chose that particular door, but I was looking for the restroom. I wasn't really thinking about where I was going. I was on auto-pilot."

"Did you deliberately choose Dr. Mackie's office?"

"No, it was a mistake. Haven't you been listening to anything I've said? I said I accidently chose that door."

"Hmmm." Hunter made a disapproving noise, clear enough for the jury to hear, but not loud enough for the prosecution to object. "Were you waiting in the same waiting room as Miss Jennings before your appointment?"

"Maybe, I don't know. I didn't see her before my appointment, but she could've been there. I was feeling ill, so I didn't take any notice of the other people in the waiting room."

"Is it true that you only asked to use the restroom after Miss Jennings had been called into the doctor's office?"

"I'm not sure. I didn't notice her."

Hunter nodded, paused, and then leaned back in his chair. "Miss Perkins, have you met Miss Jennings before?"

"Not that I'm aware of."

Hunter waited a long moment. "Do you know a man named Joe Fielding?"

The shock on her face matched the look that Miss Jennings had given earlier. The jury saw that shock.

"Objection." Rollins scrambled to distract the jury from her reaction. "Relevance. This is a wild goose chase that currently has no direction. Mr. Hunter is implying there is something significant about this name, however he's not making the information available to us, nor do I see the person's name, or any reference to them, on any witness or evidence list. If the defense wishes to include this name in the trial, then Mr. Fielding should be on the witness list."

"It's hard to be a witness when you're dead, Your Honor." Hunter stated. The crowd murmured behind him. "Joe Fielding was murdered only weeks ago."

"Approach." Judge Reed waved them both forward. Hunter and Rollins approached the bench. Judge Reed turned off his microphone before looking at Hunter over the top of his glasses. "What's the purpose of this line of questioning?"

"We believe that this person, who has been charged with fraud previously, is connected to all the eye-witnesses in this case."

"And do you have evidence of this?"

"We do. We have a witness in the defense list who will testify that Joe Fielding previously paid them to lie in court, and Joe Fielding made contact with a witness in this case." Hunter was bending the truth. He was still working on getting Heather Monroe to testify.

"That's a long string to pull." Rollins argued, but the look of shock on the prosecutor's face said it all. Buried in the defense witness list were three names meant to cast doubt on the accusations. One of them was Heather Monroe. He knew she wouldn't testify, and if forced to, she would lie, but that wasn't his goal. He had a different plan for using her name.

Judge Reed thought for a few moments before continuing. "I'll allow you to continue for now, but it had better lead somewhere, Mr. Hunter." Judge Reed turned back to the witness. "You may answer the question."

"Um… the name sort of rings a bell…" Perkins fidgeted with the edge of the chair. "I might've met him somewhere."

Hunter removed a photo and showed it to her. "This man?"

"I think that's him. I'm not sure how I know him though."

"Can't remember?"

"No, I can't remember." She brushed the tip of her nose again. "I don't know where I've met him. It could've been anywhere."

Hunter placed the photo down. "No further questions."

"Your Honor," Rollins stood up as soon as Perkins stepped off the stand, "the prosecution would like to call a recess in the light of new information coming forward."

"There's currently no new information on the table, prosecutor." Judge stated. "There's no need for an unnecessary recess."

"Your Honor. I must protest. We need time to assess the name that's being presented."

"Noted, however as I said, there's currently no new information on the table. You've had months to prepare this case." Judge Reed grunted. "Now call your next witness."

# CHAPTER 23

THE FIRST thing people noticed about David Denison was the scar under his left eye. It was hard not to. His eyebrows were pointed slightly downward, the wrinkles in his forehead were pronounced, and the corners of his mouth were turned down. His nose was long but wide, and his hairline had receded to the point where he should've given up on combing it. He wore a brown suit, the only one he owned, with a mismatched blue shirt, a black tie, and black sneakers.

As the delivery driver on the day in question, he was a witness to corroborate what had already been said, someone who could help build a complete picture, although his police statement didn't provide anything new or groundbreaking. He was another piece of the puzzle, something to add to the weight of the accusations.

"Can you please state your name and occupation for the court?" Rollins began from behind the table.

"David Denison, I'm thirty-five, and I live in Bucktown. I rent a one-bedroom apartment, I live by myself, and I work as a courier driver. I own and drive a Ford Transit Cargo van." Denison was nervous on the stand—his speech was too fast, his brow was sweating slightly, and he was unable to sit in one spot for long. However, it also appeared to be his natural state of affairs. "That's my occupation. A delivery driver. I deliver packages for people."

"And Mr. Denison, where were you on November 5th at around 12pm?"

"I was delivering a package to the Gold Coast Medical Clinic on Elm St."

"And can you take us through what you saw when you delivered the package?"

"I parked at the rear of the building, in a delivery spot off the main road, and walked through the courtyard to deliver the package to reception. It was hard to find a parking spot, but one opened up as I arrived. The main entrance of the building is around the other side, on Elm St, but I walked through the back entrance. I was delivering a package for the first time to the doctor's office and I'd called the reception as I drove there. The receptionist told me it was best to deliver packages via the courtyard, so not to disturb the patient's privacy."

"Can you please tell the court what you saw when you walked through the courtyard?"

"My job is pretty boring, a lot of the time." He looked to the jury, explaining his job. "It pays the bills, but you spend a lot of time on the road by yourself, so I like to check things out as I go past. You know, look in windows, see what else is happening in the world. It's the only way I stay sane when spending so many hours alone. So I was walking through the courtyard, and I look over to my right, through one of the windows. I didn't know what to expect when I looked, but the blinds were open, and I could see everything. And I looked in. Not like a pervert or anything, just out of curiosity. And I didn't expect to see what I saw."

"What did you see?"

"I saw that doctor there, Dr. Mackie, with his hand groping a naked woman's breast. At first, I thought it must be some sort of doctor's thing, like he was checking for lumps or something, but on second look, it looked like he was groping her in a sexual way."

"And when you say 'groping in a sexual way,' what do you mean?"

"I mean he had his hand fully over the patient's breast as she was laying down." He made the action with his hand. "He was rubbing it all over. He had a smile on his face, which I thought was weird."

A few members of the jury nodded. He was nervous, but convincing. Rollins questioned Denison for the next hour, however nothing more significant was exposed. Denison talked too fast, said too much, and his evidence was becoming lost in a rolling wave of description. Hunter objected where he could, but there was nothing else to add. Yes, he saw the incident. Yes, he was sure it was Dr. Mackie. No, he didn't say anything at the time. It was simple questioning, but effective. Rollins rested her questioning and Judge Reed gave Hunter the chance to change all that.

"Thank you for talking to us today, Mr. Denison." Hunter stood and moved to the lectern. "Can you please tell the court if you have any debts?"

"Objection. Relevance. Again, Mr. Hunter is sending this court on a wild goose chase that distracts from the actual crime at hand."

"Your Honor, the defense is allowed to question the creditability of the witnesses."

"Overruled, but don't go too far over the line," Judge Reed stated before turning to the witness. "You may answer the question."

"Everyone has debts." Denison responded. "That's not a crime."

"That's not what I asked." Hunter stared straight at him. "I asked whether you have any debts?"

He shrugged. "A few."

"A few?" Hunter responded. "Do you know how much those debts total?"

"No idea."

"I have information here that says you owe more than $150,000 to various small lending agencies. Would that be correct?"

"It could be."

"It could be? Mr. Denison, can you confirm if these are your details on these loans to five different lenders?" Hunter presented five files to the witness.

"I suppose."

"Yes or no, Mr. Denison."

"Yeah, alright. They're my debts. They come to $150,000. Sure. But it doesn't mean anything."

"Have you defaulted on any of the loans in the past?"

"I don't know."

"Shall I present that information to you as well?" Hunter raised his eyebrows.

"Alright. Sure. Yeah. I've defaulted on those loans in the past. I'm not the only one to have defaulted on loans. It happens. I don't always have work, and when there's no work, I can't pay the loans."

"And on November 10th, did you make $5,000 worth of payments to five different loan agencies?"

"I don't know how you know that. That's private information."

"Again, that's not what I asked. I asked, did you make $5,000 worth of payments to five different agencies?"

Denison looked up at the judge. "You need to answer the question, Mr. Denison."

"Yeah, alright. I caught up on the loans. They were my back payments. I had some money, so I got those loan sharks off my back."

"Did you pay it in cash?"

"Yeah."

"Where did that money come from?"

"I had a big bet come in. Won some money on the horses. Someone gave me a tip. I made a bet with a bookie and won. It's that simple."

"Was this after you presented as a witness in this

sexual assault case?"

"Objection!" Rollins leaped to her feet. "This is an outrageous accusation and is completely unfounded."

"Mr. Hunter." Judge Reed raised his eyebrows to Hunter. "Do you have any evidence that these two are connected, apart from timing?"

"No, Your Honor."

"Then the objection is sustained." Judge Reed turned to the jury and explained they needed to disregard the statement by the lawyer and any connection between the timing of the debt payment and the timing of the witness statement. Judge Reed delivered a good statement about the comment, but it was useless. The damage was done. The jury were already questioning the connection.

"Mr. Denison, do you know Mr. Joe Fielding?"

"I knew him. He was an associate of mine. We'd crossed paths a few times, but I hadn't seen him in years. When we met up, we talked about the Cubs. He was a big Cubs fan. He always thought they were going to win the World Series. Every year he'd say that it was their year."

"You haven't seen him in years?"

"That's what I said."

"Can you please look at the court monitor and tell us about the people in this photo, which you posted to your Facebook profile, dated July 5th last year?"

"There's a bunch of people in the photo. Do you want me to name them all?"

"Is one of them Mr. Fielding?"

He paused. "Ok. Yeah. I forgot about that day, but I remember now. I saw him over the July 4th weekend. We partied together, but I wasn't hanging out with just him. It was a party."

"On July 5th, did you talk to Mr. Fielding about setting up a doctor to make enough money to pay back your debts?"

"Objection! Accusation!" Rollins shouted.

"Sustained!" Judge Reed's voice thundered through the courtroom. "Mr. Hunter! You will not interfere with the administration of justice through such outrageous questions. That's your final warning. Another stunt like that and I will charge you with contempt."

"I withdraw the question, Your Honor."

Hunter turned his gaze to the jury and juror five in the back row nodded. It was a coincidence too big to ignore, and as much as the prosecution was trying to avoid it, the doubt was beginning to rise.

"No further questions."

# CHAPTER 24

THE FOYER of the George N. Leighton courthouse was filled with echoing footsteps tapping against marbled floors, murmurs of lawyers and defendants negotiating, and the cries of victims and their families about the failures of justice. The inexhaustible line of people needing their day in court seemed to get bigger every year. It was a mess of noise, a confusion of sound, but Hunter didn't want to be anywhere else. The building was his second home. A place to see justice served and integrity upheld.

Hunter was exiting the building for the weekend, briefcase in hand, when he heard his name called out. He stepped through the doors into the cool breeze before he turned around to see who was following.

Detective Regina Heart jogged through the doors behind him. Dressed in a suit with shoulder-pads, she moved through the exit with confidence and elegance. Her hair was tied back tightly, she wore thin glasses that made her face look long, and she walked with a waft of perfume following her.

The Chicago PD detective looked like she'd taken

on more than her fair share of trauma, but she worked for a purpose. In the sexual assault unit, she had found her life's calling. A victim herself, she was determined to expose the predators of the world and not allow someone else to experience her pain.

"Tex Hunter. We need to talk." She was firm as she came up to him. "I know what you're trying to do in that courtroom and I don't like it."

"Are you on the witness list? I don't remember seeing your name on there."

"I'm not on the list, but one of my colleagues is. She's on the stand next week. She's the detective that took the complaint and investigated the claims of sexual assault against Dr. Mackie."

"Ah. Yes. Detective Jessica Nam."

Heart nodded to her left, towards an empty corner near the outside entrance, away from the exits or passing foot traffic. Hunter followed her to the corner. The sound of the traffic hummed nearby, the sun was dipping beyond the horizon, and the breeze was gentle. The smell of cigarette smoke was strong, with a number of used butts near their feet.

"I've been sitting in that courtroom listening to what you've had to say. What you're claiming in court is ridiculous—someone like Joe Fielding wasn't clever enough to tie his own shoelaces."

"You knew Fielding?"

She looked around and didn't see anyone within earshot. "I've investigated him in the past. He attacked a young lady on the street, she pressed charges and I took the report, but then she suddenly dropped them. I'd suggest she got paid by Fielding to drop the charges."

Hunter nodded. She'd given a whiff of information, a taste, to suck him in to try and get more information. He didn't fall for the trap and waited for her to continue.

"Listen," she drew a deep breath. "If there's one thing I hate more than sexual assault, it's people lying about it. I can't stand people using the system to get paid for false testimony. We have to be bigger than that."

"We can agree on that. It's an abomination to lie about sexual assault."

"Then you'd also be aware that any lies will undo all the decades of progress we've made. We've worked so hard to develop an environment where people can confidently come forward with accusations of sexual assault. Times have changed." She looked around. "The worst thing that can happen now is that we start having cases in court that people have lied about. That'll destroy everything we've worked so hard to achieve. The media coverage here is too dangerous. If the media reported that a high-profile case like this was full of lies, then we'd go back ten years. It would destroy all the trust we've built, not only with the courts, but with the general public. The doubt around sexual assault claims would start to increase."

"The media do love this case." Hunter replied.

"What are you asking me to do?"

"I'm not asking you to do anything illegal. It's just…" She looked around for any prying ears again. "I'd like a heads up if you think these witnesses and the defendant are lying about the assault."

"Then consider this conversation your heads up."

"Do you have evidence?"

"We've got some, but we're not presenting it to you. If we do that, you'll tell the prosecution, and then we have no tactics left for the courtroom. I'm not falling for this good guy technique." Hunter grunted as he began to walk away. "I'm not that gullible."

"Wait," Heart reached out and grabbed his forearm. "Listen, the second we get any evidence that this is a set-up, I'll convince the prosecutors to drop the case. There's usually so little evidence in a sexual assault case that we can't have people lying about these cases. If that starts to happen, we'll never be able to get a conviction for any case. You've got to look at the big picture. This is bigger than just this case. If doubt starts to creep into the national psyche, then nobody is going to believe the victim. That can't happen. Not now."

"The big picture? My big picture is that the prosecution is going after a respected doctor with a weak case full of lying witnesses."

"Two witnesses and a defendant that's willing to testify is not a weak case. That's a strong one for sexual assault. We had to take this to court. Please, at least talk to me about what you've got. Let me look into it."

"Alright. I get it." Hunter said and ran his hand through his thick hair. "If the public starts to doubt sexual assault accusations, it'll make it hard to land convictions in court. I get that. But I've got to defend my client."

"Let me work with you. Tell me what you know, and I'll share anything I find. We're on the same team here. If these witnesses are lying, I want them to be prosecuted. I'll drag them into court myself."

"And if you investigate it and don't find anything?"

"Then I won't say a word. I'll have no involvement in the case unless I find something that can help you."

"How do I know you'll keep your word?"

"I'm a person of honor, Hunter. I wouldn't be doing this job otherwise. I certainly don't do it for the paycheck. And if you're right, then I'll owe you one. Anything to do with a case, I'll help you out."

Hunter nodded. His play had worked. The detective was smoked out of the woodwork by the questions he presented on the stand. "We found that Fielding had paid an accuser previously. The claim was also against a doctor, and Fielding suggested the person should invent extra charges to strengthen their case. Fielding paid the accuser to file the report with the police, but the charges were dropped after the accuser took a payout."

"A good payout?"

"Enough to put a deposit on a house."

She nodded. "Name?"

"Well…" Hunter hesitated.

"Something like this going through court could undo a decade of hard work. The media love your cases, and if they get wind of this, they'll run it on the front page. It'll set the movement back years. I can't allow that to happen."

"You give me something, and I'll give you something. I need you to find Joe Fielding's previous assistant. She disappeared a day after Joe went missing, and all we have is a name—Rebecca White. Fielding was a paranoid man, and covered all his tracks, and it looks like the assistant did the same. We know he had an assistant, but no one knows where to find her."

"I'll contact my people on the streets. Consider it done."

"There is one person who knows this case is a set-up. I need your gentle touch to convince her to testify. If you can do that, I'll give you everything I know." Hunter nodded his response. "But you're not going to like it."

"Why not?" She squinted.

"Because the woman is your cousin." Hunter stated. "The person you want to talk to is Heather Monroe."

# CHAPTER 25

STACEY SAT in her empty house on a Friday night, a glass of wine on the table. Next to that was another empty bottle. There was a new red wine stain on the white carpet, but she didn't care anymore. She used to yell at her husband if he wore his dirty work boots in the house, but now, she didn't care at all. There were bigger things to worry about.

She closed all the doors to the rooms upstairs, and half of the doors downstairs. The house felt too big, too cavernous, without the children running around. The empty space wasn't good for her mental health. She'd been passing out drunk on the couch most nights. She didn't want to sleep in her bed without her husband there. Staying in the living room, she had a couch, which doubled as a bed, a bathroom in the next room, and the kitchen two doors away. Her own little apartment. She had barely left those four walls in weeks.

Staggering drunk, she walked to the kitchen, and looked through the drawers. There were scissors, knives, many sharp objects. They all caught her eye. She liked sharp things. Time was counting down to her trial date, and she could feel the tension building. Her shoulders were tightening, her stomach constantly clenched, and her ankles hurt. She had never felt so bad, but she had also never drunk so much, nor eaten so little. She couldn't hold the food down. Wine and ice-cream were just about her only sustenance.

When night came again, when the darkness fell outside, she built up the courage to collect the mail that had piled up in the letterbox. She grabbed one of the kitchen knives, and opened the front door. She looked up and down the street, even though it was late. No cars. No movement. No threats nor any prying neighborhood eyes to judge her appearance.

She stepped forward onto the porch, gripping the knife in her right hand. Running down the path, she threw open the letterbox, grabbed the fist full of letters, and ran back inside without looking back. She slammed the door tightly behind her, huffing long deep breaths. She locked the door, dead-bolted the top lock, and placed a chair under the door handle.

After walking back into the kitchen, she placed the pile of letters on the table. Bills, advertising, nothing of note in the fist full of papers.

Until the last letter.

It had her husband's name on it, but it was the business address in the top corner that made her heartbeat faster.

"That can't be right." She whispered to herself.

She stared at the letter for five minutes before she

opened it. An invoice for services. Five hundred dollars. Payable by the end of the month.

Her heart pounded against the walls of her chest.

"Why was Carl talking to them?" she asked herself, but she knew the truth. There was no denying it. "Why them?"

She raced to the desktop computer in the office, the one he used when working from home. She turned on the computer and looked at the website history. Her heart beat harder. The sickness washed through her again.

"How could he? How could he go to them?" She asked herself over and over, becoming quieter each time. "Not them. Why did he go to them?"

She knew things were bad in their marriage, she knew they were struggling, but she never expected he would go to her biggest rival. She never expected this level of betrayal. She checked the website history again. The questions he typed into the search engine confirmed her suspicions.

She walked out of the home office and bumped into the wall. She stumbled, before moving back into the kitchen. Out of all the people they knew, out of all the choices, he had chosen them. That had to be deliberate.

Carl had contacted Vandenberg and Wolfe Family Law Offices to discuss a divorce. The invoice was dated six weeks earlier. Only five days before she was charged with Joe Fielding's murder.

Her heart sunk. She gripped her chest. She

couldn't breathe. Was that what he wanted? To break up their family? She fell to the kitchen floor and cried.

The idea of divorce hurt. It cut her deeply.

But worse than that, worse than the heartbreak, was the suspicion it raised about the man she once trusted.

# CHAPTER 26

FIVE AM. Hunter snapped awake, his heart racing and traces of a cold sweat rolled across his forehead. His breathing was shallow and his heartbeat thundered in his ears. Even awake, his dream was still vivid—his sister, Natalie, on a murderous rampage, killing all the teenage girls from the local neighborhood. The look on the murdered girls' faces haunted him. Their faces spoke of indescribable terror. She had slit their throats. Buried them in the woods. He could see it. He could feel their pain.

He picked up his cell phone and rang the cell number he had for his sister again. It was disconnected. He called the café in Puerto Vallarta next. No answer. He'd left messages at the café before, many of them, but hadn't received a call back. They said if he called again, they would block his number.

She was refusing to talk, and refusing to even entertain his questions.

Hunter couldn't get back to sleep. The nightmare that his sister was a killer was becoming too real. The previous day, he tried to see his father in the Cook

County Prison and confront him with the new information, however, when he arrived, Hunter was told his father had been transferred to the prison hospital and wouldn't be available for days. His father didn't have long left. That was becoming clearer with each visit.

His father had secrets, many of them, but it never crossed Hunter's mind they would be family ones. If the new theory was true, on one hand, he admired his father's sense of family honor, and his determination to protect his daughter at all costs. But on the other hand, he hated the idea that a serial killer was going free without punishment. He was torn between justice and family, integrity and honor, and he wasn't sure where he stood.

At five minutes past eight, after a number of coffees and an hour of morning news, Hunter's phone rang. It was Detective Heart. She came through on her promise to find Joe Fielding's previous assistant. Hunter and Jones had been searching for Rebecca White, however, she was going under a different name. Heart had all her details— name, address, date of birth, employment, and most importantly, her current whereabouts. Since Fielding's death, Rebecca White had changed her first name to Becky and started using her mother's maiden name, Bennett, on her identification. She'd deleted all her social media profiles, changed her cell number, and moved cities.

There was seldom a quiet Saturday morning for

Hunter. His usual routine was to grab a coffee and bagel from a coffee shop, one that he only visited on Saturdays, open his laptop, and begin work before most people had even thought about what to do with their weekends. There was always more work, always another lead to follow, always another client to protect.

By 10am, Hunter was on the road again, pushing to find the next clue.

The movie theatre in the small city of St. Charles, 45 miles west of Chicago, was the perfect place for someone to hide. Becky Bennett was thirty-five, had dark hair, and was clearly happy in her current employment at the front counter of the movie theatre. She had cut her hair, changed her glasses, and changed jobs since Joe Fielding was murdered five weeks earlier. She cut all ties with Fielding's past, but there was still one friend in Chicago who knew where she was. And that was all Detective Heart needed.

Hunter walked into the movie theatre and to the front desk. Twenty-five years ago, the desk was innovative, sophisticated, and cutting edge, but in the years since it hadn't been updated. However, the staff took pride in their place of employment, and it looked as if the theatre had only been erected weeks ago, in a retro-style to match the fashion of the 90s.

"Hello, how may I help you?" Becky Bennett avoided eye contact as Hunter approached.

The foyer around them was empty, with no movies near starting time. The carpet was off red and clean, the neon lights that lined the walls were slick, and signed movie posters of past blockbusters sat behind the counter.

"One ticket to prison for perjury." Hunter approached the counter, towering over the staff member.

She raised her head and looked at him confused. "That's not a movie here. I haven't heard of that one. Are you sure you're at the right cinema?"

"It's stars Joe Fielding."

She inhaled loudly, and then covered her mouth with her hand. It took her a moment to calm herself. "Ok. Listen, whatever Joe was involved with it doesn't have anything to do with me. If he had debts, then I can't pay them. His life wasn't my life. Whatever you want, I can't help you."

"My name is Tex Hunter. I'm a criminal lawyer and all I want is to talk to you, Becky. Or Rebecca White. Whichever name you wish to go by." Hunter used a calm voice. "I need ten minutes of your time to talk."

Becky bit her lip and looked across to her colleague at the other end of the theatre. Her colleague was busy refilling the popcorn machine, but was eavesdropping on their conversation.

"I can cover for you." The other girl said, aware of the tension. "It's quiet. There's not another movie due to start for the next hour. Take your lunch break now."

Becky gulped, wiped her brow, and then stepped

away from the desk, indicating for Hunter to follow her outside. She walked out the front doors of the cinema that led to a large open-air parking lot. Once outside, she looked up and down the street to see if anyone was watching, before continuing to the furthest corner of the building, to the place where the workers escaped to have a cigarette. Once around the corner, she stopped and turned to Hunter.

She looked up at the building. "There's a camera there." She pointed to the roof. "If you try anything, it'll be recorded."

"I'm not going to try anything." Hunter held his hands up. "You're safe."

"You said you're a lawyer. Who for?"

"Dr. David Mackie."

"You've got five minutes." She took a cigarette out of a half empty pack. "Ask what you have to ask."

"Why did you disappear before Joe's death?"

"I needed a change."

"We can either talk here, or I can issue you a subpoena and drag you back to Chicago."

She stared at her cigarette. "You said you were a lawyer?"

"I did."

"Alright. What's in it for me?"

Hunter reached into his coat pocket and withdrew his wallet. He took out a fifty-dollar bill and handed it to her.

"Double it and I'll tell you everything."

Hunter drew a deep breath and took out another

fifty. "For this price, I need to know everything you know."

She took the notes and shoved them into her back pocket. "Alright. Joe always had a plan for me. It was one of the first things he taught me when I started working for him. He always knew danger was coming from somewhere. If Joe was…" She lit her Marlboro, and took a long drag. "If Joe was in trouble, then I had to disappear. That was always the plan. He made sure I kept a 'run fund,' which was enough money to disappear if needed. I thought he was being paranoid at first, but the longer I worked for him, the more I realized how much I needed it. The plan was always simple—burn all the evidence in his office, change my last name to my mother's, change my address, delete social media, and change my phone number. Joe was caught up in a lot of things. He knew a lot of dangerous people. I don't know what happened the night he died, but I know I wanted nothing to do with the aftermath. Joe was always finding trouble. The cops came and talked to me the day after he died, when I was in the office. As soon as they stepped out the doors, I went through the ten-step plan that Joe put together. But I didn't kill him. I was out partying that night. I have lots of people to be alibis for me."

"I'm not here to accuse you of anything. I'm trying to figure out what really happened the night Joe died. Your plan explains why there were no records in Fielding's office after the cops came and talked to you. Do you know who Joe was working for before his death?"

"He kept a lot of that stuff away from me. Didn't want me to get involved. I was just the office help. Photocopying, taking phone calls, organizing his schedule, all that sort of thing. He said knowing too much about his business was dangerous. He gave me a few names, but no one I knew. He never took clients to the office either. I never met his best paying clients." She took another drag and looked at the cigarette in her hand. "I gave up the smokes; you know? For one year straight. Didn't touch the things. But the stress of having to restart my life was too much. They're just too easy."

"If Joe didn't bring his clients in the office, where did he have the meetings?"

"He used to meet them at a bar called the Whiskey Five. It's a dive bar, up in Wicker Park. Seedy. It's where he did most of his business and where he got most of his business. They all know each other up there. That's why there were no clients coming into our office. The bar was his second home. He wouldn't bring them into the office because he thought people were filming the entrance. I'd never met anyone more paranoid than Joe."

"Did you know any of the employer's names?"

"One of them was the law firm that gave him most of the work."

"Vandenberg and Wolfe Family Law Offices?"

"That's them."

Hunter nodded. "Was Joe acting strange before his

death?"

"Absolutely. He said... he said he was about to hit the jackpot. That he could take care of us forever. He'd do this one last job and then he'd pay for me to move to California with him. He promised we were going to live the highlife. We weren't dating, but he wanted to look after me. It was always that way with Joe. He'd promise the world. He always had the next scheme, always the next idea. That's how we first met. I was part of one of his ideas."

"Which was?"

She bit her lip again. "I was an actress. I had dreams of making it big, and now, maybe I'll become a character-type actor, if I get the chance. I'm getting a bit old for my big break, but I know I can add value to any show I'm doing."

"Joe was producing a movie?"

"What?" She squinted. "Joe? No. Five years ago, he approached me to do some acting. I did one small job for him, and after the job, he asked me to work for him as an assistant. Work had dried up in acting, so I worked for five years in his office."

"What job did he want you to do?"

"He wanted me to... you sure you're not a cop, right?"

Hunter nodded his response.

"I did a few jobs for him. The first, he wanted me to sit in a doctor's office in Wisconsin. Just make an appointment and wait in the waiting room. He wanted me to lie and say that I saw a girl run out of the doctor's office crying. Joe asked me to make a statement to the police about what I saw, but the charges were dropped. I didn't go to court for it. Easiest thousand dollars I ever made."

Hunter nodded. Becky Bennett. The witness in Wisconsin, and the third new patient that didn't show up at Dr. Mackie's office. He placed the name now. "The second job?"

"Joe wanted me to pretend to be in a relationship with someone, and then he'd organize a payout somehow. I didn't know the specifics. All I knew was that it was a good plan—he even had witnesses lined up to act like they'd seen us together. All I had to do was follow a woman out of a hotel, sit next to this woman a few times on the train, sit next to her in cafes, and walk near her while exercising. I didn't know what it was about, and I didn't break the law. I just tried to hang out with this woman, without her noticing me."

"Who was that target? Another doctor?" Hunter asked.

"She wasn't a doctor, and I don't remember her name. Joe wanted me to go up to her and make it look like we were in a lesbian relationship. To make it look like she was cheating on her husband."

"Why?"

"For a divorce case."

Hunter drew a long breath, and the puzzle became more complete.

All the pieces were falling into place.

# CHAPTER 27

HUNTER WALKED around the long wooden boardroom table, tapping the edge with his finger as he went. The boardroom in the law offices of John C. Clarke was subdued, with the blinds pulled shut, and the dark wood wall paneling added to the sense of dim lighting in the room. All the furniture could pass for antique and there wasn't one modern appliance to be seen, and, except for Hunter's nervous pacing, there was a sense of calm in the room.

"Why does she want to meet now?" Hunter asked as he turned to pace the floor again. "It can only be for a deal. She wouldn't be coming here otherwise."

"I'm not sure, but I guess we're about to find out." Clarke sat with one leg crossed over the other, hands resting on his lap. "Michelle said it was important. I'm going to guess it's a new deal for us to take to Stacey, not that it'll help her. I think Stacey's going to take this all the way, even if that's not the best decision. So, it's up to us to convince her of the way to move forward with her life. We'll have to use a lot of tact when presenting a new deal to her."

"As Winston Churchill once said—tact is the

ability to tell someone to go to hell in such a way that they look forward to the trip."

Clarke smiled. "And the hardest road often leads to the most amazing destinations. If we can convince Stacey to take a lesser deal, she can start moving on with her life."

Hunter looked at his watch as he paced the floor. 5:05pm on a Saturday evening.

"Prosecutor Michelle Law is here." The assistant leaned into John C. Clarke's office boardroom. "She's alone."

Clarke waited for a moment, closed two of the files in front of him, and then stood to welcome Michelle Law into the room. "Hello, Michelle. Please come in and have a seat."

"Thank you for meeting me so late on a Saturday. I'm sure you've got better things to do." Law walked in with her briefcase. "Hello, Tex."

"Michelle." Hunter greeted her. "You said this was important?"

"It is." Law moved to the front of the room, placed her briefcase on the wooden table, and opened it. She removed her laptop, turned it on, and then looked at the two men. "Won't you sit, Tex?"

"I'll stand." He leaned against the wall at the back of the room, arms folded across his chest. "I hope this'll be quick. I'm in the middle of a trial."

"So I heard. A sexual assault claim is always a challenge to defend when there are witnesses to the event." Michelle Law looked around the room. "This is a nice boardroom, John. Spacious. Can't afford something like this on public money. I guess that's the price you pay for defending felons."

"The innocent pay a lot to make sure they're not thrown behind bars by overzealous prosecutors," Clarke responded in a calm tone. "Innocent people like Stacey Fulbright."

"I'm sure," Law drew a breath and sat forward. "You two men obviously aren't interested in small talk so I'll get to the point then—we've got a new deal on the table for Stacey Fulbright. We're putting a deal on the table under 720 ILCS 5/9-3."

"Involuntary Manslaughter." Hunter responded.

"She acted recklessly when she attacked Fielding. She had a complete disregard for his life, and there's no doubt she would've know her actions would lead to his death. There's no sign of a struggle, so there's no chance you'll get off on self-defense. Fielding was a strong guy, and someone like Stacey Fulbright would not have outmuscled him. That leaves one option—she stabbed him when he wasn't looking."

"Sentence?" Clarke asked.

"A two-year sentence, with a year suspended. She'll serve twelve months behind bars, and after that, she's free to go. She can pick up the pieces after a rather unfortunate event where she took another person's life."

Hunter stared at her for a long moment. "What's triggered this?"

"The courts are busy, Tex. The system is

overloaded. The world is full of criminals and there's a long line of people to process. If we can take a deal on a clear-cut case, then it's beneficial for everyone. The court system doesn't need any more pressure chasing cases that can be dealt with out of the courtroom."

Clarke sat back in his chair. He smiled. "There's something you're not telling us, Michelle, otherwise you wouldn't be here on a Saturday. You would've waited until Monday, or perhaps even later in the week. You're scared we're going to find something out before you can make a deal. What've you found?"

"Nothing at all." She typed into her laptop. Her fingers looked like they were moving at the speed of light. "We're here to get the best outcome for all involved. We've got to think about justice for the victim, and those that knew him. But we're willing to start a discussion about manslaughter charges, instead of murder."

"What have you found?" Hunter stepped forward, leaning over one of the chairs. "What is it?"

"There's nothing official, and good luck digging this information up, but the deal we're willing to put on the table is two years for manslaughter. We can negotiate prison conditions if she's willing to entertain the idea of a deal. But I must warn you that this deal will only be on the table for the next five days, after that, we'll take it all the way to trial. Stacey Fulbright killed Joe Fielding, that's obvious, but we're willing to admit that perhaps she didn't intend to kill him.

Perhaps it was self-defense."

"I'll take the deal to her and discuss it." Clarke smiled. "Ultimately, it's her decision, but it's a good offer. I'm sure she'll appreciate the offer, even if she doesn't take it."

"Thank you for the free pass, Michelle," Hunter added.

"What do you mean?" She tilted her head as she spoke.

"By coming here on a weekend, so desperate to offer a new deal, you've given us a whiff," Hunter stood tall as he held the door open for Law to exit. "We're going to find the information, and then we're going to make sure this case is thrown out."

# CHAPTER 28

HUNTER LOVED Sundays in the Loop, Downtown Chicago. They were quieter, less frantic, and it gave him time to appreciate his city. There was less traffic on the roads, less pedestrians on the sidewalks, and less tourists asking for help. The weather was warming up and he decided to walk the thirty minutes from his apartment to his office. The sun broke through the clouds, bathing the city in a soft orange hue, and a few photographers were already out setting up to take photos of the beautiful city.

As he walked to his office, he tried his sister's cell number again. Still disconnected. He tried the café. They yelled at him to stop harassing her and told him to never call again. He tried to call them back but they blocked his number. He started to contemplate another trip south, but doubted whether that would make any difference. She was almost a lost cause.

He used his swipe card to enter the building, greeted the security guard, walked across the empty foyer, and rode the elevator to his office. Saturday had gone well for him. Two leads in two different cases.

He was excited by the breakthrough that Becky Bennett, Fielding's former assistant, had given him for Dr. Mackie's case. She refused to testify, and if subpoenaed, she stated she would lie and deny everything on the stand. Hunter would work on that. He would rather convince her to come to court of her own accord rather than force her to. He knew Detective Regina Heart had a better touch than he did, and she would only help if it looked like he could prove the witnesses were lying.

But it was a lead. A whiff of information. All that he wanted. The questions bounced around his head as he unlocked his office door—how many other people had Fielding and his connections tried the scam on? How many other times had he run it? By the time they got to Dr. Mackie, they had almost perfected the scam. It was dependent on the witnesses' ability to lie, but they were well chosen. Broke and good actors. The perfect scam artists.

Hunter opened his emails once he was seated at his desk. Jones had messaged to say he was working on collecting the video footage from the Whiskey Five, the bar Becky Bennett mentioned that Fielding used for work meetings, but the owners of the bar were refusing access. Privacy was essential to holding onto their high-paying customers.

As Hunter tried to gather information on the Whiskey Five bar, his phone pinged with a message. It was Stacey. She was outside the building. Hunter called the security officer, who escorted her into the building. Hunter stood and walked to his office door, waiting for Stacey to exit the elevator.

"Stacey. What a surprise." Hunter invited her in. "Come in."

She didn't say anything. She held her arms across her chest, head down, shoulders slumped forward. Her hair was frazzled, her skin was dry, and she had the odor of a woman who hadn't showered in days.

She walked through the office without further invitation or even a greeting, and sat down on the leather chair in front of Hunter's desk. Hunter squinted at her as he walked through his office, staring at the woman who refused to make eye contact. He lowered himself into the chair, waiting for Stacey to begin the conversation.

After a few moments, she shook her head a number of times, her frazzled hair shaking in one large mess, and she then tossed an envelope onto the desk. Parts of the envelope were stained yellow by tears. Hunter reached forward and removed the letter inside.

"An invoice from Vandenberg and Wolfe Family Law Offices?" Hunter questioned.

"Addressed to my husband." She snapped. "From Vandenberg and Wolfe. He had a meeting with Michael Vandenberg only days before I was set up for murder."

Hunter's mouth hung open for a moment. He looked at the invoice again. "This isn't a lot of money.

Only five hundred dollars. For that amount, you'd only get to talk to them for an initial meeting. They're not cheap."

"Don't you get it? This is more than a divorce case." She responded. "Carl was talking to them about getting a divorce. He wanted me gone. My husband, the man who was supposed to be there through thick and thin, 'til death do us part,' wanted me gone. He wanted me out of his life. And he went to talk to the people who made me the angriest."

Hunter's mouth hung open for a long moment. "You think—"

"Yes." She raised her eyes to stare at him. "He once said to me that if we ever separated, he could never let his children live with me. He would do everything to hold onto them. This is it. He didn't want to let his children go. He did this. He wants to take full custody of the kids."

Hunter stared at the invoice as the information rolled around his head.

"John called me yesterday and said there's a new deal on the table. Two years for manslaughter, with a year suspended. I have to take the deal." She continued. "Whatever deal is on the table; I need to take it. I have to. It's what's best for the kids. Carl can look after the kids, and then once I'm out of prison, I can work on rebuilding a life."

"We've still got to investigate what the prosecution knows. They know something that we don't. It's not in discovery yet, but they've got new information coming. They wouldn't have put the deal on the table otherwise. You know that." Hunter placed the invoice on the table. "We've got to find out what it is."

"I don't expect you to understand, Tex, but I need to do what's best for Noah and Zoe. If I have to sacrifice myself, then that's what I need to do. I have to do what's best for them. I know Carl would never hurt them, I know that. He loves them so much and he's such an amazing father. But…" She looked at her hands. They were shaking again. Anxiety had become an ever-present feeling that she couldn't escape from. "But I also know that Carl will fight for them. He'll torture me to get to the kids. This is a no-win situation for me."

"We don't know that he's set you up yet."

"I need to take the deal, Tex. I have to do it for my kids."

Hunter leaned back in his chair. He looked at the ceiling. "Michelle Law came to us at five o'clock on a Saturday evening with a deal. That's very unusual, Stacey. It means she's desperate for you to sign this deal before we find out what they know."

"I don't care anymore, Tex. I can do a year. It's not that long. Michelle Law wants someone to pay for Fielding's death, and she's not going to stop until I'm convicted. A year isn't bad. I can keep my head down, stay out of trouble, and then, in twelve months, everything is forgotten."

Hunter took a number of deep breaths before he leaned forward. "Give me a few days to look into it."

"Don't you get it, Tex? I don't care about that. I don't care about the case. I don't care about any of this anymore. I have to protect my children. And this is what's best for them."

"Give me a few days, Stacey. Please. The prosecution has said the deal is on the table until Thursday morning, and that'll be long enough for me to investigate the case. Let me see if I find some information about what they know. You're a lawyer, Stacey. You know how this works."

She didn't answer. She was hunched forward, leaning her elbows on her knees, hair drooping over her face.

"Five days, Stacey. Worst case scenario is that the same deal is still on the table, and you sign it, and do the time. But the best-case scenario is that we can find the information to get these charges thrown out."

She stood, looking around the office, unable to control her shaking hands. "You have five days, Tex. If you haven't got anything by then, I'll sign that deal."

# CHAPTER 29

STACEY FULBRIGHT huddled under her heavy blanket, her head resting on the arm of the couch, watching the mind-numbing television. It was another reality show. It was too fake and rehearsed to be funny. Even their moments of emotional drama seemed scripted. Another empty bottle of wine sat near her. This time, she hadn't even bothered with the glass. It was how she had spent the last five weeks—nervous, anxious, drunk, and over-thinking everything.

Never one to consume much alcohol, Stacey had avoided being drunk for most of her adult life. But as the pressure of the court case was starting to build, as the fear started to set in, she couldn't avoid it. It was an escape, a way to disappear from the rumble of thoughts that steamrolled through her head. She found that she preferred blacking out drunk on the couch to lying in bed, tossing and turning, and thinking about the case for hours on end.

The lavender flowers in the middle of the dining room table had died weeks ago, and she hadn't mustered up the strength to replace them. She used to love the smell of lavender. It was fresh and calming. For most of her marriage to Carl, the smell radiated through the house. Now, her home smelled of alcohol, sweat, and nerves. It stunk of loneliness.

After mustering all her energy, she opened her phone and scrolled through the happy photos of her children, her husband, and of her past life. They all looked so happy, so joyous. It seemed so long ago. A lifetime. As she scrolled through the photos, she imagined her children in Florida, having a vacation with their father, squealing as they went on the biggest theme park rides.

Carl had always had a dark streak. She knew that. He was a good man, a man who worked hard and provided for his family, but he could snap in an instant, with no warning at all. The fact she didn't see the divorce coming scared her. This was her world and her work—she thought she'd heard all about the signs of a failing marriage. The amount of times she'd spoken to women about their divorces was countless. They all told her the signs to look out for. It was the little things, they said. The moments where love should be.

On reflection, she had noticed the signals, but she hadn't done anything about them. She didn't think her problems were that big and she ignored them, hoping they would go away.

She was sure she could do a year in prison. After that, she could rebuild a life without Carl. They could split the custody of the children, and she would avoid

Carl altogether. But if he killed Joe Fielding, then could he do it to her as well?

As a woman dedicated to defending abused wives, she thought she'd heard the worst of the stories. The black eyes. The broken bones. The fear of death. She could sympathize with her clients, and she thought she understood their pain. It was only once she was experiencing that fear for herself that she truly understood how fearful an existence it was.

So many women had come into her office abused and broken. She'd heard the same story over and over—the husbands who beat them were drug addicts, alcoholics, or had anger-management issues. Those men were easy to spot. They almost wore their ability to abuse others like a badge of honor. It was the quiet abusers that scared her the most. The ones that would bottle up their rage and only let it explode when alone. Carl had that potential. She saw him snap a number of times, but it was always behind closed doors.

Carl was a good planner. Smart. Organized. Cunning. He'd could've lured Fielding to the parking lot. He could've used her letter opener and then planted it next to the body. He could've been planning the whole thing for months. But as much as she thought he did it, she still had her doubts. Carl had a good heart. He was once full of compassion. Full of love. He attended church occasionally, and felt bad if he had to kill an insect. He had a gentle touch. A nice soul.

The ringing of her cell phone shocked her from her half-asleep, half-drunken state.

It was a blocked number. Thinking of the possibilities about her children, she answered it.

"Hello?" Her voice was soft and cautious.

"Take the deal." The man's voice on the end of the phone was firm.

"What deal?" She whispered.

"Take the deal or your family will suffer."

The caller ended the conversation.

She shook as she stared at the phone. Her heart rate increased. Her breathing quickened. She recognized the voice but it wasn't her husband's. It was rougher. Deeper.

Staring at the phone shaking in her hands, she knew what she had to do.

She now had only one option.

She had to do what was best for her children. If she took the deal, her children would grow up as the children of a convicted felon. Of a prisoner. She didn't want that for Noah or Zoe. She couldn't imagine the pain they would suffer as children of a felon. Their reputations would be forever tainted. As children of a killer, their life paths would be altered dramatically.

That left her with only one option. There was only one thing left to do.

She had to say goodbye to her life.

# CHAPTER 30

THE PROSECUTION used the following Monday morning of Dr. Mackie's trial to refresh the juror's memory of the week prior. Rollins called a number of expert witnesses, all adding little drops of information to the available pool of knowledge and reinforcing the facts that were stated the week before.

Hunter had spent the night fueled by coffee, trying to find the information that the prosecution had on Stacey Fulbright's case. He came up with nothing. No new witnesses, no new angles, and no possible leads. He wasn't sure what new information the prosecution had found. He was running out of time with Stacey's case, and she was going to sign on the dotted line for a crime she didn't commit. He understood her decision, he understood why she needed to protect her children, but he didn't like it. John C. Clarke was continuing to work the case, and would call Hunter the second he heard anything.

Before walking into court that morning, Hunter spent fifteen minutes in the front seat of his car, redirecting his focus back to Dr. Mackie. There was always more than one case, and always more than one place for his attention to go. He had to be switched on for the courtroom. One opportunity might be all the case presented, and Hunter needed to grab even the smallest chance. He had to push back his thoughts about Stacey Fulbright and her family, as well as his sister Natalie and his father's case.

As more expert witnesses in Dr. Mackie's case testified, Hunter objected where he could, he threw shade at the witnesses, questioned their credentials, but overall, the case still was stacked against them. When the prosecution called their fifth expert witness for the day, Dr. Mackie's nerves were beginning to show. His leg jiggled under the table again, his eyes dashed all around the courtroom, and he rubbed his fingers over each other in a repeated pattern. Hunter asked him to control the nerves, but he also knew it was hard. Everything Dr. Mackie had worked for, everything he spent his life building, was on the line. There was doubt, but not enough to win the case.

Hunter had pressured Detective Regina Heart to talk to Heather Monroe and Becky Bennett. They were the real hope. They were the ones that could turn the case around, but they had to be convinced to testify. If Heather Monroe testified, she would break her non-disclosure agreement and possibly risk losing her home. The risks were high, but if she told the truth and told the court that Joe Fielding asked her to make up extra charges against Dr. Lighten, the case was over.

After the procession of expert witnesses, Judge

Reed called an end to the day's proceedings. The jury had filed out, looking bored, and starting to look like they wished the case would end. Dr. Mackie waited at the defense table until the prosecution had also left the room. "That wasn't a good day, was it? We're about to lose, aren't we?"

"They all can't be spectacular days. It's about winning the war, not the little battles. We can give the prosecution a win or two because we've got to focus on the big picture. Tomorrow will be better."

In a daze, Dr. Mackie walked out of the courtroom without saying another word.

After he had exited, Hunter sighed and slumped into his chair. The truth was so close, but he was struggling to prove it in the courtroom. He knew Dr. Mackie had been set up, he could sense it in his bones, but he couldn't prove it in the courtroom. Hunter rubbed his temples, sighed again, packed his briefcase and left the courtroom. When he stepped into the marbled halls of the George L. Leighton courthouse, his phone rang.

It was John C. Clarke. It was his fifth missed call from Clarke in the last hour.

He went to answer the call, but he noticed Carl Fulbright waiting in the hallway. Carl looked tired, his eyes were red, and his skin was dry, but his fists were clenched.

"You." Carl pointed at Hunter. "Tex Hunter."

"Carl?" Hunter squinted. "What's wrong?"

"She killed herself."

"Who?"

"Who? Who! Stacey! My wife!" Carl yelled. "Stacey killed herself!"

People around them stopped and stared. The bailiffs raised their eyebrows. They stepped closer.

"What?" Hunter whispered. "What are you talking about?"

"Stacey's dead." Carl glared at Hunter. "She killed herself on Sunday afternoon. Her mother found the note."

"No. How?"

"Jumped off a bridge into the river! It's all your fault, Hunter. It was you. You were supposed to save her. You were supposed to protect her. You let her die!"

"No. No. No." With eyes wide open, Hunter shook his head. His legs started to give way. He sat on a nearby chair. "This can't be right. Not Stacey. Not now. We were so close."

"It's in her suicide note." Carl leaned his fist into the wall, standing above Hunter. "They found her car at the bridge. I'm... There's a note."

"Why? Why now?"

"The note said the court case was too much. It said she wanted to take the deal but she couldn't hold on any longer. This is your fault, Hunter." The rage grew in Carl again. His teeth ground together. He pointed his finger in Hunter's face. "This is all your fault! You should've looked after her!"

"Me? Really, Carl?!" Hunter stood, looming over Carl. "The last time I talked to her, she was devastated that you'd been talking to Vandenberg and Wolfe Family Law Offices."

"What?" Carl's mouth hung open. "What are you saying?! My wife is dead, and you're accusing me! I was in Florida! I was with my kids. I didn't even find the note! Her mother found the note and called me. This is your fault!" Carl snarled; his fists tight. "Wait... How did you know about my meeting with Vandenberg and Wolfe?"

"Stacey found an invoice from them, addressed to you. The letter came to the house, Carl."

"No..." His voice trailed off. "No, no, no."

"Are you saying you didn't meet with them?"

"No, I mean, yes, I did meet with them, but that was five months ago. We were on rocky ground, but I wasn't going to get a divorce. After talking to the lawyers, I was determined to see us through. And after this murder charge... I was going to stand by her. Why would they send the invoice now?" He turned around, unsure of where to go next. "No! That invoice would've tipped her over the edge. No!"

He clenched his fist, and he punched the wall. The bailiffs started to walk closer.

Carl looked at Hunter. Hunter nodded and rested his hand on Carl's shoulder. Carl resisted for a moment, before he fell into Hunter's chest, and began to sob.

# CHAPTER 31

THE FOLLOWING days of the prosecution's evidence in Dr. Mackie's trial came and went in a blur. Despite an abundance of caffeine, Hunter struggled to focus on the case at hand. Expert witness after expert witness came to the stand to discuss their knowledge of sexual assaults. One expert witness, a feminist lecturer, accused all doctors of having the potential to be sexual predators. There was a commotion after the testimony, and Judge Reed told the jury to ignore every word of her statement after Hunter objected and filed another motion, but even with the drama, even with the loud commotion, Hunter's mind was elsewhere.

The police concluded that Stacey Fulbright had climbed up and then jumped off the Chicago Skyway Bridge. They hadn't found the body yet, but that wasn't unusual. It was a spot known for people wanting to end their lives. There were helpline numbers on the bridge, the police said. Another driver had seen Stacey walking along the edge of the structure. Another saw her climbing the metal frame. The police sent someone to the bridge to investigate the report, but she'd already gone. Heavy rains had recently washed through, and her body could be miles away.

She'd written a suicide note, left her car at the entrance to the bridge, and sent a goodbye message to her mother. Her purse was left in the car. Hunter retraced the steps of the case a thousand times—what could he have done differently? What more could he have said? Would Stacey still be alive if he agreed that she should take the deal? How could he have helped her?

In his state of distraction, Dr. Mackie's sexual assault case was beginning to tip in favor of the prosecution. A guilty verdict was looking likely. Under pressure, Dr. Mackie had started to consider a deal. They still had the offer on the table as Rollins knew the case wasn't open and shut. Even with the witnesses, there was an air of doubt still in the courtroom, but was it enough to convince twelve members of the jury? Hunter wanted to advise Dr. Mackie against a deal, but the last week had left a sour taste in his mouth.

Hunter's advice to continue the trial until a decision was based on logic—they still had the chance to win the sexual assault case. The jury didn't look convinced, and their minds could change in the jury room. All it took was one loud voice in the deliberation room, one strong opinion, and the case could end with a hung jury. It wasn't a win, but it was the best they could hope for. Hunter doubted whether the prosecution would try the case again without new evidence.

At Hunter's request, Judge Reed adjourned the trial for the weekend on Friday at midday. Rollins didn't object when Hunter explained he wanted to attend Stacey Fulbright's memorial.

After the morning in court, Hunter returned to his building, overwhelmed by his thoughts. He walked into his office, greeted Esther, and then removed his dry-cleaned suit from its bag. He closed the office door and changed his suit.

Hunter struggled to hold back his emotions. He hated the feeling of grief. In that moment, he was taken back to those days as a ten-year-old. The feeling in the pit of his stomach reminded him of the instant the jury members said his father was guilty. The moment the jury foreman stood in front of the full courtroom and said those words. The foreman's voice was strong, loud, and angry. It was the moment Hunter lost his father forever.

Hunter could feel that sensation again. It was a poison, an acid leaking through his stomach and infecting every inch of his being. His arms were weak. His legs could barely stand. He could taste the grief again.

He remembered the confusion he felt as a ten-year-old. People behind him cheered at the verdict. They hugged. They yelled. They high-fived. His brother, next to him, said nothing. His mother sat down on the bench and began to cry. His father didn't turn around. He didn't look at them. He stood at the defense table, head down, hands together in front of him, as the judge confirmed the decision.

The lawyers next to his father didn't care. They almost seemed happy. They had no intention of saving Alfred Hunter. They wanted to see the man the media dubbed as the 'Chicago Hunter' locked away in prison for life. In their minds, he was a serial killer taken off the streets.

The bailiffs took his father away. Still, he didn't turn around. The courtroom cleared, as did the noise of celebration. Patrick helped their mother out of the courtroom, leaving Hunter in the front row of the courtroom alone. He stared at the empty jury box. He didn't understand how they could've said he was guilty. How did they come to that decision? The feeling of illness rushed through every part of his body. He wanted to be sick. He wanted to curl into a ball and make the pain stop. He had failed. He had let his father go to prison. As a ten-year-old, he thought he could've stopped it. He thought his testimony would've proved how great his father was. He thought if the lawyers had allowed him to speak, he could've convinced the jury of his father's innocence. He could've explained to them that his father couldn't have been a serial killer. He spent twenty minutes sitting alone in the court before the bailiff yelled at him, called him scum, and told him to leave. At that moment, Hunter vowed never to feel like that again.

But standing in his office, staring at himself in the

mirror, he could feel that sensation build in his stomach. He felt ill. He blinked back the tears.

After fifteen minutes alone in his office, Esther knocked gently on the door and entered the room.

She found Hunter standing in front of the full-length mirror that was on the inside of one of the cupboards, staring at his own reflection. He was dressed in his darkest suit, the one he only wore for funerals, trying to turn his black tie into a Windsor knot. His hands were shaking, and his eyes were filled with tears.

"Let me help." Esther said softly as she stepped forward and took the tie into her hands. "I can do that."

Hunter didn't resist.

"We're getting somewhere in Dr. Mackie's trial." Hunter said, trying his best to focus on work. "We're establishing the groundwork for a major push next week. Christoph King is on the stand on Monday morning, and he'll provide a major turning point for us."

"Sure." Esther said as she untangled his tie.

"If we can prove the link between him and Joe Fielding, then we have a chance to create doubt in the minds of the jurors. Monday is our chance to win the trial."

"Ok."

"We need everything to go right. If we can prove the connection, then we have a chance. That's all we need. A chance. I can win it from here."

"Of course."

"I just…" Hunter looked away. "I have to win this case."

"Your tie is ready." Esther patted the Windsor knot. "It looks good."

"Esther?" Hunter whispered.

"Yes?"

"Can you come with me to the memorial for Stacey?" He didn't look at her. "Please."

She paused for a moment, before responding. "Of course I can."

# CHAPTER 32

HUNTER SAT at the back of the church hall, away from those who were going to outwardly display their strong emotions. The hall seated fifty and every seat was filled. At the front of the room, a small shrine to Stacey Fulbright was displayed. Photos. Her favorite red shoes. Her favorite book. They were a collection of her life, a tribute to a woman who tried to make the world a better place. To the left of the shrine, a projector screen had been set up. Flowers had been piled up underneath the screen.

Hunter was seated against the wall, near the entrance, on one of the fold-out metal chairs, watching the memorial from a distance. Carl had decided against a formal funeral until they found her body. He didn't want to bury the last remaining sliver of hope that he had. Instead, the family settled on a memorial to celebrate the life of Stacey Fulbright. It was going to be positive, Carl told everyone. We need to celebrate her life, he said. The music, while somber, was upbeat, and there were more happy tears than sad ones.

The church hall had been painted recently, and the

smell still hung in the air. The candles at the front of the church were lit, but it did little to hide the paint smell. The sun streamed in the skylights, almost a signal from above.

The police divers spent a week looking for Stacey's body in the bottom of the river, but they came up with nothing. They found her jacket, and one of her shoes, and concluded that the body washed further downstream. The rains had come through and cleaned the river. Bodies weren't always found; the police told the family. One day, she might show up.

Carl denied the request for a death certificate until they found her.

After the speeches, photos of Stacey Fulbright's life splashed on the screen at the front of the room, met with smiles, laughs, and tears. It was the photos of the family that broke hearts the most. The pictures of her babies, so lovingly cradled in Stacey's arms, didn't leave a dry eye in the place.

The memorial was full of sadness, but it was Noah and Zoe's bewilderment that ate at Hunter. He remembered that feeling. That feeling deep inside, clawing away at his stomach. It made him physically ill. He couldn't take his eyes off Noah, sobbing in the front row. As Noah sat next to his sister and father, Hunter couldn't help but feel that he had failed them. He had failed to protect Noah from the horrors of the court system.

Hunter remembered the days after his father's trial, the days when he felt most alone. He had lost his father to the prison system. His mother had been arrested in the days after the trial as an accessory. His older brother was dealing with the trauma by partying and never being home, and his sister Natalie had fled to another country.

That empty pit of loneliness filled his stomach again.

After an hour of memories and speeches, the fifty or so attendees began to disperse out the back doors of the church hall, and into the sunshine.

Michael Vandenberg walked behind Hunter as they exited, and then leaned close to him. "It's sad, our Stacey going like she did."

Hunter nodded his response.

"Stacey and I… well, we had our differences in the courtroom," Vandenberg continued. "But I never expected her to go out by her own hand. I never expected her to do it herself. I guess that's the profession we're in. There's a lot of pressure in our jobs. A lot of mental stress. I'm sure you know what that's like. It's a hard world we live in. Lots of us go that way."

"Are you here to support Carl?" Hunter's tone was flat.

"Carl?" Vandenberg looked at him in confusion. "No, I'm here because Stacey was a colleague of mine. We had many interactions over the years, and I'll miss challenging her on the rule of law."

"I know Carl approached you to talk about a divorce."

Vandenberg's mouth hung open for a long moment. "I talk to many people and not all of them follow through on the divorce. Carl and I had a chat. Nothing more. A chat doesn't mean he was considering a divorce."

"You represent people with money like Christoph King, not the little guys like Carl Fulbright." Hunter responded. "To even discuss the case with Carl, it would've been personal against Stacey."

"This isn't the time to speak of things like that. The past is the past. Let it rest. A woman is dead, for crying out loud. Let it go. Stacey was an intelligent woman and a formidable opponent. May she rest in peace." Vandenberg shook his head. "I'll be at the Whiskey Five in Wicker Park if you want to join me for a drink later. We can make a toast to Stacey."

Hunter didn't respond as Vandenberg walked away. Hunter waited a moment, then stepped to the side of the crowd, and took his cell phone from his pocket.

"Ray. I've found the link in Dr. Mackie's case." Hunter called his investigator. "But I need the footage from inside the Whiskey Five bar."

# CHAPTER 33

HUNTER SPENT all of the weekend in the office. He couldn't leave it. It was the only way to distract himself from the barrage of blame he had rolling through his head. He considered sleeping in his office on Saturday night, but decided it was best to head back to his apartment. He arrived at his apartment late, had two whiskeys, then he lay in bed for five hours, before deciding that he couldn't sleep. He was back in his office by 8am Sunday morning. By the time Esther had arrived with lunch, the whiteboard in the boardroom was filled with notes in various colors.

"There must be something." Hunter said as Esther walked into the boardroom. "There has to be something we can pressure King with. He's on the stand tomorrow and he knows more than he's telling us. The fact that he's arrogant enough to get on the stand, means he's arrogant enough to make a mistake. We can pressure him about his first divorce and how much he lost. The fact that he got burned in that divorce case so badly still hurts him. You could see it in his eyes. That's the way I have to break him."

"Good morning to you." Esther greeted him and held up the bags. "I brought sandwiches."

"Yes." Hunter turned and then relaxed. "Sorry. Yes. Good morning, Esther. Thanks for coming in."

The midday sun streamed in the windows behind Hunter. It was bright, and Hunter liked it that way. Esther unwrapped the sandwiches and handed Hunter his favorite—a pastrami sub from Manny's Deli. An institution in the city, Manny's Deli was regularly rated as one of the best subs in the state. The smile on Hunter's face said it all. "You know how to make a man happy."

"Well," her cheeky smile shone through.

Hunter grinned as he sat down next to her, silent as they bit into their sandwiches. At the same time, they both unconsciously let out a groan of pleasure, followed by a laugh.

While they enjoyed their subs packed full of meat, they talked about the memorial and the beautiful photos that were displayed. They talked about the flowers, and the sadness that the family was experiencing. Carl and the children were well-supported, but moving on would be hard.

"When I go, I don't want a celebration. None of these photos, or the touching soundtracks. I don't want any of it." Hunter said as he took a final large bite of the pastrami goodness. "Just pack me up, and ship me off. There's no use anyone being sad about it."

"I'd be sad." Esther said.

Hunter didn't respond, staring at the whiteboard instead. They sat in silence for a few moments before Hunter stood and walked back to the board. He picked up a marker and began writing again.

"Christoph King's first wife got seventy-five percent of everything, not just half." Esther said as she finished her sandwich. "She got the house, the kid, the cars, and control of his shares. He practically had to restart his business after that."

"But he fared better in the second divorce. After being burned in the divorce case, King remarried five years later, but that marriage didn't last long. It was only a few months before she filed for divorce. He married a young woman named Laura Charter, who had quite the following on social media. She filed first, but then withdrew it. King learned his lesson from the first divorce and turned to Vandenberg to represent him, and that was settled between the lawyers for only $500,000. It wasn't disputed by Charter. At the time, King was estimated to be worth as much as $10 million."

"Why the low settlement then?" Esther questioned as she licked her fingers. "What tipped the balance in his favor?"

"The wife's new lover stepped forward. She was willing to testify that they were in a relationship. A female, as well. The wife denied any cheating, but the pre-nuptial agreement stipulated that any cheating reduced the settlement to almost nothing. The second wife had to settle because Vandenberg had photos of

Charter and her new female lover together. Charter was previously in two female relationships, according to her social media posts. She denied ever being in a relationship with the new woman, but Vandenberg presented photos of them. He had photos of them leaving a hotel together, walking together along an exercise path side by side, and having lunch together. Charter denied it all—she said the woman followed her out of the hotel one night when she was traveling to New York, then was coincidently next to her on an exercise path, and coincidently next to her at a communal lunch table."

"It all sounds like too much of a coincidence. In a different city, leaving the same hotel?" Esther scoffed. "No wonder she settled for such a small amount. No judge would've believed it was a coincidence, and she would've got nothing."

"Exactly." Hunter snapped his fingers. "That's what Becky Bennett was talking about. The woman who ended up becoming Joe Fielding's assistant. That's exactly what she said. She had to follow a woman out of a hotel, sit near her, and follow her around for a while."

"What do you mean?" Esther questioned.

"It's Fielding again." Hunter grunted. "Christoph King paid Fielding to set up Laura Charter. What a plan. The photos made it look like too much of a coincidence, and even though Charter was telling the truth, no judge would've believed her. She would've got nothing in the divorce settlement, and her lawyer would've advised her to take the low settlement from King or leave with nothing."

"If it wasn't so evil, it would be genius." Esther placed the wrapper in the trash can. "Are you sure King organized it?"

"King or Vandenberg would've paid Fielding. One of them is behind it." Hunter responded. "This has to be our opening for the testimony tomorrow. It'll be an opening to pressure King on the stand, something to turn the screws tighter while he's under oath."

"Will it break him though? He's not going to reveal what he knows about this case just because we know about his ex-wife. He's smarter than that."

Hunter sat back down in the office chair closest to the whiteboard. He tilted his head up, resting the back of his head on the top of the leather chair, before tapping his head against it.

It was all there, all the information they needed to prove that Dr. Mackie was set-up, but he was going to have a hard time convincing the jury of the connections. The jury needed a plausible story, not one that was thrown together at the last minute. As it stood, they weren't going to find Dr. Mackie innocent.

"Vandenberg, King and Fielding have a history of setting people up. Who knows how long they were doing this sort of thing?" Esther took a loud slurp from her water bottle. "And Dr. Mackie's wife is currently being represented by Vandenberg's law firm in the divorce. So how do we prove it? How do we prove that one of them set this up? Fielding is dead, and Becky Bennett is refusing to testify. You said that even if we put her on the stand, she'd deny everything."

Hunter's phone rang. He looked at the number and placed his cell phone on the table.

"Jones. Tell me you've got something good."

"Are we talking about my success with the ladies last night at the club, or are we talking about your case?" Ray Jones laughed. "Because I tell you, last night—"

"Hello, Ray." Esther interrupted.

"Oh, hello Esther. I guess I won't go into details about my night in the club then."

"I don't think I need to hear that." Esther laughed.

"Give me something on the case." Hunter said. "I need something, Ray."

"The people in the Whiskey Five were tough negotiators, and they wouldn't give me the file footage. Privacy is their thing. Without it, they wouldn't have a business. They protect their clients. But the guy behind the bar was happy to talk, off the record, of course. He said Joe Fielding met with two people only days before Dr. Mackie was set-up. And you're going to like what I have to tell you."

"Tell me it's good."

"Oh, it's good, alright." The joy in Jones' voice was clear. "They're refusing to give us any footage, but they were happy to tell me about it. It might not be enough to convict someone of fraud, but it's a lead."

"How do we expose them if we don't have video or photos?" Esther questioned. "If the Whiskey Five won't release the footage, how do we prove Fielding was meeting with people there?"

Hunter smiled. "All great magic tricks are about misdirection."

# CHAPTER 34

CHRISTOPH KING walked to the stand full of confidence. His shoulders were back, his chin held high, and his stomach stuck out. He looked like he owned the place. He was well-dressed in a suit, walking with a smooth and confident swagger. The arrogance that he was above the law was overwhelming.

Rollins welcomed him and thanked him for coming to the court to testify. He'd been through the process before—twice—and appeared comfortable on the stand.

"Mr. King, can you please tell the court where you were on November 5th?"

"Certainly. After a morning in my office, I drove to the Gold Coast, parked on the side of the road of Elm St, and walked towards the medical clinic owned by Dr. Mackie. I thought I could stretch my legs before going inside. The air was nice, and I didn't mind the walk."

"And why were you visiting the medical clinic?"

"I wanted to talk with Dr. Mackie about a business proposal. And as I was walking into the clinic, just as

I was about to open the door, I saw something which I thought was unusual at the time."

"And what was it that you thought was unusual?"

"I saw a woman leaving the doctor's office with tears streaming down her face. She was walking out of the doctor's office doors as I was heading in. I went to say something to her, I thought the doctor must've given her bad news, but she avoided me. I stepped towards her, and she turned away."

"Did you know the woman?"

"At the time, no, but later I came to know her as Miss Jennings. It was only once the police contacted me after that day, that I put the pieces of the puzzle together."

"Can you please describe how the woman was crying?"

"Like a sobbing cry. The sort of cry a person tries to hide but it's clear to see. It looked like she was trying to hold it in."

"And when you saw her crying, how close were you to the victim?"

"She brushed past me. Not even five inches apart. She was trying to shelter her face, but then she looked at me as I went to ask her if she was alright, and that's when I saw all the tears."

"What exactly did you ask her?"

"I can't remember exactly what I said, but I said something like, 'Are you alright?' or 'Can I help you?' Something like that."

"Did she say anything in reply?"

"No, she didn't. She turned away from me and kept walking down the road."

"What happened then?"

"I watched her walk away crying, then I went into the medical clinic to talk with Dr. Mackie."

"And did you talk with Dr. Mackie?"

"Unfortunately not. The receptionist said he was busy."

Rollins nodded and looked across to the jury. His testimony had built a clearer picture of Miss Jennings' reaction to the event, and confirmed everything that came before.

"Thank you for your time, Mr. King."

Rollins sat down and looked over at the defense table. She struggled to hold her smile in, as the case was tipping in their favor. It was difficult to prosecute sexual assault cases, and even harder when there was no direct evidence on the victim, but the witnesses of the case had built a convincing story.

Judge Reed asked Hunter if he would like to cross-examine the witness, and Hunter accepted. He stood, and took his time to walk over to the lectern. He placed his legal pad on the podium in front of him, fixed his tie, and then looked to the witness. It was time to make a play.

"Mr. King, previous to November 5th, had you met Dr. Mackie?"

"Yes."

"And when had you met Dr. Mackie?"

"He owns a medical clinic, and I was attempting to

buy his business at the time. He also owns the building which houses the clinic, and I saw a business opportunity to expand my company, and help the clinic grow. Dr. Mackie and I had numerous discussions over a period of around fifteen months before that day. He was reluctant to sell, so there'd been a lot of negotiation. I met with Dr. Mackie many times."

"You said Dr. Mackie wasn't available that day?"

"That's correct. The receptionist told me he was busy."

"Did you have an appointment with Dr. Mackie?"

"No."

"So you thought you could just walk into a busy medical clinic, with a practicing doctor, and he would be available to chat?"

"I like to talk face to face with people. I find it easier to negotiate when I can see the person."

"Were you surprised that Dr. Mackie wasn't available?"

"Not really."

"Did you wait for Dr. Mackie to become available?"

"No. Once the receptionist told me he was busy, I left a message and went back to my office."

"A waste of your time then?"

"Not exactly. It's good to let people know you're available if you're negotiating with them."

"So it was a coincidence that you arrived at the medical clinic at the same time as Miss Jennings was leaving?"

"I guess so."

"Hmmm." Hunter paused and tapped his finger on the edge of the lectern. Some of the jurors made notes, others looked blankly at the witness. "Would you benefit from the purchase of the medical clinic?"

"Possibly."

"Did Dr. Mackie give you a reason why he hadn't sold the medical clinic to you?"

"He did."

"And why was that?"

King drew a long breath, pulling his jacket towards the middle of his shirt. "He said he wanted to continue to treat his patients in the area."

"And if you owned Dr. Mackie's clinic, you'd have a monopoly over the surrounding area, is that correct?"

"I suppose."

"Then you could raise your prices, couldn't you?"

"That's not part of the business plan."

Hunter paused, and turned to look at Esther, who was sitting in the front row of the court seats, behind Dr. Mackie. Hunter nodded, and Esther stood and moved out the doors of the courtroom.

It was time.

"Mr. King, can you please tell the court if you knew a man named Joe Fielding?"

"I knew him, but I hadn't seen him for many years."

The court doors opened at the back of the room.

Hunter held King's eye contact for a moment and then turned and nodded towards the entrance. Detective Regina Heart walked in first, and following was her cousin, Heather Monroe. She looked towards King, and then walked to an available seat in the front row. Esther Wright walked in next, followed by Becky Bennett. They sat in the second row of the courtroom, in full view of Christoph King.

King's mouth dropped open.

Hunter looked to the jury.

The pressure was on.

# CHAPTER 35

CHRISTOPH KING squirmed in his seat. He ran his hand through his hair, fixed his tie, and his eyes darted all over the room. He didn't know where to look. Hunter allowed the pause to sit in the room. The jury members looked confused. They had seen the women walk into the courtroom, and watched King's nervous reaction. Even Judge Reed looked confused.

"Mr. Hunter?" Judge Reed called out after a few moments. "Do you care to continue questioning this witness?"

"Yes, Your Honor." Hunter looked to the jury. They were waiting with bated breath for Hunter's next move. "Mr. King," Hunter's voice was firm. "You said that you hadn't seen Joe Fielding for years. Is that correct?"

"Objection. Asked and answered."

"Withdrawn." Hunter was quick in his response. "Mr. King, can you please tell the court if you have ever gone to a bar called the Whiskey Five?"

"I've been known to go there on occasion."

"And did you meet with Joe Fielding in the

Whiskey Five on November 1st, only five days before the alleged incident?" Hunter held up a still image of the video footage inside the bar. He didn't introduce it as evidence. Becky Bennett coughed loudly and caught King's attention.

"Ah. I probably did meet with Joe Fielding then. I forgot about that time. Must've slipped my mind." King responded. "That happens. I have a lot going on."

"And on November 2nd?" Hunter held up another photo. Again, he didn't submit it as evidence. Becky Bennett stood, fixed her dress, caught King's eye, and then sat back down. "Did you meet with him again?"

"I guess…" King looked at the two women who had entered the courtroom. "I guess that's me and Joe Fielding again. I'm a busy man. I meet with lots of people."

"Did you know the other person seated at the table with you?" Hunter pretended to look at the photo, placed on the lectern and shielded from King's view.

"It might've been Becky Bennett. She was a friend of Joe's."

"Do you know how Joe and Miss Bennett became associates?"

"I don't."

"Mr. King," Hunter's voice rose. "Did you purchase a medical clinic in Wisconsin five years ago?"

"Yes."

"What happened during the negotiation of that purchase?"

"Objection." Rollins stood up. "Relevance. Where is the defense even going with this line of questioning?"

"I assure you, Your Honor, this is very relevant."

"Then get to it, Mr. Hunter. The objection is overruled for now." Judge Reed leaned forward.

"Mr. King," Hunter's voice rose. "What happened during the purchase of the medical clinic?"

"I don't know."

"Let me refresh your memory. As the negotiation for the sale was happening, Dr. Lighten, the owner of the medical clinic in Wisconsin that you purchased, was charged with sexual assault. Do you remember that?"

"What doctors do on their own time is none of my business." King grunted. His mood had changed. The charming, smiling act was gone, replaced by a cold, grumpy snarl.

"Do you remember that Dr. Lighten's sexual assault charge was also withdrawn once he sold the business to you?"

"Like I said, what he does on his own time isn't my business."

"Did you have anything to do with organizing the accusation of sexual assault?"

"Objection!" Rollins rose to her feet again. "Accusation! Your Honor, the defense cannot be allowed to badger the witness like this."

"Sustained." Judge Reed said. "Move on, Mr. Hunter."

Hunter paused, made eye contact with King, and then turned to look back at Heather Monroe. King couldn't sit still in his chair, and looked like he wanted to be anywhere else but the trial.

"Mr. King," Hunter's voice rose again. "Have you ever employed, or paid money to, a person named Miss Heather Monroe?"

King looked up to the judge. "Your Honor, can we have a break?"

"What for?" Judge Reed leaned down.

"I just… well, I'd like a break to sort out my answers."

Judge Reed raised his eyebrows. "No, Mr. King. You can't 'sort out your answers.' You need to answer the questions truthfully."

"Prosecution moves for a recess." Rollins stood again. "The witness is under undue stress."

"The request for a recess is denied." Judge Reed stated. "Mr. King, please answer the questions truthfully."

"Mr. King." Hunter's voice boomed through the courtroom. "Have you ever employed, or paid money to, Heather Monroe?"

King stared at Heather Monroe for a long moment, and then turned back to Hunter. "Yes."

Hunter nodded and then turned to the jury. They looked at him with confusion, waiting for him to connect the dots. "Did you meet Heather Monroe before the purchase of the medical clinic in Wisconsin?"

"You know the answer to that question." His growl had become deeper.

"Answer the question, Mr. King."

"Yes."

"Were you aware that Heather Monroe accused Dr. Lighten of sexual assault before the sale of the medical clinic?"

"Yes."

A number of the jurors squinted as they stared at King. Hunter walked back to his table and picked up a photo, printed at A4 size. He waved it at King before he returned to the lectern and placed it down. "Did you meet with Miss Katherine Jennings before November 5th?"

King drew a breath and held it for a long moment. He had no idea what was on the photo that Hunter had in front of him. When he finally released his breath, he squirmed in his chair again.

"Mr. King," Hunter's voice rose. He tapped another photo on the lectern. "Did you meet with Miss Jennings before November 5th?"

"I don't recall."

"You don't recall?! You've told this court, in this statement, that you hadn't met her before, and now you're changing your mind?!"

"I might've met her; I might not have. I can't recall."

"Mr. King! Did you ask Joe Fielding to hire a paid actor to file a sexual assault case against Dr. Mackie?"

"Objection! Accusation!" Rollins slapped her fist on the table. "Badgering the witness!"

"Sustained!" Judge Reed boomed. "Mr. Hunter, you will be charged with contempt of court if you continue this line of questioning!"

"Mr. King! Were you aware that Joe Fielding paid women to lie and claim they'd been sexually assaulted?"

"I…" King turned to Judge Reed. The intensity had broken him. "How do I avoid answering that question?"

"Mr. King, are you saying that you can't answer that question for fear of self-incrimination?"

His mouth hung open for a moment. "Yes."

"Then you need to take the fifth amendment."

King turned back to Hunter. "I take the fifth amendment."

A gasp went through the jury box.

"Mr. King," Hunter continued. "Were you aware that Joe Fielding met with Miss Jennings before she accused Dr. Mackie of sexual assault?"

"I take the fifth."

"Mr. King!" Hunter continued. "Were you aware that Joe Fielding met with the eyewitnesses in this case before Dr. Mackie was accused of sexual assault?"

"I take the fifth."

"Mr. King!" Hunter's voice boomed. "Were you

aware that Joe Fielding made payments to these people to lie to the court?"

"I take the fifth."

"Mr. King!" Hunter slapped his hand on the lectern. "Were you aware that sexual assault charges against the doctor would result in him losing his medical license?!"

"I take the fifth!" King slammed his hand on the arm of his chair. "Listen to me! I take the fifth! How many times do I have to say it?!"

Hunter stared at the witness, before taking a deep breath and looking to the jury box. Most were sitting with their mouths open, and the ones that weren't, were shaking their heads.

Hunter picked up the photo from the lectern, moving it so King could see that it was nothing more than a stock photo of the seedy bar. King's mouth fell open when he saw the photos were nothing more than a bluff. He'd been played.

# CHAPTER 36

TEX HUNTER, Esther Wright, and Dr. David Mackie were waiting in a meeting room near the exit to the courtroom. The room was cold, as was the atmosphere. The air conditioner pumped cool air into the room, rattling above their heads, providing at least some distraction. The round wooden table that took up most of the space was stained through years of use, and rocked a little when someone leaned on it. The chairs were uncomfortable and equally as uneven. The cushions were full of bumps. The air smelled stale. Still, no one was leaving the room.

"What's taking so long? It's been two hours since Judge Reed called the recess." Dr. Mackie's brow was deeply furrowed. "What are they doing? Shouldn't this be over already?"

"Detective Heart is re-interviewing the witnesses, and she's talking to Katherine Jennings at the moment." Hunter was calm. "We should allow them to take all the time they need. Let's not rush them."

Dr. Mackie stood and began to pace the small room. He punched the wall gently. He repeated the action a number of times, before he started to tap his forehead against the drywall. "I can't believe it. King wanted to set me up so I'd be forced to sell the clinic? That's what you're saying? And he's done this before in Wisconsin?"

"That's right." Esther said. "Our theory is that King wanted the company so he could hold a monopoly over the area, and he saw the opportunity to expose you in your divorce. He seems like the type of guy to kick a man while he's down."

"So it was all to do with King." Dr. Mackie shook his head as he began to walk around the room again. "Were the others in on it as well? Vandenberg and my ex-wife?"

"We're not sure yet," Hunter said. "But that's the theory we're working on."

A knock on the door made them all jump. Hunter stood and opened the door. Detective Regina Heart and Prosecutor Rollins were waiting at the door. They didn't smile.

Hunter opened the door wider and allowed them into the room. They didn't say anything as they sat down on the two remaining chairs. Rollins opened her laptop, typed a few commands, and then looked up from the screen. Dr. Mackie leaned against the wall at the far side of the room, arms folded across his chest, head leaning against the wall.

"The prosecution is moving to withdraw all charges against Dr. Mackie." Rollins began. "We've re-interviewed Katherine Jennings and she's changed her statement. At this point in time, there's not enough evidence to continue with this case."

"She can do that?" Dr. Mackie became breathless. "She can just change it like that?"

"Our job is to find the truth." Detective Heart said. "We're not out to get people. We just want to find the truth. That's our job. We've welcomed the new statement from Ms. Jennings. We told her that Becky Bennett, or Rebecca White as she was formerly known, had information about Joe Fielding's activities. Ms. Jennings came clean when we said we would investigate the payments into her bank account. She admitted she was paid by Fielding to make up the sexual assault allegation. It was all a lie."

"So that's it? I'm free? This nightmare is now all over?"

"Yes, Dr. Mackie." Rollins responded. "All the charges have been dropped. You're a free man."

Dr. Mackie looked at the ceiling. He made the sign of the cross, and mouthed the words, 'thank you.'

"Perjury for the witnesses and Katherine Jennings?" Hunter asked.

"The full force of the law will land on Katherine Jennings, Daisy Perkins, and David Denison." Heart said. "The almighty dollar tempted them to lie about sexual assault. They won't walk away from this. We have to make an example of them so other people aren't tempted to do the same."

"And once their charges are released to the media, their names are going to be splashed all over the country. They're going to pay for what they've done."

Rollins added. "I'll call my media contacts and make sure their heavy penalties are reported in the news. We have to discourage others from acting in the same way."

"And what about Christoph King?" Dr. Mackie asked. "He was involved in this. He set me up."

"Unfortunately, all he actually said was that he saw a woman crying after leaving the doctor's office, which appears to be true. Katherine Jennings may have been acting at the time, but she did leave the medical clinic in tears." Rollins looked at Hunter. "Unless you've got something else to link him to all this, something concrete, then King walks away untouched."

Hunter shook his head.

"Dr. Mackie," Rollins closed her laptop. "For what it's worth, I'm sincerely sorry this happened to you."

Detective Heart and Rollins stood, neither with a smile to offer. Esther nodded her thanks, and opened the door for them to leave. Dr. Mackie didn't say goodbye.

Hunter followed them outside the meeting room and closed the door behind him. "Regina."

Detective Heart looked across to Rollins. "I'll catch up with you in a minute."

Rollins walked away without another word. Once the prosecutor was out of earshot, Hunter leaned closer to the detective. "What's going to happen to your cousin?"

"Nothing's going to happen. Her claim against Dr.

Lighten was real. It was unethical to follow it through for money, but he was still guilty." Heart placed her hands in her pockets. "I hate it, and I told her that, but she didn't do anything illegal. Hopefully, the penalties that will be handed down to Katherine Jennings and the witnesses will act as a deterrence to anyone that's tempted to do something like this again."

Hunter nodded. "Thank you."

"Don't thank me. Like I said in there, I'm not out to get people. I'm out to get the truth." She paused for a moment, before offering Hunter a half-smile. "No matter what that is."

Hunter leaned against the wall, and watched her walk down the hallway, before he drew a deep breath and re-entered the meeting room.

"What happens now?" Dr. Mackie asked. "Is that it?"

"That's it. It's over." Esther closed her laptop. "Isn't it, Tex?"

Hunter shut the door, but kept his hand on the door handle.

"For you, yes. It's over."

"Not you?" Dr. Mackie quizzed.

"I'm not done yet." Hunter stood tall. "Whoever killed Joe Fielding caused Stacey's death, and there'll be no justice until I find the real killer."

# CHAPTER 37

THE TRUCK stop on the outskirts of Minneapolis, Minnesota, smelled of diesel fuel. The odor filled the air to the point that it was overpowering. The woman didn't mind, though. It masked the smell of her body odor. Her cap shielded her face, protecting her from the gentle rain, and her backpack was full of the few remaining possessions she had left. She walked with her arms folded across her chest, dark hair dangling over her face. She had dyed her hair black and wore dark sunglasses. She struggled to recognize herself in the mirror.

She'd been able to cut the ankle bracelet off. It wasn't hard. She smashed it on the rocks and tossed it in the water under the bridge, ensuring it would be the last signal the cops received. That would seal their decision that her body was trapped somewhere under the murky water.

She tried not to think about her children, but she couldn't avoid it. They filled her thoughts while she hitched a ride. The truckers she rode with didn't talk much. She liked that. She had stared out the window of the trucks, watching the world wash past. For the past week, she had been living in a nearby motel, formulating her plan, working out the details, but something was holding her back. Crossing the border into Canada would make her decisions real. That was the point of no return. She still cried herself to sleep each night, but the tears were beginning to dry up. She had enough cash for a month of supplies. After that, she would need to find work.

Stacey Fulbright walked into the truck stop diner and ordered a coffee and a raspberry muffin. Using a new cell phone, a cheap second-hand one from another trucker, she logged onto the diner's Wi-Fi, and checked her new fake Facebook profile. 'Eden Malls,' she had called herself. Her profile picture was of a flower. She could've been male or female, young or old, or of any race. It was the perfect cover. Despite the knowledge that she had to cut contacts with her past life, she couldn't resist the urge to check on her children. She logged onto the private Facebook group for her memorial, looked at the profiles of the attendees, and scrolled through the photos. It was comforting to know that people went to her memorial. There were photos from her friends, celebrating the life that was her past.

Her mother looked heartbroken, as did her cousins. Some of her old clients were there, paying respects with their heads down. Her friends looked shattered, although they could've seen this coming a long way off. John C. Clarke was there, as was Michael Vandenberg and Tex Hunter, and there wasn't one smile to share between them.

Then she saw a photo of Noah in the background of another picture. He was hugging his Aunt Melissa tightly. Her breath was taken away. What had she done? Was losing a mother worse than growing up the child of a killer? She thought she'd done the best for them, but the look of distress on Noah's face broke her heart.

"Are you ok, sweetheart?" The server placed the coffee and muffin down in front of her on the stained table. "Need anything?"

Stacey Fulbright avoided eye contact. "I'm ok."

The server nodded, turned and reached across to the diner counter, before pulling out two tissues.

"Don't worry about the tears. We get lots of tears out here." She nodded outside. "Don't know what it is. I guess when you're on the road, you're going somewhere, but when you stop, that's when things hit you. That's when things become real."

"Thanks." Stacey whispered, and the server moved away.

Stacey knew she had to get across the border to Canada. She'd managed to hitch-hike this far, and she was sure she could get across the border without being detected. Once there, she could build a life again. Start all over. She could build a life without a husband determined to set her up for murder.

She'd come to the truck stop looking for a ride close to the border. She left nothing in the motel room that she paid for by the day. A man at the counter stared at her. His eyes lingered for far too long. He had a moustache, and had arms that looked like he worked hard for a living. He was missing a few teeth.

"Going somewhere? Need a lift?" The man moved into the seat opposite her in the booth. "Pretty girls like you don't hang out in places like this unless they want something."

"Where you heading?" Her voice was quiet.

"Detroit. Got myself a truck full of motor parts to deliver. I could use the company on the road."

"Sorry, I'm going the other way."

The man stayed at the booth, staring at her. She looked up at him, and he licked his bottom lip. In one swift movement, she grabbed her muffin from the table and walked away.

"Not tonight." She whispered to herself. "Not tonight."

She had made her choice. She had made the decision to leave her home. She had made the decision to leave her past life behind her. She had made the choice for the benefit of the children.

She only hoped that it was the right one.

# CHAPTER 38

"THINK KING will do it again?" Ray Jones cradled his beer. "He got away with it a few times and made a lot of cash out of it. You could argue that the Wisconsin medical clinic is what set him off on his path to success."

"King?" Hunter stared into his whiskey. "I don't know. He's arrogant enough to think he could get away with it again in five years' time. If setting up someone worked a number of times, then he'd be tempted to do it again. But with Fielding, his go-to guy, dead, he'd have to find a new person to trust."

The sports bar was half-filled, mostly at the rear end of the bar, near the television screens. The bar was a local Cubs fan hangout when games were on, and when the Cubs were playing well, it was packed. But this time of year, without much hope for the season ahead, the bar was only a quarter full. Only the die-hards, with their signed caps and shirts, remained. The front end of the bar was almost empty, except for Hunter and Jones sitting in the furthest booth. The table they sat at was damaged, with cracks in the dark wood, there were crumbs on the leather seats, and the blinds next to them had a number of small holes, allowing a tiny amount of daylight to sneak into the otherwise dark bar.

"Did they manage to bring any charges against King at all?" Jones turned to look at the nearest television screen, hanging above the liquor shelf. The Cubs were deep in the fifth and winning. The game was close, but nobody seemed to have much confidence in the Cubs' ability to close out a game.

"No charges yet, and I'd be surprised if they're able to find anything. There's not enough to prove that King set it all up. Jennings and the other witnesses have all been charged with various offences, but King kept an arm's length away from it all. All he said was that he saw a girl leave the medical clinic with tears in her eyes. Without proof he set this up, then he walks." Hunter watched the next ball. A slider. Swing and a miss. "King is going to keep running his business, keep making money, and keep pressuring Dr. Mackie to sell. The unfortunate thing is that even though Dr. Mackie was found innocent, his reputation has taken a hit. His name was splashed all through the papers, and that sort of mud sticks to a man. If his clients abandon him and stop coming to the clinic, then he still may have to sell the business."

"So King wins either way." Jones watched the next play. He made a humming noise when the batter swung hard and connected, but the ball landed in the stands. "Do you think the witnesses will turn on King?"

"Even if they did, it wouldn't be enough. There's no proof. The only person who could've proved anything was Joe Fielding and he's not testifying any time soon." Hunter sighed. "I hate to think what else King has done. This case could be the tip of the iceberg. The only person who could turn on King's operations was Joe Fielding."

"On the bright side, you won a case." Jones said as he took a large gulp of his ale after the batter struck out. "Another one in the win column."

"We won one case, but we lost another."

"You can't count Stacey Fulbright's case as a loss. It never even made it to court."

"It's a loss to me. I let an old friend walk a dark path because I wasn't able to save her. I wasn't able to prove that she was set up. I failed when someone needed me the most." Hunter's voice was somber. "If we'd been able to prove that Stacey had nothing to do with Fielding's death, I could've saved her life. I should've saved her."

"Sorry, man. I shouldn't have brought it up."

They both stared at the nearest television, not really watching the game, but looking for a distraction. Jones finished his beer and pointed at Hunter's drink. Hunter nodded. Jones took his empty glass back to the bar and ordered two more drinks—another pint for himself, and a whiskey for Hunter.

"I can still do something about it." Hunter stated as Jones placed the drinks on the table. "The way I see it, the person who killed Fielding killed Stacey.

The murder charges led to Stacey's death. The person who organized this set up is responsible for Stacey's passing. I won't fail her twice. I won't stop until we find the person responsible. I need to do it for her."

Jones waited a moment, and recognized the look in Hunter's eyes. He'd seen it many times before. He hesitated before he took a long sip of his beer. "What do you think Fielding was going to give Stacey that night?"

"He had to be going to Stacey with something to blackmail King with. King was looking down the barrel of another divorce, and I'm sure King would've been looking to get out of it with as little damage as possible. Fielding must've turned on King and offered Stacey a slice of the pie."

"It would've been for a lot of money." Jones suggested. "King is now worth around $50 million, and he built that success during this last marriage. Half of that would've hurt. If he was willing to set a guy up to buy his business, I'd hate to see what he'd do to a person that dared to betray his trust."

"And that's how Fielding was going to strike it rich. Becky Bennett mentioned that Fielding had a plan to make a lot of money. He was going to blackmail King." Hunter's jaw clenched as he pieced together the final pieces of the puzzle. "And Fielding went to Stacey to see if she wanted in."

"And it got him killed."

"But it's only a theory." Hunter nodded. "Even if we'd seen this earlier, we couldn't have proved it in court. There's too many missing pieces."

The people at the rear of the room cheered. The Cubs had hit another homer. Two runs up. They were holding onto a small amount of hope, something that Hunter still had.

"So what do we do now?" Jones asked. "Fielding is dead, Stacey Fulbright is dead, and Christoph King just walked out of court a free man. How do we prove any of it? We've already exhausted every avenue."

Hunter knocked back the new glass of whiskey in one shot. He stood. "The quickest way to find out the facts is to go straight to the source."

# CHAPTER 39

HUNTER'S HAND slammed against the black door, echoing the sound through the neighborhood.

The two-story mansion on Lincoln Ave, Winnetka, fifteen miles north of Downtown, was soulless, a place to stare at, not to live in. There was a black Mercedes in the driveway, polished so much it was almost a mirror, the grass was clipped like a golf course fairway, and the house was painted a dull gray. The porch, painted ashen-gray, was devoid of furniture, and the garden didn't have one personal touch.

A maid answered the door. She was Latino; young and pretty. Hunter was sure King hand-picked her personally. "May I help you?"

"I need to talk to Christoph King." Hunter didn't wait for an invitation to come inside. He stepped around the maid, and onto the white marble floor of the spacious, bleak entrance. Jones followed behind him. With a glass of red wine in his hand, Christoph King stepped out into the foyer. King was dressed in a red and green shirt, running shorts, and socks with sandals. It seemed no amount of money could buy good taste.

"Tex Hunter?" King questioned.

"You think you can get away with this?" Hunter grunted. "I'm going to prove what you did. I'm going to prove that you've set up many people in the past."

"What?" King chuckled. "I get away with whatever I want. I do what I want, when I want. That's my life. You can't touch me."

"Stacey is dead because of what you did." The rage built inside Hunter until it was almost overflowing, every muscle in his body tightened into a spring ready to explode.

"Stacey Fulbright? She did that herself. Silly little girl."

In a moment of rare emotional intensity, Hunter cracked. With one swift motion, he slammed the smaller man against the wall, his forearm pressing into the short man's neck, the wine glass smashing onto the floor.

Jones stood behind Hunter, and nodded to the housekeeper that everything was going to be ok. Jones peered outside, then closed the front door.

"You think you can play me, King? I'm the best player in the whole game." The bone of Hunter's forearm pushed hard into King's windpipe.

"And yet, here you are, threatened by me." An air of infallible confidence leaked off King. He grinned as Hunter pressed his arm deeper into his neck. "Go on. Do it, Hunter. Strangle me when there are witnesses. See how long you'd last in prison."

Hunter growled, pressing tighter.

"Go on, Hunter. Let me see what you're made of. Choke me out."

With restraint, Hunter released the pressure on King's neck, but his left hand still gripped the collar of his shirt. "I should smash you into the ground, King. Setting Stacey up for Fielding's death was low, and I'll prove you did it. I won't rest until you're charged with Fielding's murder."

King squinted. "Stacey Fulbright was a nasty soul. Imagine representing women who are going through divorces? All she wanted to do was destroy us men. I thought you would've understood that, Hunter. You're a red-blooded male, just like me, and us men have to stick together. We've got to have each other's back."

"I'm nothing like you." Hunter growled and pressed his forearm back into King's neck. King's smile disappeared. "And I won't fail her twice."

King struggled to take a breath, gasping as Hunter's thick forearm pressed deeper. King felt his face beginning to turn red, and his smugness disappeared. He began to squirm. Exactly what Hunter wanted. Struggling, King brought his hands to Hunter's forearms, trying to force him back, but it was no use. The lawyer was too strong, and too powerful.

King gasped. He didn't have much air left. Tears began to fill his eyes. Panic began to set in. King tried to knee his attacker, but Hunter didn't flinch.

Adrenaline and fury had engulfed him.

"Tex." Jones' voice was composed. "Ease back."

The calm voice of his friend snapped Hunter out of his determined rage. Just as King was about to pass out, Hunter released his forearm, and King fell to the floor, gasping for breath. Crouched over, King wheezed deep breaths, holding his neck, trying to suck oxygen back into his lungs. He coughed loudly, desperately sucking in breaths. When his breath returned, he moved to sit up. Leaning against the wall, still sitting on the ground, King began to chuckle.

"You think this is funny?" Hunter stepped over him. "Stacey Fulbright is dead because of what you did."

"You think I did that?" King sniggered. "I had nothing to do with her death. Although," he raised a finger in the air. "I must admit that I danced when I heard she'd killed herself. It was a win for all red-blooded males."

"You set her up for Joe Fielding's death, and when you did that, you signed her death certificate." Hunter growled. "I'll make sure you pay for that. You're going down for the murder of Joe Fielding. I'll find evidence you did it."

"I didn't kill Fielding and I didn't set her up." King continued to laugh. "That wasn't me. You really think I did that? Fielding was dirty, and he had more enemies than I did. Take your pick—half of Chicago wanted him dead. He wanted out of the game, but he had too many secrets to be cut loose. There could be a hundred guys that would've stabbed him."

"Fielding was trying to blackmail you." Hunter bent down to stare King in the eyes. "We know he was going to take the information about your set-ups for sexual assault to the highest bidder. We know he wanted to take you down."

"Blackmail me? Not likely." King shook his head as he rubbed his throat. "I didn't set up any of those doctors. I bought the clinics, and I knew about the plans, but I didn't set it up."

Hunter squinted. "Then who did?"

"Vandenberg. Michael Vandenberg. He set them all up for the divorce payouts." King rubbed his throat. "Michael Vandenberg was being blackmailed by Joe Fielding. Not me."

# CHAPTER 40

"ESTHER, GET me everything on Michael Vandenberg." Hunter used his cell phone to call Esther as soon as he was inside Jones' truck. "We've got a lead in Fielding's death."

"Michael Vandenberg? The divorce lawyer?" Esther questioned. "You really think it was him?"

"Fielding was trying to blackmail Vandenberg. That's what got him killed. And that murder caused the death of Stacey Fulbright. Vandenberg needs to pay for this."

"Ok." Esther replied. "I'll have everything we currently know compiled in fifteen minutes."

She ended the call as Jones roared the engine of the truck, slammed the accelerator, and left King's mansion behind them. He drove aggressively through the streets, racing back towards Hunter's office.

Hunter stared out the window at the passing buildings. He hated that he hadn't seen it from the start. If he had seen the connection, if he had found the truth, he would've been able to save Stacey. That failure ate at him. While the police couldn't charge anyone with Stacey's death, Hunter wasn't going to leave it as a dead end. He owed it to her son, Noah. He needed to find the truth and he needed to expose it.

"Why was Fielding in Fulbright's parking lot?" Jones asked as they raced through the streets towards Hunter's office. "And why was he stabbed with her letter opener? How did Vandenberg get his hands on it?"

"If only Stacey were alive to tell us." Hunter quipped.

Hunter's cell phone buzzed. It was Esther.

"That was quick." Hunter answered.

"Well, I have something to add. I think it'll be of interest to you." Esther said as Hunter placed her on speaker. "It might be nothing, but to me, it looks like something. It's a hunch."

"What do you mean?" Hunter quizzed.

"I was being nosy, looking through the photos of Stacey's memorial. Just scrolling through. I… It would be better if I showed you. Ray, do you have your laptop there?" Esther asked.

Jones pulled the car over to the side of the road, stopping in a strip mall parking lot. Jones reached over the back seat, and removed his laptop computer from a bag. He connected to his phone's hotspot. "We're ready."

"I was looking through the photos of the memorial for Stacey and something struck me as unusual. Based off a hunch I had, I did a little bit of preliminary digging. Not much, just twenty minutes of surfing online. Just the easy stuff to check." Esther said. "Stacey's friend set up a Facebook page for her memorial and made it a private group. It was touching stuff—photos of Stacey's life, comments from friends, memories that had been long forgotten and were now shared worldwide. Lots of smiles and good times. But whoever wanted to join the private group, needed approval from the administrator, which was Stacey's best friend, Ursula. She approved my request when I said I had worked with Stacey. I looked through the list, and most were people known to us, but there were five profiles that I was suspicious of, so I looked into them a bit further. Four of the profiles checked out to be real people, but there was one profile that looked like a catfish."

"Catfish?" Hunter asked.

"A catfish is a deliberately fake online profile, and this one looks like one to me. Ray, can you bring up the Facebook profile of Eden Malls?"

Ray typed into his laptop as Hunter looked over his shoulder.

"Have a look." Jones turned the laptop towards Hunter, highlighting the social media profile. "I think she's right."

"Looks legit to me." Hunter scrolled through the profile. "I can't see anything wrong with it. It looks the same as all the other profiles."

"The best ones look legitimate, but there's always little giveaways that show it's not real." Esther said. "Whoever made this profile has done it well, but look at the start date for the creation of the profile. It's the same day as the group approval. The person made this profile just to have access to the pictures."

"Interesting, but that says nothing."

"There were over a hundred photos added to the group page, and around twenty photos of the children. The person from the fake profile liked every photo the children were in. And they also left one comment— 'My baby.' That's on a picture of Zoe, the youngest child. And nobody else in the memorial group is friends with Eden Malls." Esther waited for a response, but when there wasn't one, she continued. "Stacey Fulbright may still be alive. She may have faked her own death to save her children. They still haven't found her body in the river."

"Any idea of the location?" Jones asked.

"I was suspicious, so I tracked the IP address of the user. It's a public Wi-Fi address from a motel outside Minneapolis. I called, and after some sweet talking, they confirmed a single woman who matches Stacey's description checked in there a few days ago. The woman only had a backpack." Esther said. "It's a hunch, and it might be nothing, but I don't think she jumped off that bridge. I think she's on the run."

"What does your gut say, Esther?" Hunter asked. "Do you think Stacey is alive and this is her?"

"I do."

"Ray, turn the car around." Hunter said. "We're driving to Minneapolis."

# CHAPTER 41

THE MOTEL outside Minneapolis was a stop for the lonely and desperate, a place to escape a life once lived. The street lighting was poor, the parking lot was littered with potholes, and the screams of the mentally ill occasionally cut through the night air. The front rooms of the motel were only a small strip of grass and a five-foot wire fence away from eight lanes of traffic on the Interstate-94 highway. The outside of the building, once painted cream, was now covered with grit, grime, and car pollution.

It was past midnight when Jones and Hunter arrived after the six-hour drive. Jones parked the truck outside in the parking lot and walked into the twenty-four-hour reception desk. Hunter waited inside the truck, watching the rooms for any activity. There was an older couple stumbling into a hotel room on the second-floor balcony, a homeless man pushing a cart past the parking lot entrance, and a lonely figure leaning against a car smoking a cigarette, but no sign of Stacey Fulbright.

Within ten minutes, Jones returned. "It's amazing what money can buy." Jones said as he climbed back inside the truck. "The motel had a person book in two days ago under the name of 'Jane Black.' No return address, and the lady matches the description of Stacey Fulbright, except for the hair color. I showed the guy a picture of Stacey, and he confirmed it."

"The first thing she would've done is dye her hair." Hunter responded. "Room number?"

"Number five." Jones pointed across the street. "Bottom level."

Hunter opened the door and went to step out of the car, but Jones reached across and grabbed his wrist. "She'll run the second you knock on her door. She's a fugitive."

"You're right." Hunter nodded his agreement and closed the door. "It's past midnight. We'll have to wait until morning."

Jones looked at his watch. "If we stake out the room, we'll see her leave to get something to eat tomorrow. I can't imagine that we'd see much at this time of night, and I'd suggest she won't go far for food, perhaps the diner across the road. The sign says it's open twenty-four seven, and by the looks of the place, I don't think it's going to be booked out. Take it in two hour shifts to sleep?"

"You want a room in the motel?"

"Not a chance. You'd be eaten alive by bed bugs, if you weren't first kidnapped by the rats. It'd be more relaxing here." Jones nodded to the back seat. "Not a lot of room, but it's comfortable."

"You sleep first." Hunter said.

Jones didn't need to be asked twice. He climbed into the rear seat of his truck, his large frame barely fitting on the seat, but he curled his legs up, and was out within ten minutes. His snoring kept Hunter awake. For the next five hours, they took it in turns to watch the motel room, switching every two. Hunter couldn't sleep. His long legs didn't have enough room to stretch out.

They were both awake by 5am, sitting in the front seat of the truck, a large coffee each from the nearby diner.

"If there's no movement by 10am, we go in." Hunter reasoned. "I'll go in quietly, because I don't want to spook her, but I'll still get you to cover the back of the motel room. I'll go over and knock on the door and explain to her what we're doing there. If there's no answer, I'll break in."

"That's a good plan, but I say we go in at 8am." Jones responded. "I'm not a patient man when I'm tired."

They watched the motel as the minutes ticked past, and almost on the stroke of 7am, the door to room number five opened. The figure was under a hood, moving quickly, heading for the diner across the road. A gust of rain drifted through, loud as it hit the top of the truck, but the men kept their eyes on the woman.

"Did you think it's her?" Jones asked. "Matches the description."

"Hard to tell from this distance." Hunter

responded as he opened the door to the truck. "And there's only one way to be sure."

Hunter jogged towards the diner, followed by Jones, watching for anyone else following them. The diner was as expected for a place opposite a road-side motel. It stunk of burned bacon, old coffee, and stale bread. The lights were too bright, the tables were dirty, and the country music was too loud. There were two truckers at the counter, hunched over their breakfast, grunting about the weather.

The woman from number five had sat in the furthest booth from the door, away from any wandering eyes. Hunter approached the woman. He sat down.

"Hello Stacey."

Stacey Fulbright gasped and then froze. She was speechless. She had no idea what to say next. Jones followed Hunter and sat down.

"How…" She composed herself. "How did you find me? How did you even know I was alive?"

"I have the best team in the criminal justice system, Stacey."

"Do other people know I'm alive? The cops? Carl?"

"Not yet."

"But if you've found me, then Carl will find me as well. I can't risk that. Not now."

"Carl?" Hunter questioned. "Your husband?"

"Don't you get it?" She said. "He killed Joe Fielding and made it look like me. He set me up. He never wanted the divorce, but he wanted me out of his life. He killed Joe Fielding to get rid of me."

Hunter leaned forward. "Do you have evidence?"

"He went to Michael Vandenberg to talk about a divorce. See? That's all the evidence I need."

"We don't think that's right, Stacey." Hunter lowered his voice. "We think it was Michael Vandenberg who killed Joe Fielding."

"What?" She whispered. "Not Carl?"

"Vandenberg was using Fielding to set up Dr. Mackie for sexual assault. He needed Mackie to sell the medical clinic to profit from the sale." Jones said. "There was ten million dollars involved. We think Fielding was coming to you to see if you wanted to buy the information about the fraud. Fielding was going to turn on Vandenberg and blackmail him. You were going to be a pawn in Fielding's plan."

"I don't understand." Stacey shook her head. "I'm sure it was Carl."

"Fielding was turning on Vandenberg." Hunter replied. "His assistant, Becky Bennett, told us that he had leverage on someone, and they were going to pay big. We thought it was Christoph King all along, but it wasn't. It was Michael Vandenberg. Stacey, you said you were on the phone late at night in your office just before Fielding was killed. Who were you on the phone to?"

"I was discussing a divorce case." She looked at her hands. They were shaking. "I was on the phone for an hour before the person hung up. The person on the other end of the line just didn't want to let me go, like they were waiting for something. They called me from their car at 10pm. I thought it was unusual, but they said it was important. They were talking from their car… almost like they wanted to keep me in the office. They wanted to make sure that I didn't leave the office until after 11pm."

"That person didn't want you to leave the office until Fielding had walked into the parking lot. They knew the lot only had cameras outside. They needed you to stay in the office until after Fielding arrived." Hunter pressed. "Who was on the phone, Stacey?"

Stacey looked into the distance. Her world had come tumbling down again. "I was on the phone with Michael Vandenberg."

# CHAPTER 42

THE SIX-HOUR drive back from Minneapolis was long. The roads were mostly clear, except for the large semis hauling loads of goods. Hunter stared out the window, the thoughts pounding through his head as tiredness started to kick in. Jones had the cruise control on past the speed limit, but the drive was still draining.

They'd talked to Stacey for an hour. Once the shock subsided, she agreed with their theory. Michael Vandenberg had always hated her. He was a man on a power trip, a man with a chip on his shoulder. He was sexist, racist, and heavy-handed. She never thought he'd be a killer, she said, but she didn't doubt it.

Hunter had a theory, but no evidence on Vandenberg. Nothing. Not a note, not a clue. Not even a lead. The only hint they had came from Christoph King, and he would never turn on Vandenberg.

As Hunter and Jones drove back to Chicago, they discussed their options, but there weren't many. Stacey Fulbright was still officially on bail, still charged with murder in the first degree. The fact she faked her own death to skip bail wasn't going to look good for her, no matter the outcome of the Fielding investigation.

"She looked determined to run over the border and start a new life." Jones said as the blues hummed on the radio. "She was ready to disappear. Had it all planned out. Get a job in a small town. Start a new life. She looked shocked that we left her there."

"She needs time." Hunter responded. "She wasn't ready to come back yet. We've just re-calibrated her world by telling her it was Vandenberg that set her up. She was running because she thought it was her husband. She was running to protect her children, not herself."

"Do you think she had a point? That her husband could've done it? We don't have any evidence that Vandenberg did it yet. He could've been a part of it."

"Evidence is the key. Stacey's not going to come back to Chicago until there's evidence that Vandenberg was involved, and we don't have one shred."

Hunter stared out the window as they passed another truck. It was only on the open road that a person began to comprehend the size of the country's population. Miles upon miles upon miles of once empty land was now consumed by the spread of suburbia. Farming land was disappearing, empty space was vanishing, and cities were becoming joined by the coverage of new developments.

"Do you think she'll keep running?" Jones tapped the steering wheel. "Even with this new information?"

"I don't know. I really don't know. Most people in her situation…" Hunter paused to work through his thoughts. "Most people would cross the border, and start a new life. Forget about the past. She's made it this far, and the cops think she's dead. They're not chasing her."

"But you wouldn't run?"

"Not me." Hunter agreed. "I'd fight until the end. I'd fight until I had nothing left. That's the only way I know how to handle things, and that's what I'm going to do for Stacey. I won't let this pass. But we need a plan. We have to be able to prove it was Vandenberg."

For the next hour, they discussed their options. Every possibility was raised, and discussed. By the time they had reached the outskirts of Chicago, they had an idea. Hunter picked up his cell phone.

"Tex Hunter?" Detective Regina Heart asked. "This better be good."

"You owe me a favor, Regina."

"Already? The court case was only resolved a few days ago. I didn't expect you to be calling this soon."

"You asked me to contact you if I knew about the sexual assault case and who set it up. I did that for you, and now I'm calling in the favor."

She paused, and then sighed. "I'm reluctant, but go on. Tell me what you need."

# CHAPTER 43

STACEY FULBRIGHT waited near the entrance to the motel. It was dark and cold again, but the people of Minnesota seemed to be used to the long winters that stretched into early March. In the twenty-four hours since her world was rocked by Hunter's ideas, she had gone back and forth between her options. She was only five hours away from the Canadian border. The crossing would be easy. There were places she could walk across.

She had one last chance to change things. One last chance to move the game into her favor. With one last roll of the dice, she called him. She told him where to meet her. 10pm. Minneapolis Roadside Motel. Outside of the I-94.

He agreed. She wasn't sure if it was the right decision, but she needed to take the risk. It was her last chance to see her kids grow up.

She waited near the corner of the motel, in view of the entrance to room 5, and watched the cars come and go in the night. The noise of the highway was a constant drone, but she was becoming used to the rumbling of trucks. It was becoming a comforting white noise.

If the meeting didn't work out, she was still going to run. Canada wasn't far away, and once over the border, she had contacts that could help her disappear.

The black SUV rolled into the parking lot just before 10pm. The new vehicle looked out of place in such a rundown area. She recognized the vehicle. It had parked outside her house on a number of occasions. There were no plates.

Michael Vandenberg stepped out of the vehicle, looking around for his safety. Dressed in a suit without a tie, Vandenberg searched the parking lot for any suspicious movements, before striding towards Room 5.

"Michael." Stacey stepped out of the shadow. "I'm over here."

"Stacey." Vandenberg faked concern. "How happy I am to see you alive."

"Cut the crap, Michael. You wanted me dead a long time ago. I know that car. I know you've been following me."

"Well, what can I say?" He looked back at the car. "I like to drive. And sometimes, I get into little accidents."

"I need the truth from you."

"I had to follow you, Stacey. And Tex Hunter. Add a bit of pressure here and there. But just because we were rivals, didn't mean I wanted you dead." Vandenberg was cautious. "Why don't we go inside your room to talk?"

"Answer me something first." Stacey had her arms folded across her chest, hair hanging over her face. She kept her distance. "What did you tell Carl when he came to see you?"

"Ah." Vandenberg shrugged. "You have to know that I can't talk about it due to privacy concerns."

"I'm officially a dead person, Michael. Everyone thinks I died jumping off the bridge. The whole world thinks I'm already gone. And I saw photos of you at my memorial."

"Sure. You're a dead woman." He scoffed and shook his head. "You want to know what we talked about? Ok. We talked about your divorce and how much I could take you for. We talked about custody, and how Carl wanted more than fifty percent. And we talked about what a nasty piece of work you are. That's what we talked about."

"You enjoyed that, didn't you?"

"Of course I did. I loved it." Vandenberg's jaw clenched as his demeanor changed. "The chance to kick you where it hurts? I thrived on it. I absolutely loved it."

"So you took out Joe Fielding instead."

"Ha." He scoffed again. "Is that what this is about? Let's step inside the hotel room and talk about it. It's cold out here. Come on. Let's go inside."

Vandenberg pointed towards Room 5, and as he did, his jacket lifted. Stacey saw the handgun in a holster on his belt. He'd come prepared.

Vandenberg noticed Stacey's eyes on his holster. "Stacey." Vandenberg stepped closer, moving his jacket to expose his gun to her. "Go inside. I'm not going to ask you again."

"Is that your plan? Shoot me? How would you explain that?"

"Easily."

"Humor me."

"I came up here to talk you into returning to Chicago to face your murder charge. If you're not dead, then you've skipped bail. You, of course, resisted my plan to take you back to face the courts. That's when you drew your gun," He nodded to his holster. "This is an unregistered gun, Stacey. I'm sure you picked it up on your way here to protect yourself while on the run. In a struggle between us, gun shots were fired, and you were hit. Accidently, of course. Now, if you step inside, we don't have to go through all of that. We can sort something out. We can talk about your options."

"Is that what happened to Fielding? He wanted to sort something out? He wanted to talk about his options?"

"Joe." Vandenberg scoffed and then smiled. "That dumb fool was trying to blackmail me. What an idiot. He had evidence that he was threatening to take to you. He said he could sell it to you. That's why he was waiting for you in the parking lot. He was going to sell you my secrets."

"And that's why you kept me on the phone that

night."

"I had to make sure you didn't have an alibi. For the right price, Fielding wanted to give you all the evidence of my set ups over the years. He wanted to show you all the things I've been involved in. I couldn't let him do that. Do you know how many people I've set up?" He raised his eyebrows and stepped closer. "I'll give you a hint—it's a lot."

"Including Dr. Mackie."

"Dr. Mackie? Sure. He was one of them. That one was an easy set up, but I didn't bank on him fighting it all the way. Most guys deal out before the case makes it to court. That's what the lawyers recommend, anyway. Don't take it to court, we tell them, even if the witnesses are lying. The cost to their reputation isn't worth it. How stupid."

"But Dr. Mackie took it to court, and King crumbled on the stand."

"You've been keeping up with the cases? I guess once it's in your blood, it's hard to let the courtroom go. We'll get away with it, but it was close. If we forced Mackie to settle, his divorce could've been very profitable for us." Vandenberg grunted. "And King has been on the stand before; he should've known better. We even used this ruse with one of his ex-wives. That ruse saved him millions of dollars."

"Classy." Stacey said. "How'd you get your hands on my letter opener?"

"I was in your office that day, Stacey. We were talking about a divorce case, remember? It was easy to swipe it from your desk. I'm just an opportunist." He smiled. "Now, Stacey, you can either step into the room and we can discuss this like adults, or I'm just going to have to shoot you here. That's your choice. Go out with dignity, or disgrace." Vandenberg turned around. "There are no witnesses here, and there's no cameras up there. Everyone is going to believe my story."

A black BMW sedan screeched into the parking lot.

Stacey smiled. "I wouldn't be so sure of that, Michael."

Vandenberg turned to her. "Are you..." He looked around. "Have you set me up? You're wearing a microphone..."

Tex Hunter stepped out of the driver's seat, followed by Detective Regina Heart from the other side.

"You set me up!" Vandenberg took one step towards Stacey, before turning back to his SUV.

"Michael Vandenberg!" Heart shouted. "Don't run!" She positioned herself at the front of the car, with her hand on her gun. "Vandenberg!"

In one swift movement, Vandenberg turned and ran towards his car. He leaped into the driver's seat, and roared the engine.

Before Heart could fire a shot, before she could even call his name again, Michael Vandenberg was roaring out of the parking lot in his black SUV. Within seconds, Hunter was back in the driver's seat of his BMW sedan, Detective Heart in the passenger seat.

Fueled by aggression, Hunter screeched the tires of his sedan as he raced onto the street.

# CHAPTER 44

"WE DON'T have to chase him!" Heart gripped the safety bar as Hunter roared around a corner. "I'll call it in. Let the professionals deal with this. This is a local police job!"

"I won't let him get away." Hunter gripped the steering wheel as he yanked the BMW sedan onto the four-lane highway. "If he gets away now, we'll never see him again."

Vandenberg was four cars in front. Hunter floored his car to make up the distance. The speedometer moved past 125 miles an hour. The SUV in front took the next ramp, screeching in front of another vehicle. Hunter followed.

"Stop the car!" Heart gripped the edge of her seat. "You're not a cop, Hunter! Stop the car!"

"But you're a cop." Hunter gritted his teeth as he yanked the steering wheel. "And you should hold on tight."

Hunter roared his car past the slow-moving traffic at the off-ramp, flying across the intersection. The traffic from the left and right broke hard, horns wailing through the night air. One car slammed into the back of another. A scooter slid on the wet road. A van pulled to the side.

But they were across.

Vandenberg was barely a few hundred yards away from them. His SUV weaved through the traffic on the main road. Hunter followed, determined to catch him.

"That car has been following me for weeks." Hunter grunted. "And now the tables have turned."

Hunter dropped the car back a gear, roaring through the gears with an unabated aggression, fueled by his need to deliver justice.

The SUV turned sharply onto a side street. Hunter gripped the handbrake, yanked the steering wheel and followed. His BMW slid across the road, almost out of control, until the tires gripped and raced them forward.

The speed bump in front of him did little to slow him down.

Lights flashed past. Cars pulled out of the way. Vandenberg was closer now.

Hunter floored his sedan, thundering past cars on both sides of the road. He got close, and clipped the back corner of the SUV. Vandenberg's vehicle slid and weaved, until he regained control. Vandenberg wasn't stopping, and nor was Hunter.

"Tex!" Heart yelled as they narrowly missed a pole. "Stop the car!"

He ignored her. Vandenberg was his target. They raced through the streets, block after block disappearing behind them. Hunter overtook cars around blind corners, full of adrenalin. He hit the accelerator with hostility. Floored it. Pushed everything out of it. Heart continued yelling, but Hunter could no longer hear her.

With his foot on the floor, with no margin for error and no chance to make a mistake, the harmony began. Hunter was testing destiny, pushing past the limits of sanity. Past the edge. Past what was considered reasonable. The SUV was slowing around the corners. Hunter closed the gap again. His car was faster, lighter, more efficient. He pushed the car harder. Dropped it back another gear. Forced the engine to roar.

There was a pool of water on the road. The SUV hit it at speed. It lost control.

The back end of the car was beginning to fishtail down the road.

"Hunter!" Heart screamed. "Watch out!"

The tires of the SUV slipped.

The weight of Vandenberg's car began to move sideways.

He had lost it. The SUV hit the side of another car.

The front corner of the SUV caught the edge of a pole, launching him into a spin.

Then came the impact.

It was deafening. The SUV flipped. Crunched onto its roof. Bounced back into the air. Rolled sideways. The sound of crunching metal was thunderous. The

SUV bounced again. Rolled once more.

Hunter slammed on his brakes. His car slid to a halt.

The SUV was upside down on a sidewalk, not in the same shape it was only moments before. It barely resembled the same car. The car was broken. No windshield. The roof smashed downward. Tires turned inwards. A missing door.

Hunter leaped out of his car, searching the smashed wreck. He could see blood. A lot of it.

Heart stood next to Hunter. She pulled out her phone and dialed 911, but they were already coming. She could hear the sirens in the distance.

When he saw the car was safe, Hunter scrambled under the wreck. He tried to help Vandenberg. The roof had collapsed. Vandenberg was squashed by the impact with the ground.

Heart was soon next to him, assisting him. Other cars stopped to help. The local police arrived. So did the ambulance.

The place was soon buzzing with lights, people, and activity.

Michael Vandenberg was alive. But only just.

# CHAPTER 45

AFTER THE Minneapolis Police Department officers took their statements, Hunter drove Detective Heart back to the motel. It was early morning, and Stacey was waiting for them. She barely reacted to the news that Michael Vandenberg was in the hospital after a car accident. She was still in shock.

Every word of the conversation between Stacey and Vandenberg had been recorded by Heart, and it was the admission of guilt the police needed to charge him with the murder of Joe Fielding. The Minneapolis police were keeping Vandenberg guarded until Detective Heart returned. He'd be processed and taken back to Chicago once he recovered in the hospital.

"The crash left Vandenberg with suspected broken ribs, a broken arm, a broken ankle, and a possible skull fracture. His recovery will take time, but he'll serve that time in a prison hospital." Heart told Stacey. "The important thing is that he's under arrest and he's admitted everything and it's all recorded. It's what we needed. He's going to prison for a long time after this."

Stacey nodded. There was little joy in her face as she tried to work out her next steps.

"But you're still officially on bail. You skipped it," Heart continued. "I have to take you in until all this has been sorted out. I'm sorry but that's the process. Vandenberg has admitted on tape that he killed Fielding, but we still have to get you cleared. You're currently a fugitive, and you'll face penalties for skipping bail."

The look on Stacey's face was of pure disappointment.

"Or Tex can drive you back." Heart said. "It's early morning. If you drive back now, you'll be there before midday. Go and see your kids. I'll call my partner in an hour, and then we can take you back into the station to clear this up tomorrow."

"Thank you," Stacey whispered. "Thank you."

Hunter thanked Detective Heart, and she left in a Minneapolis Police Department squad car to check on Vandenberg at the hospital. Formal charges would be forthcoming, but Vandenberg wasn't going anywhere quickly.

Hunter consoled Stacey and then began the drive back to Chicago.

At 5am, as they were driving the dark roads, Stacey Fulbright called her husband. She could barely speak when he answered the phone. She didn't know what to say, but she couldn't have said much through the tears anyway. There were tears coming from the other end of the phone as well. Hardly a coherent word was spoken between them, but the communication of love was clear.

Stacey Fulbright barely said another word on the drive back to Chicago.

Hunter asked her a number of questions and Stacey answered them as best she could, but her mind was elsewhere. It was with her children, and her husband. Her family. Her friends. Her past life. She longed to hold and hug her children again.

It was after ten o'clock in the morning when they arrived in Naperville. The air was cold and damp, but Carl didn't care. He was sitting on the edge of the front porch, looking like he'd barely had a moment of sleep. When the BMW pulled into the driveway, all that had gone before had been forgotten. All Carl wanted to do was hold his wife in his arms.

When Stacey stepped out of the car, Carl embraced her and held her tight. The tears flowed freely.

Hunter waited next to the car, and after many tears, Carl offered his hand to Hunter.

Hunter nodded and shook it firmly. Stacey walked closer and hugged Hunter, before walking into her house, Carl's arm wrapped around her.

Hunter looked at his watch. 10:50am. It was time to catch up on sleep.

# CHAPTER 46

IN THE days since the accident, it had emerged Vandenberg had a fondness for driving his large SUV around Chicago. He was already known to police. He was known to follow rival lawyers and intimidate them, in the hope they could cave on any potential deals between clients. Vandenberg was transported back to Chicago under guard, and would serve his time in the prison hospital until his trial. His injuries would take years to heal, and that healing would have to take place behind bars.

Hunter stood outside the 18th District Police Station on North Larrabee St. Next to him was Esther Wright, and behind her, Dr. David Mackie.

"They're going to ask you questions about your interactions with Christoph King. That's who they're going after today." Hunter said as he held open the door into the police station. "They've gotten information from Stacey Fulbright, and Vandenberg has talked to the detectives already. Vandenberg turned on King the moment he realized he was done; in the hope they would offer him a better deal for Fielding's murder."

"It feels good to be on this side of the fence, giving evidence and statements about the truth to the police." Dr. Mackie said. "On the phone, they said the evidence was strong against King?"

"Vandenberg has made statements about their joint fraud activities, and those statements are enough to see King spend a considerable amount of time behind bars." Hunter responded. "Your testimony is going to add to the weight of evidence against King and ensure that he doesn't see the streets for a long, long time."

Esther smiled as she followed them into the building. They spent hours by Dr. Mackie's side, guiding him as he was questioned by police. They were his security blanket. Dr. Mackie's trust of the force had diminished after his latest case. He detailed everything he knew, speaking to the police for two hours while giving evidence against Christoph King and Michael Vandenberg. Once his statement was taken, Dr. Mackie couldn't wipe the smile from his face.

"So this is it? All done?" Dr. Mackie questioned after they stepped out of the police building and into the bright sunshine. "We're all done?"

"All done." Hunter responded.

Dr. Mackie offered his hand. Hunter shook it firmly. They held the handshake longer than usual, a subtle sign of thanks and respect.

"Thank you." Dr. Mackie said. Hunter nodded, before Dr. Mackie stepped into the waiting cab.

Esther smiled as she and Hunter walked back to their cars, both parked further up the street.

"What about Joanne Wolfe?" She asked. "Was she involved?"

"It appears not. It seems she just wanted to see her rival Stacey Fulbright suffer. Vandenberg has admitted he asked Wolfe to follow Stacey for a while, just to scare her, but she claims that she didn't know the extent of Vandenberg's crimes."

"Surely, she must've known what he was doing?"

"I'm not sure." Hunter said as they stopped outside Esther's car. "But her firm will take a massive hit over this. Perhaps it's even the end of her career."

"And the other doctor?"

"Which doctor?" Hunter asked.

"No, the normal doctor."

"What?" Hunter squinted with confusion on his face.

"Which doctor? Witch doctor? Get it? As in, 'No, I don't need the normal doctor, I need the Witch Doctor. Like voodoo. Oh, never mind. It was a terrible joke."

"We can agree on that." Hunter laughed. "It's never good when you have to explain a joke."

"It's not my fault if your comedic understanding is a little slow." Esther smirked. "A smarter person would've understood it."

"But to answer your question—Dr. Lighten was guilty. He got away with his crimes by signing a non-disclosure agreement, even if Heather Munroe was

303

encouraged by Joe Fielding."

A fresh gust of wind blew down the street, and Esther patted her hair back down into place. "Did you hear anything more from Natalie?"

"Nothing. No response, and no answer. It's a dead end. I've tried to call her, but she's blocked me. Short of kidnapping her and dragging her back over the border, there's nothing else left to do."

"Does this mean it's over? The crusade is done?" There was hope in Esther's voice.

"It appears that way." Hunter put his hands in his pockets and leaned against Esther's car, parked in front of Hunter's on the street. "There's no other avenue left. It looks like an innocent man will die in prison."

Esther let the pause sit between them for a moment, before she took her car keys from her purse. "Then the answer is yes."

"Yes?" Hunter squinted. "To what question?"

"Dinner." Esther said. "I'll say yes to dinner."

"With me?"

"Yes. With you."

"Wow. Um…" Hunter stood up straight and ran his hand through his hair. "I guess… well… um… sorry, you've caught me off guard."

"I'll give you a hint about how this works—you should ask me which night I'm free, and then you ask me what sort of food I like."

Hunter smiled. He already knew the answers to those questions. As he went to respond, his phone rang. He removed it from his pocket.

"It's a Mexican phone number. Excuse me a moment," he offered Esther another smile, and stepped away from her car, further down the street. "Hello?"

"Tex. This is your sister. Natalie." The voice on the other end of the line was soft. "I need to talk to you."

Hunter inhaled. He looked back to Esther. She looked so happy and peaceful and calm and stunning. The breeze was blowing, and her hair was dancing alongside her face. She smiled as she leaned against her car, taking in a moment of sunshine.

"Tex?" Natalie questioned. "Are you there?"

He drew a breath. His stomach filled with nerves. He took one last look at the smile on Esther's face, and stepped further away.

"I'm here."

"I have a friend here in Mexico. She's been so good to me. Her son has been locked up in a prison in a small town in Illinois. He got in some trouble, but he didn't do it. He's just a kid and he won't survive behind bars. He's not much older than my eldest boy." Natalie paused, but Hunter didn't respond. "I told her that I have some family in Illinois, and then I said that my brother was a lawyer. You're a criminal lawyer, aren't you?"

Again, Hunter didn't respond.

"Her son didn't have any defense." Natalie continued. "The poor kid had to go up against a racist cop and a racist judge in a racist town. He didn't stand a chance. He was arrested because he was Mexican. And well…"

Hunter's heart pounded in his chest as Natalie paused. He turned and looked back at Esther.

"And well," Natalie continued. "Maybe you can get him out. I looked you up. My baby brother did alright for himself, didn't he? Big time city lawyer. Name in the paper. Face on television."

"I can't help you, Natalie."

"If you do…" Natalie paused again, and then drew a deep breath. "If you get him out of prison, I'll tell you everything. I'll tell you exactly what happened and why our father shouldn't die in prison. If you can get my friend's son out of lock-up, then I'll come back to the US. I'll come back and tell you and Patrick everything I know."

Hunter didn't respond. He looked back to Esther, gazing at a life that was so close, so near, but so emotionally far away.

"Tex?" Natalie pressed.

Hunter looked at the ground. Ran his hand through his hair. He looked up and caught Esther's gaze.

She was looking at him with confusion. Hunter hesitated. Esther shook her head. She could sense what the call was about. She opened the door to her car.

Hunter turned around. "It's a deal, Natalie."

Natalie gave him the details of the case, and the run-down of what she knew.

When Hunter turned back to look at Esther, she'd already driven away.

# THE END

# AUTHOR'S NOTE:

Thank you for reading Saving Justice. I hope you enjoyed the twists and turns of this plot. I certainly enjoyed writing it. Sometimes the twists in the plot made my head spin.

I love the city of Chicago. It's such a beautiful city filled with interesting characters. I started this book sitting in a café in the Downtown area, which I often do, watching a mother embrace her young child after a day away. There was so much emotion in the mother's hug. I sat in the café for hours after that, pen and paper in hand, scribbling notes and fueling myself on five cups of coffee, two muffins, and a sandwich, watching people come and go. Those people formed the characters in this novel.

From the moment I put pen to paper for the first Tex Hunter story, I've been looking forward to writing the next two books—Natural Justice and Freedom and Justice. These two books resolve the saga of Alfred Hunter's life. If you've read any of the other Tex Hunter books, you know that I love a great twist or two, or sometimes even three, and there's a number of big twists to come in this family tale. Those twists have been hinted at right from the first book in the series. Each story has included little hints about what happened in Alfred's past, a lot of which will make sense when all is revealed in the next two novels.

I love hearing from readers, and a question I'm asked a lot is what will happen to Alfred—is he guilty or innocent, or somehow involved, whether Alfred Hunter will leave prison, whether he'll pass away in his cell, or whether something else will happen to him. I avoided answering those questions, because if there's one thing I love, it's a plot twist. So expect another few twists in his story...

I've loved writing this series, and telling the world about the Hunter family, and hopefully, you've loved coming along on this journey as well.

Stay safe and well.

Much love,
Peter O'Mahoney

# ALSO BY PETER O'MAHONEY

*In the Tex Hunter series:*

**Power and Justice**
**Faith and Justice**
**Corrupt Justice**
**Deadly Justice**

**\*\*\*\*\***

*In the Bill Harvey Legal Thriller Series:*

**Redeeming Justice**
**Will of Justice**
**Fire and Justice**
**A Time for Justice**
**Truth and Justice**

**\*\*\*\*\***

*In the Jack Valentine Series:*

**Gates of Power**
**Stolen Power**

Made in the USA
Las Vegas, NV
02 July 2022

51028933R00187